Praise for **BLOOD FUGUES**

"Yunqué is a dazzling writer with a distinctive and vital literary voice."

—*San Francisco Chronicle*

" . . . The author is a bravura storyteller with an extraordinary ability to create fascinating, emotion-engaging characters."

—*Booklist* starred review

" . . . Not even a disciplined plot, centered on the stories of just two families, can tame Yunqué's ambitions or his boisterous voice."

—*Details*

"An exceptional novel . . . thematically disciplined, intense, complex, moving."

—Robert Friedman,
Scripps Howard News Service

"Ambitious . . . a page-turner. Yunqué's latest work, *Blood Fugues*, has Faulkner's fingerprints all over it."

—*New Haven Advocate*

"Yunqué writes with grace . . . a moving family portrait."

—*Publishers Weekly*

EDGARDO VEGA YUNQUÉ

BLOOD*fugues*

A NOVEL

rayo *An Imprint of* HarperCollins*Publishers*

THIS BOOK IS DEDICATED TO
MATTHEW

HarperCollins books may be purchased for educa-
tional, business, or sales promotional use. For information, please write: Special Markets Department,
HarperCollins Publishers, 10 East 53rd Street,
New York, NY 10022.

FIRST EDITION

Book design by SHUBHANI SARKAR

Library of Congress Cataloging-in-Publication Data
is available upon request.

ISBN-10: 0-06-074278-1
ISBN-13: 978-0-06-074278-2

06 07 08 09 DIX/RRD 10 9 8 7 6 5 4 3 2 1

READ INTO IT! Join ClubRayo by e-mailing rayo@harpercollins.com.

He keeps the sorrow alive for the sake of memory . . .

COLUM McCANN

This Side of Brightness

The Modern Era has nurtured a dream in which mankind, divided into its separate civilizations, would someday come together in unity and everlasting peace. Today, the history of the planet has finally become one indivisible whole, but it is war, ambulant and everlasting war, that embodies and guarantees this long-desired unity of mankind. Unity of mankind means: no escape for anyone anywhere.

MILAN KUNDERA

The Art of the Novel

A fugue generally consists of a series of expositions and developments with no fixed number of either. At its simplest, a fugue might consist of one exposition followed by optional development. A more complex fugue might follow the exposition with a series of developments, or another exposition followed by one or more developments. Fugues that are tonally centered will expose the subject without venturing out of an initial tonic/dominant constellation.

TIMOTHY A. SMITH
PROFESSOR OF MUSIC THEORY
NORTHERN ARIZONA UNIVERSITY
"The Canons and Fugues of J. S. Bach"
(May 20, 2001)
(jan.ucc.nav.edu/~tas3/bachindex.html)

PARTS

prelude

KENNY ROMERO placed his red hockey bag in the luggage compartment of the Trailways bus, gave the driver his ticket and got on. He carried a knapsack with sandwiches, a bottle of orange juice, a package of Raisinets, two Almond Joy candy bars, a toiletries bag his mother had bought him, a paperback copy of *The Return of the King*, third in Tolkien's Lord of the Rings trilogy, and a small metal picture frame that held, in an oval, a color photograph of Claudia Bachlichtner. The hockey bag didn't hold his pads, gloves, uniform or skates, but his clothes. They were summer clothes: jeans, polo shirts, underwear, some sweaters and a mackinaw lumber jacket, bought for him the previous summer by Gabriel Brunet. Last year when the early mornings and evenings had grown colder at the end of the summer, Gabriel had driven him to Utica and urged him to pick out a jacket. On his jeans he wore a wide belt with a large cowboy buckle, which Gabriel had also given him as an end of summer present. Now, as if he were ready to begin work immediately upon his arrival, he wore heavy work boots. Kenny settled into his seat and a few minutes later the last of the passengers boarded. The door of the bus closed and they were moving out of Port Authority terminal in midtown Manhattan and heading north to upstate New York.

Kenny had the soft, delicate looks of his mother, a girl whose grandparents came to America from the severity of rural Ireland to the harshness of New York City in the 1890s from Roscommon, family lore said. He was brought up quietly and respectfully by loving parents. His mother was Frances Ann Boyle, an Irish girl from the Bronx, whose family was unable or unwilling to escape to the suburban tranquility of two-family houses and front yards in the outer boroughs of New York City. Instead, like other Irish families in their situation, they remained obstinately in neighborhoods like Hell's Kitchen, the Upper West Side, the South Bronx and Inwood, touting apartment living as devoid of pretense. Most of the offspring of these families, detesting their condition, diligently sought a place in the middle class. Some struggled and failed. Most attained stability through service to the city. Others surpassed their assigned status and rose to positions of influence in many areas of the society, reaching as far as the U.S. Senate. Still others perished along the way, succumbing to the ills that all ghettos, in spite of their dubious romance, provide in abundance.

Kenny's father was Tommy Romero, a Puerto Rican boy born in East Harlem, a different kind of ghetto that produced some successes although its myth persists as a cradle to great accomplishments. Before he was ten the Romero family took flight to the Williamsburg section of Brooklyn known as Los Sures because of the numbered streets, such as South 6th and South 7th, which carried their direction. In time the south streets became Puerto Rican, displacing the Italians, who moved deeper into Brooklyn. The north streets remained Polish, extending into Greenpoint. His parents purchased a house cheaply and over the years created a home that was a welcome place for their children and grandchildren. This haven was of such serenity that Kenny often felt the same respect and awe that he experienced when entering the fragrant solitude of a Catholic church, the incense replaced by the pungent aroma of his grandmother's cigars, a feminine peculiarity, to be sure, but a small matter compared to the delights of her kitchen, which produced, generously, confections of unequaled flavor, whose smells dissipated that of the tobacco.

Fleeing went the Irish seeking refuge from the advancing Harlems, the dark skin of the people making unrecognizable the prejudices they had endured when they arrived in America, the defect of memory driving them forward to separate themselves from the shadows that follow all immigrants. Fleeing went the Puerto Ricans escaping the same blackness, but impelled by the fears of blood, both physical and hereditary. Fearing with greater horror the prospect of losing themselves in the anonymity that America forces on all of its people, both groups fought the country's wish for that homogeneity that destroys language and culture. As an antidote to assimilation they both retained fiercely their Irishness and their Puertoricanness. Each side of the family spoke of its ancestral homeland poetically, as if it had been the land of milk and honey. This stance was staunchly defended even though the deprivation endured by hundreds of thousands like them had been immense for too many years and had forced them to leave their island homes. And yet, inflexibly, they remained branded in their hearts, the one with a green shamrock and the other a blood-red flower, a *flamboyán*, each year their pride celebrated by marching in pageants of ethnic excess.

Tommy and Fran, as they called each other, were drawn together when Jerry Boyle, her brother, asked Tommy to her twenty-first birthday party one late August. Jerry Boyle, working Narcotics in the 23rd Precinct, was assigned Tommy Romero, who played with undercover brilliance a Puerto Rican junkie. So convincingly did he carry out his role that eventually it earned them commendations and innumerable busts and convictions. Jerry Boyle was as gifted in his deceit, playing with equal verve a hippie-like, Nordic, blond, out-of-control, richboy honky, consistently high as a kite with a gift of gab, and the insane charm that the dark ghettos respect in white people. Tommy, ever in character, was the direct opposite: quiet, brooding, dark eyed and Moorish, mysterious and dangerous, appearing doped up to the unsuspecting until they were caught in the snare of mendacity the two partners had constructed. They did well for a while and then through missteps their life in law enforcement came to an end. They then turned to other endeavors, politically admirable, clandestine and dangerous, and not without some nobility, a quality which in spite of their mistakes, they both possessed amply.

The invitation to the birthday party came about suddenly and naturally after they gained the conviction of a gang of thugs from First Avenue. After a few beers of celebration with others from the squad at a saloon in Upper Manhattan, they were hugging each other and horsing around and Jerry Boyle looked at Tommy Romero and admitted what he'd known for a while. This Spanish kid was special and much more than a partner. It was one of those things that happen between men when they recognize love for one another. He asked immediately if Tommy wanted to come to his sister Frances's birthday party the following Saturday. Jerry said that Frankie, as he called her, had graduated from Hunter College and would start teaching in September. Maybe he would understand her, since she was a bit weird and the first one in the family to graduate from college. Maybe he, who had also attended college, could help him understand her. Tommy had shrugged his shoulders and wondered if Jerry Boyle was being polite. In spite of his doubts he said he'd go and wondered all week what Jerry's sister looked like.

Now, as Kenny Romero, the first offspring of this Dublin–San Juan union, rode the bus upstate for his second summer working at the Brunet dairy farm, he thought again about his father. He was gone for days now. When he returned he was withdrawn and unapproachable. When his father was away his mother would often go into the bedroom and cry and his sister Mary Margaret, Peggy to the family, two years younger than Kenny, would take over the household, feeding the other children and caring for Tommy Jr. who was four years old. Peggy was a near replica of her mother in looks except that she had black hair and coal dark eyes. In temperament Peggy was brusque and resembled cigar-smoking Grandma Rosa Romero, who treated the subject of Catholicism like most people treat ghosts, as quaint and not to be believed in or trusted. But Kenny and the other children were raised devout and went to church, their mother, Frances, instructing them on Christian goodness.

His little sisters would knock on the bedroom door and call their mother and sit outside crying in sympathy: Rose, Katherine and Diana. He would go to them and coax them into the living room, turn on the television and sit with them, Diana on his lap and the other two on either side, holding them close until they relaxed. His father would eventually show up and his mother was happy again, glad that he had returned safely. His father would ask him how things were going with hockey or baseball and he'd nod an okay, just looking at him cool and game faced, directly into his eyes as his father always looked at others, not displaying any fear. He was respectful of his father's quiet anger even though the anger was never directed at him or the family, and instead was aimed at the injustices of the government toward poor people. At times he mentioned the treatment of Puerto Ricans and what the United States had done to the island, a mystery to Kenny. The same poverty against which his father stood did not permit visits to this island of his paternal grandparents, Pablo and Rosa. Cacimar, where they had been raised, remained shrouded in their countless anecdotes so that the town appeared a fiction.

Although his father had accepted his decision without protest, Kenny knew that he was disappointed that he'd chosen not to play baseball and instead was going upstate to work at the farm. Reluctantly his father went along with Kenny's rationale that he needed to be away from the frenzied pace of the city because it tore at his nerves and caused him to feel constantly on guard. His parents were never unkind but there was a pressure to please them and he wanted to be free of the obligation. Although he loved and respected them, he didn't want to be like them, not quite knowing why he felt as he did.

He turned away from thoughts of his father and focused on Claudia, his girl last summer. He wondered if she still liked him. She had written him some letters, a Christmas card and then another for Valentine's Day. Although everything was signed "Love" that had been it. They promised not to date anyone else. He wasn't able to keep his promise completely and had kissed Nancy Martínez, his cousin's friend, the time a group of them went to the skating rink in Prospect Park. There had been nobody else. He went to school, practice, games and back home. As the bus picked up speed he looked out at the city buildings along the highway and then watched the landscape change to suburban dwellings. In another half hour they went through the tollbooths and onto the open highway and the long stretches of trees and large grazing fields, the highway becoming steeper and in the distance, shrouded in the summer haze, the mountains.

As one travels northwest toward the Adirondack Mountains, the upper regions of the State of New York are nothing like its southern end. Upstate, beyond the Catskill Mountains, one could mistake the landscape for that of Pennsylvania or Ohio, where there are vast expanses of grazing terrain, forests and farms, and the land is still invested with the innocence of what was once the United States. This was important to Kenny Romero, for it gave him a sense of belonging that was absent for him in the city. In New York City he was Irish or he was Puerto Rican. Upstate he was just Kenny Romero. There, in the country, was an opportunity to be away from the harshness of concrete and noise. Absent in the country was the benevolent parental rule that was a constant of his existence, their concern genuine but suffocating. There, beyond Albany, near the Mohawk River he could think calmly and work and spend his leisure hours walking and imagining what both sides of the family were like as farmers. When he learned that the Iroquois tribes had hunted and fished the area, he decided that the land had a power he wished to acquire. The history of the land fascinated him, much as if that part of the American mythology were also part of him.

In summer the land in the region is fertile and verdant. The woods are dense and often devoid of trails. In this part of the state the wildlife is plentiful and hunting is good. There are black deer and quail and pheasant abound. Wolves are now extinct but their strains remain in the large coyotes that yip and howl in the night, become bold and at times come close enough to farms and towns to kill small dogs and cats and cause hunters to say, unfairly, that they've depleted the deer population. There are foxes, and as in song and tale, they raid chicken coops. In the deeper woods there are black bears, although not many. Their presence is a certainty, their spoors and droppings apparent if one ventures into the higher reaches of the mountains. Woodchucks, squirrels and chipmunks are ubiquitous in farms and small towns. Raccoons and skunks are plentiful and from time to time appear in the towns. There are also songbirds of many kinds, and aloft, hawks dance in the summer currents as they search the ground for prey. At night, owls fly nearly silently through the forest and fields hunting rodents. Beavers build their dams on brooks and lakes. On them ducks and turtles flourish. Fishing is good and geese stop off on the lakes during their trips north and south, signaling the changing of the seasons.

Kenny was a big boy with his mother's good looks and the quiet disposition of his father. At the age of seventeen he was six feet one inch tall, strong and rangy, his body naturally muscled and his hair brown and slightly wavy. At the end of the summer, when it had grown long, the hair acquired dark blond streaks from exposure to the sun. Together with the golden hue that his skin took on because of his father, he appeared exotic. His last name, Romero, caused adults to whisper that he was Spanish. This was confirmed one Saturday afternoon while he was in town during his first year when the police stopped two migrant families on the way to a farm. The old station wagon was carrying four adults and a dozen children of different ages. In his English-speckled Spanish Kenny was able to translate for the farm workers. The policeman permitted the families to continue their trip.

The girls around the town said he had dreamy blue eyes. His eyes were, in fact, a greenish blue, which made his maternal grandmother, Mary Katherine Boyle, née Grady, a generally unsentimental woman, often say wistfully that they were Irish eyes, the way Kenny smiled easily under the most difficult situations. His attractiveness heightened young girls' whispers when he and the other boy from the city working on the farm rode into town to go to the movies or the town diner on Saturday nights. Because she had gotten to know Kenny, some girls in the town often questioned Claudia Bachlichtner, a tall Lutheran girl who wanted to become a nurse. To the consternation of her peers, she was closemouthed about her relationship to Kenny. Equally athletic, Claudia was thoughtful, worked hard and did well in most of her subjects at the town's high school. Her academic proficiency and quiet dignity caused both teachers and counselors to encourage her to set her sights higher and consider preparing herself for medical school during her time in college. Politely, almost apologetically, she explained that she simply wanted to become a nurse and assist doctors in helping patients.

When Kenny Romero spoke, he addressed everyone as politely as he did the brothers and lay teachers at his Catholic school in New York City, where he excelled at ice hockey in the winter and baseball in the spring. There was little doubt in the minds of all concerned that scouts would have rushed to see him play in the Brooklyn league where other New York baseball stars had played in their youth, had he not made his decision to quit playing baseball during the summer. He enjoyed ice hockey in the fall and winter and it was enough for him to play soccer, which his grandfather Martin Boyle had loved.

The schools of the Archdiocese of New York did not offer scholarships, but there were alumni who provided funds to help disadvantaged boys. Kenny certainly was that, the two sides of his family scraping by even though both his mother and father had attended college: she at Hunter College, he at

Brooklyn College for two years. To compound their financial situation, Fran and Tommy adhered not so much to their Catholic upbringing as to the one entertainment they didn't have to pay for in the immediacy of their ardor, but which, because of their desire, produced five more children before his mother was thirty-four years old.

Kenny made friends easily and during the summer older boys often invited him to the bars in the town. He was underage and didn't like having to lie to Gabriel, who had made it possible for him to come to the farm and work. He didn't know how long he had believed that he should be honest, but he suspected that he decided to do so in order not to feel the overwhelming guilt of going to confession and having to admit that he had sinned. For it was as much a sin to lie as it was to commit other acts against God. There was a distinction about lying that he hadn't quite grasped but decided that in time he would do so. Both his mother and father appeared to feel it was all right to lie to protect others. Perhaps that type of lying wasn't a sin but simply a secret.

Kenny loved hearing the old man, Mr. Brunet, talk about the land. He was Gabriel's father and although it was his farm, as he aged, he could do less and less. Other than feeding the poultry, smoking meats, cooking and doing some of the administrative tasks of the farm, his bent, arthritic back kept him inactive most of the time, his face a permanent grimace. Kenny had asked about Gabriel's mother but obtained little information from either Gabriel or his father. He was told she had died shortly after Gabriel was born. Her name was Marguerite Bouillet, a French Canadian girl. He'd asked if there were any photographs. He was told that there was too much grief in her passing and Henri Brunet had destroyed all traces of her. He once asked the old man if she was a beautiful woman. He was told that she was a good woman, beautiful in

EDGARDO VEGA YUNQUÉ

many significant ways. He wasn't sure if he was being told the truth. The adult world was like that, filled with secrets and vague explanations. And so the trip went. He ate the ham and cheese sandwiches his mother had made and drank orange juice. He read Tolkien and chewed his candy bars and napped, waking up aroused and thinking of Claudia Bachlichtner again. He wondered if they would finally make love. He had yet to touch her intimately and wondered what that would be like. It would be his first time. He hoped she had kept her word as well.

He fell asleep again, half waking when the bus made its stops on the way north. When he next opened his eyes the bus was traveling through familiar terrain. Fifteen minutes later he was in the town with its old houses, picket fences and neat yards, the shops small and painted brightly, the streets narrow and the trees old. Gabriel Brunet was standing by the red pickup that he had taught him to drive the previous year. A new boy with glasses was standing by Gabriel. He was a Spanish-looking boy. Gabriel introduced him and said the boy had come from Mexico and didn't speak much English. His name was Carlos Zamora. The way Gabriel looked so lovingly at Carlos, Kenny wondered if the boy was related to the girl Claudia said Gabriel had loved many years ago. He knew it was a wish to ease his mind about Gabriel's loneliness. Gabriel had pictures of the girl. She looked Indian. The photographs had snow-peaked mountains in the background. He asked her name and Gabriel painfully told him it was Carmen. Kenny wondered about Carmen but Gabriel wouldn't talk about her except to say that she spoke Quechua, an Indian language that Gabriel began learning while in Peru. Just as he wouldn't talk about his mother, Gabriel was equally silent concerning Carmen, the sorrow of his memories etched into his eyes.

obsession

*Kenny had the soft, delicate looks of his
mother, a girl whose grandparents came to
America from the severity of rural Ireland
to the harshness of New York City in
the 1890s from Roscommon, family lore said.*

THE SUMMER had gone well. He arrived at the beginning
of July and fell once again into the six-day routine of rising at five o'clock in the morning to help Gabriel with
milking, tending to sterilizing the teats of the sixty milking
cows, mixing the solution of iodine and scrubbing the long
nipples gently, and then flushing, with a similar solution, the
pipes that carried their milk to the tanks for eventual trans-
portation in the tanker trucks from Cloverleaf manufacturing
dairy. There, the thick raw milk was pasteurized and con-
verted into the different products that appeared in the dairy
sections of the state's stores, the abstract Shamrock of its logo
an even greater obscuring of the cattle ownership that centuries before determined wealth and position in Ireland but

that meant little to its present investors. By five-thirty in the morning they had placed eight cows into the milking stalls and fifteen minutes later they were done, had swabbed the cows' teats again, a precaution against infection and contamination. The cows were returned to the corral and the open bales of hay that had been scattered there. Eight more cows were then ushered into the milking stalls, the routine repeated until they were done. If it rained the hay was left in covered pens and the cows gathered there, the pungent smell of their waste filling the air to mix with the smell of the rain. Each shift took approximately fifteen minutes, with the milking taking eight to ten minutes and the rest of the time spent in preparation and cleanup.

Seven times eight was fifty-six and then four more and they were done by eight o'clock and came in to eat a breakfast of sausage and eggs and fruit juice, and pancakes or French toast and cold milk and if you wanted, coffee, which he liked. His appetite was prodigious. It was not unusual for him to have fruit juice, three eggs, six pieces of sausage, four pancakes or French toast, and a quart of cold milk. The mornings were cold even in midsummer, the air dry and fragrant with the smell of the grass in the fields as if the evaporating dew carried with it the aroma. When he was done he saddled a horse and began herding the milking cows out into the fenced pasture, which extended a half mile to the edge of the woods and had a brook running through it where the cows gathered to drink. The bulls remained in another pasture that the old man, Henri Brunet, called their den.

When Kenny returned to the farmhouse he helped the other boy feed the calves, heifers and the ten dry cows. He liked tending to the cows and felt as if he were doing something of importance because milk helped people to be healthy. He recalled his mother breast-feeding his sister and wanting to know how her milk tasted. He was three years old and she removed Peggy from her breast. Pressing her nipple she collected a bit of the thin, yellowish milk and placed it on his lips. He had tasted it but was not drawn to it even though he'd been breast-fed until he was nearly eighteen months. This information was provided by relatives. He had no memory of tasting his mother's milk.

Counting the sixty milking cows, the two bulls, the ten dry cows, sixteen calves and nine heifers there were ninety-seven cattle on the Brunet farm. There were also four goats, which roamed about in their pen and were permitted grazing in an enclosed area. There were also three horses, two mules and a small, elderly donkey that brayed in his sleep, often tottering as he stood. There were countless laying hens, rabbits, some pigs, including a pregnant sow, a flock of turkeys that gobbled constantly as if they were laughing at their eventual fate, and ducks that waddled down to the stream below the farmhouse. Lastly there was a peacock and two peahens that were kept in a large wire cage and permitted to roam about the enclosed yard once a day for exercise, the pavonine carriage of the peacock offensive to the lesser fowl, which upon his entrance and display of his feathers immediately segregated themselves from the magnificent bird.

The farmhouse was large and comfortable with lots of bedrooms, a television room and in the basement a pool table. The barn was immense and had a hayloft into which he and Claudia Bachlichtner often climbed for privacy. He liked the smell of the barn with the aromas of the hay and the animals. The barn held the horses and the dry cows and it was where the heifers and calves were kept and protected. Beyond the barn there was a silo, and beyond it a curing house where the old man, following the tradition of the previous owners of the farm, the Vanderveers, prepared his hams and sausages.

Kenny often worried about the old man, who was frail and walked with difficulty. He also worried about his son, Gabriel Brunet. The son's only concern appeared to be the farm and the care of the animals, and keeping extensive charts of their well-being and production. Aided by itinerant workers and a veterinarian, he worked seven days a week from four in the morning when he rose until ten at night when he finally rested. Gabriel said he slept soundly those six hours, but at times it didn't seem as if he'd slept at all. Kenny knew that twice a year, during the springtime and fall, Gabriel Brunet traveled northward through the state and drove into Canada and east toward the Quebec of his ancestors. Gabriel remained there for a week, speaking French and eating in the fine restaurants in Montreal. He later regaled him with tales of La Belle Province which Kenny loved hearing about since as a boy, he had traveled with his father to Granby for a Squirts Ice Hockey tournament. Kenny had stayed with a French-speaking family in Granby and had learned to say *bonjour, bon soir, bonne nuit* and *bonne chance*, which meant good luck and which he liked because it meant you had a chance, and if you had a chance you could always win.

After that first night at the other boy's home he met his father at the rink before they went into the locker room to get dressed. He had cried and his father held him and asked him why he was crying. He said that the family was nice to him but he couldn't speak to them and thank them. When his father was tightening his skates and taping the laces, he smiled and said he should ask the boy how to say thank you. He nodded happily and said he would. He scored two goals against the team from Syracuse and afterward he said he had seen the French boy as he was getting dressed for his game and he'd learned how to say *merci beacoup*. That evening they went to a restaurant and had hamburgers. When he said *merci beacoup* after the food was brought to the table, the French waitress smiled, tousled his hair and said he was a handsome boy, pronouncing the word "andsome." When he told Claudia the story as they were walking from the motel to the cars she had grabbed his butt and said he was certainly "and *some.*"

He was nine years old that year. Coming back to Brooklyn he was sad that they hadn't won the tournament. Gabriel said that someday he would have to come up to the farm in the winter and he would take him to see the Montreal Canadiens, Les Habitants, at the Forum in Montreal and they could see the city together. Kenny said he'd like that. Gabriel said he'd probably end up playing at the Forum someday. He shook his head and couldn't imagine being able to play at the speed at which the professional players did everything: the stick handling, passing, the way they could shoot the puck, lightning quick and with deadly accuracy. He knew he was good but not that good. Maybe he would go to college and play and that would be it, but Gabriel smiled and said he should keep working hard. Kenny had been First-Team All City the past year but the school hadn't made the playoffs.

Had Gabriel played as a boy? No, his father was too busy and Utica was too far away. Where had he gone to college? Syracuse University. He had studied Geology and Spanish. And then Gabriel talked about his time away in school and then graduating and his father coming to the college and standing proudly with him and his aunt's family and his aunt Simone saying that he would no longer need to be a farmer but could have a regular job. His aunt Simone was married to a man who drove a lumber truck for a company in Maine. They had two daughters, one of whom they talked about a great deal and another one they never mentioned, since she had run away from home and lived in Hell's Kitchen in New York City. He asked what Gabriel's cousin Marie did in Hell's

Kitchen. Gabriel shook his head. He closed his eyes, sighed, opened them and explained that she was a prostitute, but that he didn't judge her.

Gabriel changed the subject that first year and talked about dry cows, explaining that the term meant that the cows had been heifers until they were impregnated by a bull and could not produce milk until they had their calves. The milk came in then and they could join the milking herd. He had asked about the calves and Gabriel explained that they were fed by hand out of big baby bottles that held a formula with nutrients. He had watched as Gabriel filled the bottles and in a wire basket carried them to the barn and one in each hand, Gabriel and the other boy, Angel, last year, fed the calves. Angel had returned to the Bronx and had been shot in a gang dispute. Gabriel had given him two bottles and he held the bottles and watched the calves' soft eyes, the lashes reminding him of those of big dolls. The calves' tongues were large and thick. He felt sorry for the animals, knowing they would be fatted and sold for veal, a few of them raised to heifers, spared to increase the milking stock.

Gabriel was an enigma to Kenny. He was a wiry man, now forty-five years of age, the same age as his uncle Jerry, his mother's brother. Mr. Brunet had shown him Gabriel's birth certificate. After graduating from Syracuse University he remained in the city, found work with an insurance company and traveled across that area of New York, crossing into Vermont and New Hampshire attempting to get farmers to switch insurance companies. After a year, growing tired of the long days and lonely nights, he went to work for the State of New York as a farm inspector and traversed the middle region of the state making sure health standards were being observed at the farms that grew products for human as well as animal consumption. Gabriel was attractive enough that women gravitated naturally to him, but he spoke about subjects that were foreign to the women, his reserve and intellectual interests making him appear arrogant to them. He eventually tired of the bureaucracy and paperwork of his job, returned home to the Vanderveer farm and announced to his father that he was thinking of joining the Peace Corps. His father said President Kennedy had been right in establishing such a program and it was a shame he hadn't lived to see its flourishing. He applied, was accepted and after Peace Corps training and because of his knowledge of Spanish he was assigned to South America. After a week's orientation he was sent to a community in the highlands of Peru, the air thin and the people more austere and silent than he was, their faces impassive and untelling.

For Kenny the two summers working on the farm had made him feel as if his life was now in his own hands. His second year had been better and he was grateful that things had gone so well with Claudia and she was now truly his girl.

One day in late August of that second year, when the days grew shorter and the chill air began to descend on the land earlier, Kenny had looked at the birthing chart and reminded Gabriel Brunet that Cow 571 was due to calf early the following week but that she was missing and maybe she was going to give birth sooner. The cows wore lead tags the size of a playing card on their ears. When they no longer could yield milk their eartags were removed and saved as a remembrance before they were sold to be butchered. There was a pile of the heavy lead tags in a bin near the barn. He felt sorry for the cows. They were useful and people took them for granted. Gabriel told him many things about cows. The spots on a cow, he said, are like fingerprints. Gabriel photographed them and matched their photographs to their tags. The cows generally weighed about fourteen hundred pounds and gave roughly fifty thousand quarts of milk in a lifetime. A cow drinks about forty gallons of water a day. Once upon a time when a cow was butchered the gelatin was used to make film for photographs and phonograph records. Gabriel said that the Pilgrims brought cows to the United States.

Carlos, the boy from Mexico, squinting through his glasses, had nodded and smiled, his English improving steadily. Gabriel had spoken in Spanish and explained that Cow 571 was giving birth next week. The boy nodded and Kenny was again amazed by the Spanish term for giving birth: *dar a luz*. *Parir* was the verb for birthing but the other phrase was poetic and delicate. *Dar a luz*. To give light, but more properly, Gabriel had explained, to bring into the light. The cow would bring the calf into the light, he thought. The idea pleased him. He imagined his mother holding him a few minutes after she had brought him into the light, her eyes smiling with satisfaction. He was her first child and the idea pleased him as well.

*K*enny finished driving the manure out of the barn with the skid loader and piling it up to be carted away. It was now noon. After lunch he wouldn't have any other tasks until four in the afternoon when he would ride out and bring the cows back for their evening milking at five. He ate lunch and asked Gabriel if he could drive into town. Gabriel nodded and, after making sure he had his driver's permit in his wallet, Kenny retrieved the keys from Gabriel's desk in the small room where he conducted the business of the dairy farm. He showered, put on all clean clothes, clean socks, his new running shoes, and his International Harvester cap, and stepped out into the afternoon sun. He wore sunglasses, and as he drove he looked at the rolling hills and in the distance the mountains.

Utica was only twenty miles beyond the town but it seemed an eternity getting there because the closer he got the more excited he was about seeing Claudia. He would park the pickup, walk to the hospital and meet her in the lobby. She would be wearing her candy-stripe uniform and in her car they'd drive to a motel where she had rented a room. They'd spend almost two hours or so together. She would drive him back to the pickup and they'd drive, one behind the other to her house, get out of their vehicles, kiss good-bye and he'd return to the farm. Sometimes he went into the house and said hello to Eva Bachlichtner, Claudia's mother, who was tall and slender like her daughter. She was attractive but seemed consistently worried, her eyes narrow in the same Teutonic way as her daughter's, but devoid of Claudia's joyfulness.

Everything had been totally unexpected this year, totally different from the previous summer. Soon after unpacking that first day he had called Claudia. On the phone she told him that she was working as a volunteer in the hospital in Utica for a few hours Monday, Wednesday and Friday. He and Carlos had driven into town on Friday and they'd met Claudia and the three of them had gone to the movies. He had kissed her and held her hand but Carlos's presence inhibited them. The following day she called him and then came to get him in her VW. He had been startled by the change in her. Physically she was the same, but something in her personality had changed. She was five feet nine inches tall, dark blond, rawboned, the skin tight to her face, the cheekbones so high that she looked Asiatic, her ancestry from that part of Germany that borders Poland, reaching back into the centuries to highlight the influences of Genghis Khan and his Mongol hordes or perhaps the Lapps farther north. She wore shorts, a cutoff Buffalo Bills sweatshirt and clogs. She no longer seemed shy and she looked at him cagily like a large feline, he'd thought. She said hello to Gabriel and his father and shook Carlos's hand, speaking to him haltingly in Spanish. Carlos laughed and Gabriel congratulated her. They drank lemonade and then she asked him if he'd like to go for a drive. Kenny nodded and they'd gone off. They drove on the dirt road for a short while before she turned off and drove onto another narrow dirt road that led to a nearby farm and into a secluded place near the woods.

She stopped the car, faced him and asked him if he had been with any other girl. He shook his head and then said he had kissed a girl. *But no sex,* she said. *No, no sex,* he replied. *Not even touching?* she asked. *Nothing. Top or bottom. And you?* he'd asked. She had gone to the movies in Utica with a boy twice and held hands but nothing else. *Not even a kiss? Not even a kiss,* she had answered. *Are you angry that I kissed a girl? Is it like going back on my word?* She wanted to know if he loved the girl. He shook his head, the question impossible for him to consider. She said she wasn't angry and it was not like going back on his word. Immediately after that they were kissing, and his hands were lifting her sweatshirt and touching her breasts until she was telling him that they should leave the car. She had brought a blanket and they hurried through the woods until they had climbed higher into the hills and the air was dark and cool. They found a clearing where there was a bed of pine needles.

The sunlight barely penetrated the small clearing. She spread the blanket on the pine needles and lay down, seemingly melting from standing into lying down, so fluid and agile were her movements. He went to her and they again kissed desperately. He removed her sweatshirt and loved immediately the small breasts. He then removed her shorts and underwear and marveled at her magnificent hips and buttocks, which when she was dressed made him want her at all times. He parted her legs, amazed by her smallness and fragrance and the softness within, kissing her belly, licking her like she was the sugar from cotton candy. Instinctively, but aware of its acceptance from novels and films, he went to her, his tongue searching for her within the wiry hair until she was tearing at him and undressing him. He rose and undressed fully. She then stared at him in awe, astonished, later telling him that she wanted to die he was so beautiful and frightened at how his hardness could possibly fit into her. He had gone into her fiercely, both of them hurting from the violence at first until he was deeply into her and she was holding him and crying and he was spent. The entire time elapsed was no more than two minutes from the time he entered her. She cried some more and told him she loved him and he said he loved her and they held each other in the cool of the woods until he was once again erect within her. He then moved against her, this time more slowly, savoring the sensation until he was again spent and now he withdrew and lay next to her, touching her and smelling the blood on his fingers until she brought his hand back to her and he stroked her gently until she too was sated and they slept in each other's arms, the blanket wrapped around them. Later he would see that he had also bled, noting the diminutive cuts on the inner skin of the prepuce of his uncircumcised penis.

They woke up forty minutes later and they kissed again and again made love, this time the girl insisting on holding him in her mouth with clumsy desperation as he caressed her face and hair, watching the inverted cones of her breasts until he urged her atop him, his hands on her buttocks, which forever would hold his interest. She grasped him inside her and lay moving slowly with her own rhythm until the desperation became too great. She then drove against him gasping. Her cry startled the songbirds and they fluttered away as she sank against his chest, her mouth slack and her nostrils expanding like those of a racing mare. Shortly thereafter he again came and literally wanted to swallow all of her, devouring the thickness of her lips and tongue.

When they were dressing he looked at his watch and said that he ought to get back and start getting ready for the afternoon milking. He explained about the giving of light and she smiled at him, her Mongol eyes nearly closed but their dark blue color filled with delight. When they returned to the car they kissed some more and he wanted her again. She touched his jeans to see if he was aroused and said: *Oh, my, you are so passionate, Kenny Romero, I love you so much. We'll have to find a place to be together. The barn at the farm?* he'd asked. *Maybe,* she said. *But more private. I'll think of something. Do you really love me?* she asked, leaning against him. *Yes, I'm sure I do,* he said. *I love you, Claudia.*

*h*e'd left Claudia and had returned to the farm. He parked the pickup and went into the barn. At four Gabriel was already mixing the iodine solution and flushing out the pipes. He nodded at Gabriel and Carlos, went to the barn, saddled the horse and without changing rode out. Most of the cows had come in and were gathered outside the gate. He galloped into the meadow and rounded up part of the herd that had tarried and drove them back to their pens. Carlos held the gate open and then closed it. He again counted the sixty milk cows, but only nine dry cows and told Carlos to close the gate. He tied the horse's reins to a post and promised himself that he would ride out later and look for the missing cow. He told Gabriel that 571 was missing and once again reminded him that she was the first one on the birth list. Gabriel told him not to worry, that she would come in on her own when she was ready.

They continued working through the late afternoon, checking the temperature of the tanks, flushing the milk lines with steaming hot water and then disinfectants and then once again with hot water. By seven o'clock they were done and were sitting down to supper. At seven-thirty Kenny went outside and checked around the property looking for 571 but the cow was nowhere to be found. He checked all the gates to make sure she had not wandered out. When he was done he rode down to the stream and walked the horse alongside the water to make sure she hadn't gone there to birth the calf. As he had learned when things became uncomfortable and he could do nothing he tried thinking about something else and remembered his uncle Jerry telling him to make himself concentrate on other things. Jerry was the one who had brought him to St. Mark's High School to play ice hockey. His mother had protested, since they couldn't afford the tuition, but Jerry smiled and said she shouldn't worry, that he'd take care of it.

Jerry Boyle had attended St. Mark's and was an end on the football team. He was a defenseman for the Brooklyn ice hockey team that played in the Garden before New York Rover games. He was tall and had the same blond hair as his mother. His eyes were steel gray, his face wide and his nose crushed from boxing in the Golden Gloves. His hands were huge and his wrists thick. Jerry Boyle had been a policeman like his father but Kenny didn't know much about why they were not cops anymore. He asked him but his uncle made a motion as if he were washing his hands. *Finished,* he'd said. Both his uncle and his father were the kind of men you didn't ask the same question twice. They simply ignored you.

Jerry was his mother's older brother and Frances Boyle Romero spoke about him worshipfully. Five years older than she was, he was her hero, and no one could say anything wrong about him. He had taught her to swim and skip rope and not be afraid of monkey bars by telling her she was his monkey, which made her laugh. He was the one who had encouraged her to go to college and always protected her and her sister, Maureen, and their brother, Michael, who was a bit slow. She was the baby.

He remembered being seven years old when Jerry suggested to his father that he let him play ice hockey because he seemed like a talented athlete. His father said that baseball was good enough for his son and his uncle said that maybe Tommy Romero was afraid his son wouldn't be any good at white sports. He wanted to know what his uncle meant, but he said: *Never mind. Sorry, Tommy.* His father had ignored the apology. Jerry Boyle played for the Police Department ice hockey team and they'd gone to Madison Square Garden for the game against the firemen later that month.

He sat behind the bench with his father and his cousin, Christopher, who was Uncle Jerry's youngest son and his same age. Patrick, who was three years older, was already playing and sat with another boy whose father was also on the team. The game was billed: New York's Finest vs. New York's Bravest. He was dazzled by the speed of the game and the bright colors of the uniforms: the firemen in red and the policemen in blue. He loved the gleaming white surface of the ice with its circles and lines and wanted to be skating near the pipes and nets of the goals, touching everything and hearing the slashing and hissing of the skates on the ice as they stopped and sprayed snow. The popping sound as the puck was passed or shot was loud. The most fun was when someone scored and the other members of the team who were on the ice raised their sticks. Each time the policemen scored he raised his arms as if he were holding a stick. After the game, in the corridors below the stands, he and his father went to the locker room and in front of his uncle, who was dressed and showered and was placing his equipment into his hockey bag, he'd said he wanted to play ice hockey. His father and uncle laughed and nodded and his uncle asked Christopher if he wanted to play and his cousin said he also wanted to play.

The following weekend they went to Gerry Cosby's Sporting Goods store at Madison Square Garden and they bought skates and everything: helmets, shoulder pads, elbow pads, shin pads, pants with suspenders, gloves, jockstraps and cups, and sticks with a couple of rolls of tape. He was right handed but he held the stick like a lefty, which meant from the right side. He was a righty who shot right. But in baseball he could switch hit, so that wasn't so strange. That's when he began playing ice hockey, but his uncle stopped playing for the NYPD team and maybe that's when his father and uncle quit being cops.

One time his uncle and father came to their apartment and they were both dressed raggedy, his sister Rose said. His uncle was a hippie with bell-bottom pants and a bandanna keeping his long hair from falling over his eyes. His father looked like a junkie and had blue marks on his arms and they were talking like the black kids in school, which frightened his mother, and she took all of the children into the living room and said his uncle and father had to talk. A short time later Jerry left the apartment and his mother and father went into the bedroom and argued and his mother said why was he coming in the house with him and Jerry dressed like that and scaring the children. His father said something had gone down and then his mother was crying and after a while they were quiet and an hour later they came out of the room and she wasn't crying anymore.

When his mother gave birth to his little sister Diana,

Peggy, Katherine and Rose had to stay at his grandmother's and he'd gone to stay with Uncle Jerry and his aunt Sheila. He slept in bunk beds with his cousin Christopher, who said he could sleep on the bottom bunk, but he said it was okay because he wanted to climb the ladder. His uncle and his wife hardly ever spoke. They were totally different from his parents, who talked to each other all the time about books and movies and things they'd heard on TV and the radio. Sometimes in front of his sisters and his brother, they spoke privately in big word English they didn't understand. Other times they spoke in Spanish. But his uncle and his wife hardly ever spoke.

He once asked Jerry Boyle what it was like being a policeman. His uncle shrugged his shoulders and said it was just a job. Did he like it? Sure. Maybe he'd be a cop like his father and him. *No, you should go to college and play hockey and then go to law school and earn good money,* Jerry Boyle said. Other than that, his uncle was a mystery. After they stopped being cops his father got a truck and started moving people. They stayed in their apartment in Brooklyn. His uncle and his family moved to Long Island, where they had a big house and a big boat and he was a fisherman. They had a smaller house on the sand dunes near the beach. Sometimes during the summers his father drove all of them out there and they swam and had cookouts and got to go barefoot all weekend.

*A*t eight o'clock, when the sun had set and the temperature had dropped considerably, Kenny went into the TV room, where Gabriel and Carlos were watching a program on sharks with Gabriel translating for the boy. Kenny waited until Gabriel finished speaking and then said that 571 was lost. Gabriel said that sometimes cows went away to have their calves and maybe she had done that. Shouldn't they go and find her? No, it was fine. She was the smallest of the heifers. *Very little chance of dystocia,* he said. *Dystocia?* he asked. Gabriel explained that in larger cows the calf would get stuck or presented a shoulder delivery and then they'd have to assist the cow. He explained that 571 would calf small. Maybe forty pounds, maybe fifty, but no more. The other cows could go as high as seventy-five pounds a calf, the male calves born heavier. *Anyway, she's not due until next week. She'll return in a few days and the calf will be fine, Kenny. You shouldn't worry. Are you sure?* he asked. *Yes, please don't worry,* Gabriel said. *Suppose she needs help, Gabriel? She'll be fine, Kenny. They can handle things on their own. And bears? They don't come down this low. What about coyotes? A cow's too big for them,* Gabriel had said.

He'd left the room and sat out on the porch listening to the crickets, every once in a while sensing the shadow of a bat as it flew close hunting insects. He watched the stars and the quarter moon rising in the sky and thought about Claudia, still amazed at how beautiful she was and how much they enjoyed each other. He would marry her and then they wouldn't have to worry about keeping everything a secret. They wouldn't have children right away but go to college. And then they would have children, lots of them like his mother and father. But Claudia was so little down there. How could the baby come out?

He couldn't imagine what giving birth was like and he thought about his mother coming home with Peggy that first time when he was two years old. He couldn't recall anything, but his grandmother said that she had given him a bath and dressed him in a new striped shirt and jumper overalls with snap-on buttons on the inside of the leg so mothers could change their diapers without taking off their pants, which Mary Margaret had worn after him and then the other girls, each time the jumper becoming more frayed and being patched until now when Tommy Jr. wore it, it was thin but he had new little sneakers and new tiny polo shirts, which his sisters borrowed to dress their big dolls.

His mother had given birth to the six of them and she still looked pretty and bright except when she cried and then he asked her what was the matter and she would say nothing and when he insisted she said she missed their father and he'd reassure her that he'd be back soon. After he stopped being a policeman he'd be gone three and four days at a time and when he returned he brought them little presents each time and they'd ask where he'd been and he'd mention places and show them on the map and teach them geography: Michigan and Wisconsin were next to each other and next to that was Minnesota and beyond that the Dakotas. He'd ask if he had driven there and he said he had. *In the truck, Daddy? Yes, in the truck. By yourself? Yes, by myself.* And then they'd eat together and each one, at their mother's urging, got to tell what they were doing in school and what they were reading. *Tell Daddy about the diorama, Mary Margaret. Tommy, it was just like the ones at the Museum of Natural History,* his mother would say. And then he and the other children would go to bed and he could hear them talking softly to each other in the living room and then all the lights would go out and his father and mother went to their bedroom and he couldn't imagine what it would be like to see his mother without clothes, which his father could.

Does Daddy love you, Mommy? Yes, Daddy loves all of us. But does he love you in a special way? Never you mind, Kenneth Romero, you wise guy. Go and finish your homework. We're not paying good money for you to attend Catholic school for nothing. Scoot, nosy. He does, he does! he would chide his mother. *Daddy loves you in a special way.* And she would smile, shake her finger at him and swat his behind, which made him laugh and go skipping out of the kitchen. She was never angry with them and when they did something really bad, like the time that he poured the nearly full five-pound bag of Domino Sugar on the dinette table to see if he could make a mountain, she would say things like: *naughty, naughty, and shame on you.* He was only six but she told him to go to his room and kneel. *Mary Margaret Peggy,* which is what he called his sister for a while, said that their mother cried and scooped the sugar back into the yellow bag with a spoon and then her hand and told Peggy that they were not rich as she swept into a dustpan the sugar on the floor, nearly a half a cup, that had fallen in a straight line through the division of the dinette table. She debated whether to keep it for her own tea and finally forced herself to flush the sugar down the drain in the kitchen sink.

When she was finished she came into the room where he slept. He on the top bunk bed, Mary Margaret on the bottom, Rose in his old baby bed with the slats halfway to the bedstead, and Katherine in her crib. He was proud that he could look over his sisters and keep them safe with his presence. His mother knelt next to him and they both said the Our Father together. She told him that he ought to ask God for forgiveness and said that he shouldn't do such things because they hurt her and she loved him so much. *I'm sorry, Mommy,* he'd said. *I'll be good. Please don't cry.* And she hugged him to her, kissed his cheeks and he could smell how good and beautiful she was, and he truly loved her.

Sometimes he asked her if she would become a teacher again and she said that her children were her pupils now and one by one she taught them to read before they were in kindergarten and she read to them at night, even to Tommy Jr. now. She had read to them from big books, starting them and reading a few chapters and then they had to read the book on their own. She had once read to them from Tom Sawyer but warned them that they shouldn't use the word "nigger." *Why not, Mommy? It's not a good word,* she'd said. *It makes Negroes feel bad. It's an ugly word. But they use it, Mommy,* Peggy protested. *They, who?* she'd asked. *Negroes, Mommy. What are Negroes?* Rose had once asked and Peggy explained that Negroes were dark people. This was before Katherine and Diana and Tommy Jr. were born and they sat on the linoleum floor of their living room and Rose asked if Grandpa Pablo was a Negro and Peggy said he was Spanish and Spanish people were not the same as Negroes. *But he's dark,* Rose insisted and Mary Margaret said it wasn't the same and he'd waited until everyone had spoken, and quietly, with dignity like his father, said that Pablo Romero, their grandfather, was Puerto Rican. His mother had smiled and said that he was correct. Rose asked about Puerto Rico and their mother said that the following morning after they walked to school with Kenny and Mary Margaret, which is what she always called his sister, even though Grandma Mary called her Pegeen, and he and his father, Peggy, she would take Rose to the library. They would see if they had books on Puerto Rico, which it turned out they did not, since they lived in Brooklyn and there were not many Spanish people in their neighborhood and even fewer Puerto Ricans, which were a special kind of Spanish people that nobody cared about because they spoke English, his grandmother Rosa said, and that's why they had to learn Spanish. Charlie Peccorino, his friend, said that Puerto Ricans were always loud and they were criminals, mostly, and he had come home and told his mother and she said it was not true because look at his father who was a policeman and worked hard, and his grandfather who was a carpenter, and they were not criminals. But then his father was not a cop and he didn't know why. He sensed that something had happened, but he didn't know what.

The following week his mother called their aunt Evelyn, his father's younger sister, and even though Evelyn didn't like her, she explained that the children wanted to learn about Puerto Rico and did she know of a library where she could find books about the Island. Their aunt said it was about time they started learning about Puerto Rico and how come she had been in college four years and hadn't learned anything about Puerto Rico? At one point during the conversation someone at Evelyn's house had asked who Evelyn was talking to and his mother heard Evelyn say: *la rubia boba.* Evelyn knew his mother understood Spanish and the words "dopey blonde" would hurt her. She never told anyone but their cousin Nilsa told Peggy years later and Peggy told him. He could hear his aunt talking loudly on the telephone, berating his mother. She eventually thanked his aunt and hung up the telephone. There were tears in her eyes. He asked if his aunt had been angry. His mother said that his aunt wasn't feeling well.

She began looking through the telephone directory for Spanish bookstores. Frances Ann Boyle, now Fran Romero, a good Irish girl, blonde and ruddy, with shy blue eyes went with her little dark Puerto Rican daughter, Rose, to Spanish bookstores on 14th Street, Lectorum and Macondo, and was shown some books. They came back with two books that he couldn't remember. She translated the writing for them and read to them in Spanish. They only had Jell-O for dessert for a month and it didn't have fruit cocktail in it because the books were too expensive. She read to Rose and Rose said she didn't understand and she said it was okay and taught all of them to say things in Spanish. Their grandmother Rosa was very proud that they spoke Spanish and gave them coconut candy that was crunchy. She let them take puffs from her cigar, which made them laugh but worried his mother.

*A*t nine o'clock the lights in the house began going off. The old man was already in bed. When Kenny saw Gabriel he began to say something but Gabriel said things would be fine. The feeling that something was wrong wouldn't leave him. He nodded, but Cow 571 worried him and he wanted to say something but nothing came to him and he went to his room, took off his shoes and said his prayers. He asked God to protect the cow. He felt foolish but he prayed anyway and asked Saint Francis, who loved animals, to intercede on the cow's behalf and help God keep the cow safe. He read from Lord of the Rings and wondered if there were good and evil animals. He knew about good and evil people and although he couldn't tell easily if people were good or bad, he wondered if he could learn to recognize them like his father and uncle said they could. Maybe it was a special thing that policemen learned. But he knew what right and wrong meant to him and he guarded against doing bad things.

His father wouldn't talk about why he and his uncle were no longer policemen. He never raised his voice or got angry. One time, though, a man in a furniture store had spoken harshly to his mother while they were shopping for bunk beds for Peggy and him so that Rose could have Peggy's bed, moving from the crib to make room for Katherine. His father gave his mother Rose to hold. After his mother took his sister and placed her in the stroller his father went over and asked the man if he could speak to him privately. They'd gone to the back of the store and he held his mother's hand and Mary Margaret clutched at her dress, her head tucked beneath the large pregnant belly that would soon be Katherine. The man came back looking pale and frightened and apologized to his mother and offered her a discount on the bunk beds. His father said they would pay the price on the tag and they could deliver the beds. The man said of course and his father thanked him.

In the car, with Peggy and him sitting in the backseat, his mother holding Rose, who had fallen asleep, she asked him what he had said to the man. His father shook his head and after a while said that he had explained that the man ought to treat his customers more politely. *Was that all, Tommy?* she'd asked him. *Yes, Fran, that was all,* he'd said. *Did you threaten him, Tommy? No, I didn't, Fran,* he said. *It was fine. He understood my suggestion. They'll deliver the beds on Friday. Make sure it's the furniture store and not some nut ringing our doorbell. I'll be careful, Tommy,* she said. *Don't worry, please. All right,* he'd said and asked them if they wanted to go to McDonald's or Burger King. *McDonald's,* he and Peggy shouted and they'd gone and had gotten the children's meal and laughed a lot while they ate and then his father drove them to Coney Island and they walked around and their father bought them soft custard ice cream. They strolled on the boardwalk with his father holding his mother's hand while he pushed the stroller with Rose. He held Peggy's hand because she was his little sister. They walked behind their parents, listening to the summer crowd and talking about the Cyclone ride and the Ferris wheel and the bright lights that made everything like a circus. Before they left, his father bought them one big cotton candy. His mother held it and Peggy, Rose and he ate from it, all three of them around the blue spun sugar and he and Peggy licked the sugar from each other's face, which made both of them laugh until their father told them to stop and they did. He was sure his father hadn't threatened the man at the furniture store.

Sometimes his father came home early and they went to the playground and played catch with a solid rubber ball and the tiny baseball glove he'd gotten the previous Christmas from Grandpa Pablo. His father pitched to him and he'd hit the ball with the small wooden bat that had come wrapped in bright Christmas paper for Three Kings Day at his grandparents' house. He hit the ball all the way to the water fountain. One time he hit the ball beyond the water fountain and over the fence out to the street. The ball bounced into the traffic and was carried away somewhere toward Bensonhurst. He said he was sorry he had lost the ball. His father was laughing and tousled his head and told him they could get another ball. At dinner that night with his mother nursing Katherine at the dinner table, her full breast shining like a moon, he thought, his father said that he'd hit the ball over the fence. *That was some shot, Fran. Maybe two hundred feet, honey. He's only seven years old. Look at him. He's like a little Mickey Mantle. Do you want to learn to hit lefty, Kenny? Sure, Daddy,* he'd said. *Look at him, Fran. A little harp Mickey Mantle. A little Mick. Please don't use those words, Tommy,* his mother had said. *I'm sorry, honey,* his father had said. *What's a harp, Daddy?* Peggy asked. His father said that a harp was a musical instrument played by angels in Heaven and by beautiful girls like her and the next day he brought home an empty bottle of Harp Beer and showed them all and explained that this was an Irish harp, and Peggy said she'd like to play an Irish harp and his father said he'd see what he could do.

Peggy never learned to play the harp but she learned how to fiddle and step-dance and then she learned flamenco and her cousins Iris and Nilsa, who were seventeen and eighteen, taught her how to dance salsa and they now went places and danced and looked like three Puerto Rican girls on the prowl, their black lipstick and hair in French twists, black and slick, and their tight dresses alluring and not at all like Catholic girls, which they were on Sundays when they went to Mass and knelt with their rosaries in hand, dressed demurely and properly. The girls learned to dance and play musical instruments and he learned about sports even though he wanted to learn an instrument as well. Eventually he got a harmonica and taught himself how to play and went to his friend Bobby Grimes, whose father was a saxophone player and taught him to play blues, playing the tunes on the saxophone and he following him with his harmonica and Bobby on drums down in the basement of their house in Harlem, which was only a few more subway stops from St. Mark's, walking in Harlem with Bobby and never afraid even though he looked like a white kid, everybody said, which made him feel separate from his father and Grandpa Pablo, which he didn't like.

Later that spring after he hit the ball into the streets his father and Tony, another cop, brought him to a Little League field in another neighborhood in Brooklyn. The field had fences around the outfield. It had actual dugouts and a scoreboard. Tony spoke to a heavyset Italian man who was the coach. The man introduced himself and said he looked like a ballplayer and handed him a bat. There were other kids older than he was and the coach, who was Mr. Russo, waved his hand and they went out into the field. He stood at home plate and the man pitched to him and he missed the ball the first two times before he hit a line drive that rolled to the fence between left and centerfield. He didn't hit the ball over the fence but the man nodded approvingly as he hit line drives all over the field, the ball going over the other boys' heads, loving the sound the bat made on the ball. Later they used metal bats but he didn't like the sound. Mr. Russo waved to the boy at shortstop and asked him to go into the outfield. He took the glove from his father and went to the place where the other boy had been. Mr. Russo hit grounders at him at shortstop that he fielded and threw to the boy at first base. He told him to move to centerfield and he hit him flyballs, which he caught and threw back in. The man nodded approvingly and said he should come to practice the following Saturday.

He went to practice for the next three Saturdays and then he was given a uniform with the number eight on it and his father said that was Yogi's number. He asked his father who Yogi was. He was a great Yankee catcher, his father had said. But I'm not a catcher, he'd said. That's all right, his father had said. You'll be fine. When they got home his father went to the closet and brought out two shoe boxes of baseball cards and after going through them he showed him a Yogi Berra card. They sat on the floor and his father placed the cards as if they were players on a diamond with Yogi Berra behind the plate and Tony Kubeck at shortstop, Billy Martin at second base and Mickey Mantle in center field. His father told him stories and said that when he was a boy his father, Grandpa Pablo, took him to all the ballparks: the Polo Grounds in Manhattan where the Giants played, Ebbets Field in Brooklyn, the home of the Dodgers, and Yankee Stadium in the Bronx. He liked riding the subways with his father, especially when they went to see the Yankees. Once at Grandpa Pablo's he had seen photos of the two of them. They had on newsboy caps, Grandpa Pablo and his father. And now he had disappointed his father by not wanting to play baseball.

$\mathcal{W}$hen he could no longer concentrate on the book Kenny turned off the light on the nightstand. He wrapped himself up against the cold, thinking about his life and Claudia and how quiet the night was but he couldn't sleep thinking about the cow alone and perhaps needing help. There was something wrong but he couldn't tell what it was. Maybe he should be more trusting and listen to adults. He always listened to his coaches and his parents most of the time, but there was something wrong. It felt the same way as when he sensed that Peggy was in trouble coming home from dance class and he had rushed to the subway station. She was surrounded by a group of Italian girls who were calling her a little spic bitch and he'd gone to her, taken her bookbag and stared at the girls, not saying anything until they were laughing nervously and saying she was lucky she had a cute Irish boyfriend and they went away laughing and Peggy said she wanted to kill them. It was the first time he'd seen Peggy really angry. She reminded him of their uncle Jerry. Peggy was very quiet and polite for about twelve years and then when she hit thirteen she changed.

She was now like both of their grandmothers wrapped into one. She could fight better than some boys and in junior high school had broken a boy's nose, explaining that the boy had gotten fresh with her and tried to touch her breasts. *She just hauled off and punched him,* Pauline O'Connor said. Pauline's father was a fireman; she lived down the street and liked him. She had black hair like Peggy but had blue eyes and said that she and Peggy were black Irish and were both good step dancers and were learning to speak Irish. *Punched him right in the face, the fuck,* Pauline said. And nobody touched their little sisters because Peggy went up to them and yelled that she was going to break their face if they even looked funny at Rose or Katherine and then Diana. In spite of her toughness he always felt protective of Peggy, sensing she was vulnerable in spite of her hard exterior. And that's how he felt now. Like the cow was in danger and he ought to do something in spite of what Gabriel had said.

He often thought about his grandmother and wondered if Mary Boyle missed his grandfather Martin, who had died the previous year of cancer, unable to work anymore at the butcher shop he hoped someday to own. He asked her if she did but she shook her head and said that Grandpa Boyle was in Heaven amusing the angels with his laughter and blarney, telling them jokes and making them blush when he asked them where he could get a pint. She had wiry, reddish blond hair now graying and always uncombed and unruly, which she tamed when going out by wearing a kerchief. She rouged her cheeks and wore lipstick and smoked cigarettes, which she fanned away from her grandchildren and toward open windows, the lipstick-smeared butts piling up in a large ashtray that was seemingly never emptied. She had an enormous bosom against which she held him fast when she hugged him, making him feel always protected. She laughed easily and everything about her was light, as if nothing bothered her.

She talked about everything and like her husband told outrageously long stories. She was born in the South Bronx where they lived in an apartment on the fourth floor of a six-floor tenement on 141st Street between Cypress and St. Ann's Avenue across the street from the Emerald Store. There was a German Lutheran church up the street where it was rumored Nazis came to plan attacks on New York. There were Irish who sided with the Germans but most of them did so because England held part of Ireland captive for the sake of the Protestants in the North, she told him. She detested war and violence but more than war and violence she abhorred injustice and had she been a man she would have joined the Irish Republican Army and fought against the British, which to him sounded contradictory.

What was it like when you were a girl, Grandma? he'd asked when he was ten years old and he and Peggy had gone over to stay with her while Diana was being born because her mother had complications and had to go into the hospital for a week. Rose and Katherine had gone to stay with Grandpa Pablo and Grandma Rose and returned saying things like *gringos hijos de puta* and *yankis desgraciados,* which made their father laugh but which appalled his mother, who decried all sorts of prejudice. When Rose's attack on the American Way of Life was recounted to Mary Boyle, she laughed and said that the girl showed real promise and she wished the girl's mother, Frances Ann Boyle, had a bit more fire in her heart and would quit pretending that life was peace and love like she was a flower child, which she had never been, instead keeping to the straight and narrow, which was good only up to a point because life was not a bowl of cherries, which when they asked, she explained was a song and sang a little bit of it.

But what were you like as a girl? Mary Margaret asked. *Pegeen, you don't want to know,* she'd say and explain that she still had knots on her head where her mother had struck her with a big wooden hairbrush because of her craziness. *But what did you do, Grandma?* Peggy had pestered her. His grandmother would explain that she was crazy and wanted to play roller hockey and she climbed fences and stole coal from the coal yard down by the railroad tracks near the East River. She said she painted her face black like a nigger, hid behind the stairs of the buildings and scared other girls and even younger boys. Peggy said her mother had told her that was a bad word. *What word?* she asked, puzzled. *The one you said about painting your face black. Mommy said not to repeat it.* Their grandmother nodded and said their mother was absolutely correct and they shouldn't use such a word. She went on and said she played pranks on boys and once squirted her fountain pen in a boy's face who was making fun of her because she had big boobs even though she was only twelve. The boy began yelling that she had blinded him, which earned her a good beating from the nuns at school and a worse administration of justice when she came home and handed her mother the note explaining what she had done and how she was to be suspended for a week.

Her mother had fallen on her with all the fury of a dozen banshees. *What are banshees, Grandma?* he'd asked. *Oh, they're awful beings who yell and scream and are supposed to mean that someone is going to die but they're full of beans. Full of beans, Grandma? Yes, they're bean fairies. And that was what my mother was like, wailing that I had the devil in me and hitting me with her brush and me yelling back to stop and telling her she was crazy, which you should never do because you should always respect your parents. But I was a crazy girl, which the two of you should not be.*

And then what? he asked. *Oh, it would go on like that for a while and my two brothers cringing and my sister, Rosemary, snickering with her evil little grin and my mother hitting, and talking incomprehensibly in Gaelic, which everyone now calls Irish like the poverty is going to disappear because they give the language a new name, but the poverty remains there like a specter, always watching the misery and laughing, but hitting and cursing me to eternal damnation and farting awful cabbage stenches that smelled worse than when it was cooking because it had gone through her system, which manufactured bitterness twenty-four hours a day, may she rest in peace. That's how I knew she was in league with the banshees and was a bean fairy,* she'd say, talking like that and neither he nor Peggy understanding words like "malevolent" and wanting to ask but becoming lost in the effect of her words that, like a flight of roof pigeons, flew from her so that you didn't concentrate on individual birds but how they traveled together like they were connected, turning one way and then the other against the brilliant sky and the tall buildings like they had one soul.

Did you like dancing, Grandma? Peggy had asked. *Oh, I loved dancing,* she'd said, *but not damhsa and ports,* she added. *What, Grandma Mary? Oh, that means dances and jigs. What they're teaching you now, Pegeen. No step dancing for this girl. I was Mary Katherine Grady and I was a lost girl. I liked real dancing. We lived in the Bronx but then moved to the Upper West Side of Manhattan, which was all Irish, and we loved dancing the jitterbug, so by the time I was fifteen years old, Christine Flaherty, Peggy Killigan, who was a terrific singer, and this Jewish girl, Miriam Kantrowitz, who played the piano, and I would dress up and I'd tell my mother we were going to the movies but instead we rode the subway up to 125th Street and met boys and we went to Harlem to the Savoy Ballroom and other dance halls and clubs like Small's Paradise to listen to jazz. We learned all the steps from colored boys, who talked in a strange way that we liked. Oh, we were horrible girls and hated coming home early. When was that, Grandma? Oh, I don't know. Maybe 1927 or 28. But we loved jazz.*

They asked what jazz was and she played thick 78s on her old Victrola and taught them to jitterbug to Count Basie and Benny Goodman. He liked best Duke Ellington's "Take the A Train," which had a girl named Betty Roché singing words like *badebop* and *shadubia*. He asked what the girl was singing and Peggy said the girl was singing in Negro. His grandmother laughed and said it was called scatting. They looked at each other and then asked why and his grandmother standing in the middle of the floor shimmied, fluttered her fingers, waved her hands and said scat, scat, scat like she was waving someone away.

And when did you meet Grandpa? Peggy had asked. *Oh, that's a long story,* she'd say and ask them if they were hungry and they always were but it was a way for her not to talk about Martin Boyle. She gave them bologna sandwiches with mayonnaise on Wonder Bread and big mugs of root beer.

It was so obvious she had a secret and would never tell what it was. They all had secrets. Every one of them had secrets and now he had a secret and it was about Claudia and in his bed he wished that she was next to him and he was stroking her smooth, taut body instead of himself. He was erect but he fought against the other sin, which was even more abominable because it led to insanity and abuses more grievous like alcohol and drugs. That's how it started. *In corpore sano, mens sana.* If he was to participate in athletics he must remain clean, which meant no cigarettes or alcohol, and definitely no self-abuse, Father Mahoney, who was the athletic director, had told all of them. He and Claudia had passed a Catholic church in Utica and he'd wanted to go inside and confess his sins but he changed his mind and they went ahead to the motel room. He didn't want to think about Claudia. He thought instead of the cow lying in a field, waiting for the calf to come, but nothing could make him fall asleep and in the darkness he shook his head and wondered what he ought to do.

preparations

*His eyes were, in fact, a greenish blue,
which made his grandmother Mary Katherine
Boyle, née Grady, a generally unsentimental
woman, often say wistfully that they were
Irish eyes, the way Kenny smiled easily under
the most difficult situations.*

K ENNY WAS NOT her first grandchild, but none of
her other fourteen grandchildren could displace him
in her heart. Not Jerry's four, not Fran's other five,
not Maureen's three, nor Mike's twin girls, who were the
youngest. Although she couldn't say why, Kenny was her favorite like Jerry was her favorite child even though she loved
them all and would never admit her preference. She thought
this as she waited for the water to boil, the radio provid-
ing news and weather. She thought again about her visit to
the doctor. There was no pain, just the small lumps near her
underarms.

The tests had come back positive and the doctor said that

they would have to operate, the sooner the better, and both had to be removed. Thank goodness, she had joked, they've always been a hindrance and lately I've been thinking of ordering a wheelbarrow, since they've been dropping increasingly lower each year since I turned thirty-five. Derisively, she sang in a finely brogued alto voice: *In Dublin's fair city, where girls are so pretty, 'twas there I first saw sweet Molly Malone, as she wheeled her barrow through streets broad and narrow, crying cockletits and musselboobs alive alive-o.*

The doctor laughed with embarrassment and said that the best cure for illness was laughter. She said that perhaps she ought to get a second opinion but was certain that they would say she still had the figure of a Gibson girl. Pre-op, of course. Post-op she'd look like Olive Oyl with nice hips. *How long do I have to live, Doctor?* she'd asked, which was the obvious question. The doctor said: *If we operate soon and the disease doesn't spread you'll have a long life because you're an otherwise healthy woman. Does Medicaid cover falsies, Doctor?* she joked. He had laughed again and said that the social worker would discuss all of that with her and she should go home and talk over the issue with her loved ones.

She had come home and rather than cry she had raged and wondered with whom she should discuss this latest disaster of her wretched life. Which of her daughters should she discuss this with? Neither of them was secure enough and each had children to raise and didn't need the aggravation. There was no sense complicating their lives. What would Martin have said? *Maybe you'll sprout wings because never has there been a more saintly woman and may God not strike me dead for telling such lies. Ha!* she'd say and they would both laugh and figure out what they would do. She had never truly liked Martin but had grown to appreciate his good humor when he wasn't bedeviled by his doubts. He was a passable companion and other than his failings, a good man. But he was gone now and there was no one she could talk to. She was alone and she'd have to walk these next long steps by herself. The family was in turmoil and she had no idea what would happen. She didn't believe Jerry would stay in his marriage much longer and heard from her cousin, Moira Hanratty, who lived near him, that he was seeing a Spanish girl who was working for a dentist in West Islip, out in Long Island where he lived. They were a horny bunch, these Spanish. But who the hell was she to talk. Frances hadn't called in a week, which meant that, as had been the case on other occasions, she was expecting again. Why didn't she protect herself? Damn being Catholic! A vasectomy was not a sin. They were hell-bent on repopulating the earth with Mickoricans, as Jerry and Tommy called the children. She had called Frances and asked her point blank if she was pregnant again. Frances had laughed and said of course she wasn't. *Why haven't you called me? Oh, just busy with the kids, Ma. I'm sorry.* That had been one piece of good news. Maybe Jerry wanted to make Mickoricans too. Everything had turned upside down and now word had come about Kenny. How had Henri and Gabriel let this happen?

*h*e had been unable to sleep and rose, pulled on his jeans, put on his socks and work boots and began planning how he would go looking for the cow, first in the meadow and then maybe the edge of the woods if it was necessary, hoping it had already birthed the calf so that he could bring them back. He pulled on a sweater over his T-shirt and grabbing his mackinaw lumber jacket and a wool cap from a hook he stepped out of his room and closed the door.

Before he had taken three steps Kenny returned to the room, retrieved his hunting knife in its sheath and an old Boy

Scout compass and thinking of having to go into the woods, tried recalling Scout skills about tying knots and making fires. He went back down the hall past Gabriel's room and into the den, where the rifles were kept. He undid his belt, pulled it out from the first loop of his jeans, placed the belt through the sheath holder, into the loop, and secured once again the big cowboy buckle Gabriel had given him.

*h*e was an angel and if she went to Heaven she wanted all the angels to look exactly like Kenny. She knew that there were probably ugly angels and there had to be Negro angels, but not very likely Puerto Rican ones because they would be dancing somewhere in Purgatory trying to convince wayward Irish Catholic girl angels to take off their robes and fold their wings so they could lie down on some fluffy clouds in the Caribbean. But she wanted the angels to look like Kenny because that is what he had always been. It was a horrible thing that had befallen him and she shuddered again at the thought of his ordeal. And here she was thinking of angels as if she had already given up hope. They had finally transferred him to New York. She was there when he was born, and at his baptismal and first communion, and at each of his graduations, all joys, and now for the first time, sorrow. Fran was near collapse with worry. What had gotten into him?

He had been a perfect baby, hardly ever cried and always looked up at his mother with soulful eyes as if he were thanking her for feeding him. *Isn't he beautiful, Mom?* Frances had asked. *He's a wee bit thin, Frances. Are you feeding him enough? I know you're not me,* she'd say, propping up her bosom, *but you should be more generous. Oh, Mom,* Fran would say and then ask her if she smelled him. *Oh, he'll let you know when he needs changing, the little stinker. You'll know, all right.*

But his skinny legs filled out and before he was six months

old he was a fat, smiling baby with big blue eyes and margarine-colored hair, thick and curly, and never had she seen such a perfect baby. And when he started walking and talking he was always offering others his food or candy. Always thinking of other people. Two years later, when Pegeen was born, she expected to see another tow-headed baby but this one had hair the color of coal and eyes a shade darker. She was her mother, Frances, all over again: a smart girl in school but a large dummy running around inside of her until she was suddenly transformed into a devil teen.

Jerry gave his little sister a boy's nickname, always calling her Frankie because maybe he wanted her to be a little tougher. When they brought Pegeen from the hospital Fran had sat down in a chair with Tommy standing proudly behind her. *A little girl, Ma,* he'd said to her. *Aye, a wee lass,* she'd replied. Wishing Kenny to welcome his little sister properly, she had bathed and dressed Kenny and made him a bottle that he was working on and was halfway through when his mother pulled back the blanket to reveal his little sister, Mary Margaret Romero, sleeping and fragile. *This is your baby sister, Mary Margaret,* his mother had said. Kenny had taken the bottle out of his mouth and brought it forward against his sister's lips. *Baby's hungry,* he'd said sweetly. They had all laughed and shook their heads, not believing the boy's generosity. That is how Kenny had remained his entire life. *Later, sweetheart,* Fran had said and touched Kenny's face. *We'll feed the baby later. She's sleeping now. Baby's sleeping,* he'd said and returned the bottle to his mouth.

Who does he get that from? his father had asked. *Certainly not my side of the family. Oh, maybe my grandfather Grady,* she'd said. *He and my grandmother eventually came from Ireland and lived with my parents and he worked day and night to help us out,* she'd said. *He was a farmer and had no other skills and could barely read and write and talked more Gaelic than he did English. Irish, Mom,* Frances would say, being she was a college graduate and had learned such distinctions. *Yes, Irish,* she'd said. *But he had no skills except cutting sod, tilling land, milking cows and other handy things like butchering animals. Here he swept out saloons and mopped them at night. He eventually got a job with the Sanitation Department sweeping up horse droppings into a barrel with a big tough broom and a shovel and was very proud to come home with a pay envelope, but he was kind and thoughtful and he always gave of himself and asked nothing in return, thanking God and being obedient to other's wishes. He was a big, craggy-faced, troll-looking man who was not very bright.* Kenny was like that except that he was bright in school matters, getting stars on all his notebooks because he had a writing hand like his mother's, delicate and neat, the letters penned exactly as one sees painted on a blackboard. That is how Kenny made her feel. Kenny's looks were delicate, feminine almost. God, he was a handsome young man.

When his mother held him at his baptismal he didn't cry and Father Marciano said that he had actually smiled up at him. *Oh, he's a little gentleman, Father,* she'd said. Except it was likely that the boy had gas, she'd said when they returned to the house and were preparing lunch. *Oh, Mother,* Fran said, refuting her theory. *Well, at least he waited until we were out of the church to let his gas,* she'd said. *It was a pity he couldn't go then and had to wait until we were back in the car. He sounded as loud as his grandfather, who had no compunctions where he farted. Mom, that is so crude,* Fran said prissily, and she responded that farting was a God-given right of the poor and Fran finally laughed raucously and said some dopey college thing like: *flatulence along class lines.* She said she had always wondered if Karl Marx had written about this, to which she'd said that she hadn't heard about this new Marx brother. Was he given up for adoption? *Oh, Mom, you're so silly. Please don't make tuna fish salad. Tommy doesn't like it.* Fran took Kenny to the bedroom and she'd gone off into the kitchen to make Campbell's tomato soup with milk, and cheese and bologna sandwiches on Wonder Bread, which she had been making all her life, it seemed. For the first time in many years she thought about her life as a young girl and her life away from home, interned, cloistered and silent.

*K*enny put on his mackinaw, found a flashlight, took down a 30-30 Winchester carbine from the cabinet, searched for ammunition but only found six cartridges, checked their caliber, dropped them into the right-hand pocket of his jacket, went into the kitchen and out the door, only to return seconds later and retrieve twenty or so self-igniting wooden matches, which he dropped into the left-hand pocket of the jacket and went back outside.

*S*he remembered the countryside and the snow falling endlessly as she prayed at all hours of the day. No one spoke except the Mother Superior and some of the nuns who were on the staff, but none of the novices could speak even among themselves except when they attended class. She had been such a crazy girl and no matter what anyone said, family, teachers or priests, she loved life and wanted to dance and carry on and feel boys' hardness in her, even though nothing had happened before she went to the convent and she was twenty, the aching down there awful so that in her senior year in high school she had let a handsome colored boy going to Columbia University touch her in Riverside Park where they went after going to a jazz party in Harlem with Christine Flaherty. He'd talked sweetly to her and recited poetry that was beautiful. He had wanted to put his small thing in her but she asked him to stop and he had. Coming home she had hurried up the stairs of the elevated train at 125th Street. She raced up, placed the nickel in the slot and stepped through the turnstile and ran to make the train. In her haste she stepped between the car and the platform. The doors began closing and she screamed, her leg stuck above the ankle. Someone inside the car pulled the emergency rope and the doors snapped open and people helped her pull her leg out, the heel of her shoe ruined.

She thanked everyone and then she sat down, closed her eyes and thanked God for saving her, the train doors opening and closing at each stop and she shuddering until she got off at 86th Street and walked in the cool late summer evening with the fragrance of Central Park coming at her until she got to her tenement building and climbed the four flights and her mother asked her if everything was all right and what was the matter with her leg that it was scratched and her stockings ripped. She said she had fallen going down the subways stairs. *Clumsy girl,* her mother had said. She had risen early the next morning and was at the church to be confessed. She told Father Corrigan everything and the old priest said that perhaps it was a sign from God, which she agreed it had to be.

She'd gone to school and told Sister Agnes that she was thinking seriously of a religious life. Sister Agnes had said: *Oh, that is admirable* and smiled kindly, but with as much amusement as disbelief, as if she were saying: *You, Mary Katherine Grady? Heaven help us if the Good Lord has chosen to call you.* But in spite of the doubts of everyone concerned she became a model of Catholic behavior and stopped touching herself and prayed constantly until graduation came and eventually the nuns, seeing a miracle in the making, recommended her and she was accepted to the convent in upstate New York for her initial year as a postulant in the spring of 1931, the year after she graduated from high school.

Once there, her hair was shorn. She was issued habits and underclothing and shown her room with the large wooden crucifix and bare walls, the bed neat and a basin and pitcher made of porcelain on the night table, and a Bible on the bed. She was fine for a year and a half, well into the beginning of her novitiate, her thoughts on service to God and her studies, hoping someday to be a good teacher. And then she and the milkboy had noticed each other and her life was upside down again. Sisters and novices, especially young ardent ones, should be exempt by God from love at first sight. No matter how hard she prayed he was there, his dark eyes boring into her and his small, even teeth glimmering behind his curiously inviting but insolent smile. He spoke with a French accent and sisters said he was a French Canadian boy, not very smart but a hard worker, who had left home after an altercation in a village outside of Montreal.

That spring of 1932, her twentieth year, in the midst of the Depression, she was working in the kitchen and was given the task of receiving the deliveries, counting the groceries, noting everything in an accounts book, signing the receipts and paying for the goods. The Canadian boy came every morning and delivered the two large galvanized cans of milk from his wagon and tipped his cap. Sometimes he tarried, removed his newsboy cap, looked at her and smiled a bit insolently and said she was *la plus belle soeur,* which she knew she was not because she was rather ordinary in looks, with plain features, especially a nose too large for her face, hooked and ugly, even though Mary Margaret, her granddaughter, said she was beautiful and looked exactly like Meryl Streep, pointing at the old photos in her trunk when she was a young girl and after she married Martin Boyle. *Did you see her in* The Deer Hunter *last year, Grandma?* That was crazy because her own lips were hardly apparent and her only saving feature was her eyes, which danced with the joy of her life and which nothing could ever dim, except perhaps death, which lately seemed to be knocking more loudly.

And then that spring the wicked French boy said that she should come with him to walk in the moonlight. *The moon is not as beautiful as you,* he'd said boldly, first in French and then in English. She shook her head and said he should go, her face becoming red and her body warm. *Tonight I will come and wait for you by the well,* he'd said. It was like he knew she was burning to be touched but she could not sin again as she had before and remained on her knees all night, praying. He came again the next day and again pled with her. She was studying French and said: *J'aime seulement Dieu. I love only God. Moi aussi,* he'd replied. *Me too. Mais, Dieu sait que je t'aime. But God knows I love you. He knows. I'll wait for you by the well. Tonight after the lights have gone out, I'll wait for you. Go,* she had hissed at him. *You're crazy. I will pray that you'll stop torturing yourself.* But rather than waning, his ardor grew with each rejection and he wrote her verses about the loneliness of a heart without love and birds that flew endlessly without a branch on which to land. She read the verses, felt her heart skip and in painful and private autos-da-fé she threw the versed notes into the fires of the stone oven where bread was baked, wishing she had the courage to grasp the burning iron handles of the oven doors and scar the palms of her hands to punish the transgressions of her heart, never once considering confession but letting the flames of her desire consume her soul.

She held out for a month and then one night, when the moon was full again and the flowers in the garden of the convent were in full bloom, enveloping the grounds with their fragrance, she rose and quietly after all the lights were out she let herself out and walked into the fields like a somnambulist, no longer praying but her body calling out for release from her own torture. She was certain that he had grown weary of waiting for her, but he was there by the well, standing in the moonlight like a shadow and her heart leapt up at the sight of him. No one knew of this, not Martin, and not her sister, and not one priest and certainly none of the nuns. Only one person knew—him—and God. And now someone else because he was dying and wanted his son to know his mother's identity.

*h*e didn't know how long he'd be gone but he was sure to get hungry. Quietly Kenny found a backpack in the toolshed, placed a small ax in it and returned to the kitchen. He opened the big industrial stainless steel icebox with the large cuts of meat and chickens, and butter and milk, and vegetables and juices. He unsheathed his knife and cut a large wedge of ham, perhaps a pound or so, wrapped it in aluminum foil, placed a half-dozen biscuits in a bag and took a long plastic bottle of water and put everything in the backpack. He came back outside, his heart beating with anticipation. He buttoned his mackinaw against the cold and continued preparing himself to go and look for the pregnant cow. Rover, the old Labrador-Shepherd mix, came up to sniff at him. He patted the big dog and told him to go back to sleep. The dog pushed his big body against his leg and followed him.

*t*he girl had come to her and apologized as if it had been her fault that this fate had befallen her grandson. She was tall and gangly and said she loved Kenny and knew they were too young but that she hoped she would forgive her. *There's nothing to forgive,* she'd said. *Does your mother know you're in New York? She knows. How old are you? Six-*

teen. Where are you going to stay? I don't know, the girl said. *Maybe I could stay with you. I'd do chores and anything else you'd like. I can pay you a little. I brought my savings. I have almost five hundred dollars and then I can get a job and if I can't I can go back and live upstate at my mother's house and finish school afterward.* She told the girl she could stay and she should take Frances and Maureen's room down the hall. *Did you bring a winter coat? It'll be cold soon.* The girl nodded and said she had a good ski jacket and plenty of sweaters and pants.

She was a sweet girl, pretty and delicate even though she was so tall. She was so scared by everything that had taken place over the past month. They had talked about someday getting married but now she didn't know whether that was possible because Kenny may never wake up. *He'll wake up,* she said, daring Heaven to go against her will. *Give him time,* she'd said and held the girl's hand, not quite knowing whether she should take her into her heart just yet. *How will your father respond to all this, you coming down from up there?* She said that her father hadn't lived with them for a long time. He'd moved to Buffalo when she was six and lived with a Polish woman and had other children. Two boys and a little girl whom she saw first when she was twelve after she traveled north at her father's invitation, making herself not hate her siblings because they'd done her no harm. She wondered why her father had left her mother and robbed her of a father, choosing instead these other children as his own. Maybe she'd grow to love them, but she didn't know. She'd see.

The third evening of her stay when she felt more at home, the girl offered to cook dinner for them. She went out and came back with kielbasa and made potato pancakes and fried the sausage and made a blueberry pie, the crust delicate and flaky, and made tea and served it to her. She made her laugh with her industriousness and she thought that if Kenny loved this girl as she said he did, then he was spoken for, at least for the next fifty years. When they were done eating she asked Claudia if she wanted to watch television. The girl shook her head and said she didn't like television very much and preferred reading instead. *Will you go to college?* she asked. *Yes, to study nursing,* she'd replied. Mary Boyle had nodded and asked her why she wanted to become a nurse. The girl answered that she had always wanted to be a nurse even when she was a little girl. *I played that my dolls were sick and took care of them until they were well again. Sometimes the dolls had very bad illnesses like tuberculosis and cancer.*

Cancer? she'd asked matter-of-factly. *How would she make a doll feel better about cancer?* The girl smiled and said: *Oh, just making their life easier and loving them and always helping them to smile and be positive,* she'd replied. *You're a positive thinker, then? Yes, I am. And do you pray? Yes, I pray. Are you Catholic? Lutheran,* the girl had said. *That's between a Protestant and a Catholic,* she'd said. The girl had laughed for the first time. *Something like that,* she'd said. *You're not going to go down the street to St. Ignatius and hammer edicts on the door of our church, are you?* And the girl laughed some more and said she was glad that she was so funny because living with her mother she had to paint with her lipstick little happy faces on the corners of their mirrors to give herself a hint that she ought to smile once in a while. The image of the girl drawing happy faces made her laugh and say that the two of them were two of a kind and if she was going to be a nurse she had to curb her enthusiasm because if the patients in her care had stitches and she joked like this she'd make them laugh and break their stitches and a fine mess that would be. They had laughed even harder and then she looked at Claudia and said: *You're not much in the breast department, are you?* Without missing a beat Claudia said that compared to her she was an ironing board.

Mary Katherine Boyle, approaching septuagenarian status, had laughed and said that she'd soon be as flat. *What do you mean?* Claudia had asked and then as if she'd known the girl all her life she was talking about her diagnosis and what she'd have to endure and likely chemotherapy if the cancer spread. *Double radical mastectomy,* Claudia had said. *I'm too big to be a doll, but what do you think?* she'd said. *What are your chances? Did the doctors say?* She explained that she was otherwise healthy. *I'd go through with it and take my chances,* Claudia had said, *but I wouldn't be losing much. Oh, hell, why not, then! Let them carve away. The social worker said I could get a fitted bra. I'll ask for just a touch. Just enough to make men wonder. We'll be itty bitty titty twins, you and me,* she'd said and they laughed and Claudia stood up and held her and smoothed her wild, wiry graying hair, talking to her softly and loving her as she did Kenny. When the outpouring of sentiment was over she'd told Claudia Bachlichtner, junior nurse, that she would prefer if this was not discussed with anyone, since everyone had too much worry already on their minds. Was that okay with her? *Our secret,* the girl had said, and she felt a great weight lifted from her shoulders being in the presence of such a fine young woman. Where did the goodness come from in them? Frances was the same way. She felt it had always been missing in her.

*K*enny left the house knowing that no one had heard him. He retrieved the large square flashlight from the shed, and together with the smaller one placed them in the backpack and slung it over his shoulder. He pulled down a kerosene lamp, checked to see that it had enough fuel, changed his mind and placed it back on its hook.

*K*enny seemed as brave but not as crazy as his uncle Jerry. When Jerry was growing up she heard stories from others that he and the Dolan boy, whose father worked for Liam Casey and died holding up a bank in New Jersey, who was just as crazy, went to the railyards and hopped on trains and when the trains picked up speed they jumped off and rolled in the bushes to come out bloody but laughing and the other boys cheering. He'd come in scratched up: his arms, legs, face and he impervious to the pain, his head with clumps of bloody hair. Her heart broke looking at him and seeing the same wildness that raged inside her. She knew it couldn't be tamed, so she prayed extra hard for him. She enjoyed swabbing his scratches and cuts with iodine and hearing him scream and cry, hoping that he'd come to his senses. She relished telling him calmly that he would die if his wounds became infected and was that what he wanted? He'd howl *no that isn't* what he wanted and then she'd tell him that he'd end up going to Hell if he kept being so bad but loving him just the same because he was one brave little son of a gun even when he was ten years old. Though she crossed herself and murmured prayers, her heart swelled with pride upon hearing of him fighting bigger boys and making them cry. He was just like the Dolan kid except that the Dolan kid ended up like his father, working for gangsters, and Jerry went to the police academy, became a cop and went on the job as they said. Jesus, men were an arrogant lot. And now Kenny had been brave and foolish. What had gotten into him, alone like that in the woods at night?

She had no idea what the hell had happened for Jerry to leave a job that he loved. *What happened, Jerry? They set me up, Ma. Set you up, how? Too complicated, Ma. You don't want to know. I'm sure your father and I would understand, and you with children and a wife to support. What are you going to do? I'll be okay.* And his father offering to help him since he had almost five thousand saved up. *I'll be all right. Maybe I'll go to work for Mickey* and his boys in Hell's Kitchen. They always have work for someone like me. Jerome, don't even mention those people in my house, son, his father said. They give the Irish a bad name. A worse one, I'd say, Jerry had joked and she laughed, which Martin hadn't liked. Maybe I'll go and see Spillane at the train yards and get a job. He's another, that Bobby Spillane, his father said. She'd asked what it was about Bobby Spillane that was objectionable. He's a union steward and the subway is not a bad living, she'd said. What's the matter with that? Nothing, Martin said and Jerry shook his head. She was left wondering about Spillane until later that night after Jerry had returned home to Queens to break the news to his wife. She said nothing all evening and then she couldn't contain herself. Martin Boyle had gone to sleep but she poked him awake, turned on her night table light and demanded an explanation on why Spillane wasn't acceptable.

Why don't you leave it alone, woman, he'd said angrily. He always called her "woman" when he was upset. I'm his mother, she'd responded, the anger rising in her as well. I have a right to know. Spillane's with the Army, he'd said, his voice dropping as if his words would travel through the walls and word would eventually get back to Bobby Spillane. Oh, she'd said, I thought he worked maintenance with subway trains. He collects money for their activities over there, Martin said. A patriot, she'd said worshipfully, knowing it would anger him. Something like that, he'd said, ignoring her taunting. Go to sleep or go pray for his soul if he gets involved with them. Do you think he will? she asked. He's more Grady than he is Boyle, he'd said and turned over and went to sleep. She'd wanted to question him further about what he thought had happened with Jerry, but she figured she'd wait until he was in a better mood. She switched off her light and turning to him stroked his back gently until she felt him relax and settle into a sound sleep. He worked hard and didn't need the aggravation of a nosy woman, she thought, mediating her dislike of his flaws against his good qualities.

She worried about it all day and toward afternoon she called Sheila, Jerry's wife. She was in a panic. *Ma, they set him up,* she cried into the phone. *What are we going to do? No pension, no nothing. Ten years and nothing to show for it.* She'd calmed the girl down and told her things would be all right. *He can handle himself. Don't you worry,* she'd said. *Who set him up? Spics and niggers,* her daughter-in-law said. *Friends of his partner. Of Tommy's? Are you sure? Did he say it was Tommy? No, but I know it was them. They protect each other. What are we going to do?* She asked Sheila if she wanted her to come out and help with the kids. *No, Ma, that's all right.* She could hear the kids screaming in the background. She told Sheila to call her if she needed anything. They hung up and she called Fran and asked her what she knew. Fran said she knew nothing because Tommy wouldn't say anything other than to tell her he was no longer on the job.

She asked her if there had been problems between Jerry and Tommy. *None that I know of,* Fran said. *They're more like brothers than Jerry is with Mike or his cousins, you know that. Do you know where they are?* she asked. *Probably at McMullen's in Inwood. That's where they go,* Frances had said. Jerry was so crazy there was no telling what he'd do. He had enlisted in the U.S. Army before he was out of high school and became a paratrooper and went to Korea and made jumps and fought and it was like he lived a charmed life. *We just killed gooks, Mom. That's it. Nothing like Calley in Vietnam, but Communist bastards anyway you know,* he'd said. *And what are you going to do now?* she'd asked when he returned in uniform, a beret instead of a regular army hat. *I don't know. Take the police and fireman's test and go on the job. Find a girl. Get married, have kids, send them to Catholic school and hope they'll grow up to be Irish saints.* Talking crazy like that, his eyes wild and smiling at the same time like he was one of the horses her cousin, Seamus Grady, took care of at the racetrack.

McMullen's in Inwood? Yes, I think so. She got dressed, put on her kerchief, took the bus and marched into the bar. They were both sitting at the bar, not yet shit faced but close to it. She said she had to talk to them, so they went to a booth and she ordered a boiler maker. She downed the shot and drained half the mug of the cold beer and asked them what the hell they were going to do now that they were off the job. *We'll make do, Mom. Don't worry about it. You have kids to raise,* she'd said. Tommy wouldn't say anything but Jerry kept reassuring her that he wouldn't go to work in Hell's Kitchen for the gangs on the docks. *And promise me that you'll stay away from Spillane,* she'd said. *I'll stay away from Spillane,* he'd said, but she was now sure that he hadn't.

That was nine years ago and he had done all right and now owned a big trawler and fished the Sound and had a big house and his older boy, Patrick, would be starting his second year at St. John's University in the fall. Patrick helped his father in the summer. How old was Jerry now? Forty-four. July 11, 1935. This was September, so he was forty-five. What did that make her? Sixty-seven, and in a few weeks she'd be a flat young girl again, her ribs showing on her chest like she was malnourished. It had to have been horrible with people starving to death on those farms. Everything so green and nothing to eat, she thought again recalling her grandmother's stories.

*k*enny came out of the toolshed with Rover following him. He told the big dog to stay. He had next gone into the fields, the air cold against his face, no moon now, but the sky filled with stars. He walked perhaps two hundred yards into the meadow before he shook his head and turned back, walking quickly, the rifle pointed downward as he climbed the corral fence and headed for the barn, knowing he would accomplish little by walking. It was like his mind was a muddle of thoughts and he didn't know what things would be like. It wasn't like ice hockey, he'd thought, where he could see the entire ice surface in front of him and could anticipate what would happen next. This was different.

in that regard Kenny was like his mother, quiet and polite and not very aware of the consequences of his actions, much as if they were being guided by some inner goodness. Jerry had taken everything out of her. He was such a difficult boy those first few years, colicky and hard to handle, fighting her even when she held him. It was as if she had invested all of her rage in him. She was pregnant again the following year and Maureen was born, and then Michael two years later. She then had a miscarriage and hemorrhaged. The doctors said there had been some damage and maybe she wouldn't have any more children. She was relieved but protected herself against pregnancy, letting Martin have his pleasure periodically, making excuses to him about not feeling well whenever she felt as if she was ovulating until one night about six months later when he had grown tired of her excuses he threw her on the bed as she was pulling the nightgown over her head. He propped her up against the side of the bed and went into her from behind, without removing his pants, latching brutally onto her breasts and his huge organ smashing into her, grunting until he was finished and he pushed her away and she lay facedown on the bed, violated but strangely calm and as if she had defeated him.

She had convinced Martin that she enjoyed sex as he had done it when he raped her, that perhaps this mode of sexual union would curb the Grady meanness that she had forced

Jerry to inherit, but knowing she didn't want to face Martin because she didn't like him very much. If someone had plumbed the depth of her soul she would have admitted that she loved her husband but she did not like him and hardly ever faced him in kindness.

When she found out she was pregnant again she prayed it would be a little girl and a placid satisfaction came over her. Nine months later, on August 20, 1940, she delivered Frances Ann Boyle, a little blond baby with a pouty mouth and gentle little eyes. *She's just fooling me, Ma,* she'd said to her mother. *Lulling me into believing that she's not going to be a hell-raiser like Jerry. Quiet,* her mother had said. *Is it harm that you're wishing your daughter?* Frances had been a perfect baby. She slept when she was supposed to sleep, ate hungrily, first from her breasts and then cereal and baby formula until she could eat mashed vegetables and a little meat broth, each day growing healthy and strong, her blond curls like those of Shirley Temple but more beautiful. She hardly ever cried, except when she was read a book and a bird had fallen from its nest or the tigers melted into butter in "Little Black Sambo." *Poor wittle tigers,* Mommy, she'd cry. *Poor wittle black Sambo. Now he has no tigers. But he has butter,* she'd say. And Fran would nod and then she'd tell the little girl that little black Sambo had butter but no toast and she'd laugh and Jerry would laugh, which was a good thing, since he was always upset with something and smashed his toy soldiers against the wall, nicking the plaster. Whenever he got angry his little sister would go to him and hug him and tell him she loved him.

Before she was four she knew the Lord's Prayer and the Rosary and would sit with her and pray, kneeling beside her, her little hands clasped to her chest and her eyes shut tight until they said amen and then she'd smile up at her. She was bright and loved learning.

Maureen and Michael had grown up with even dispositions, neither of them interesting enough to make a difference. But the extremes of Jerry and Frances were an enigma. Frances did well in high school, earning honors and receiving a strong recommendation that she should attend Hunter College, which was not too far from where they lived on the Grand Concourse. A walk down the hill to take the Jerome Avenue train to the Bronx campus of the college. They had moved to a large apartment with mostly Jewish people around, glad to be away from her mother. Her mother returned to the old apartment near Cypress Avenue, creating a rut on the sidewalks to St. Luke's on 138th Street, so frequent were her visits, much as if she were attempting to make amends for her meanness. The witch, Monica McGraw called her. Monica was a scrawny, pale girl with mousy brown hair who had married her youngest boy, Michael Patrick Boyle, another poor dumb mick. Jesus, where in Heaven did they make the bastards? Her father, Michael Grady, never picked up a hand to hit her, but never did he stay his wife's against his children, letting her employ the back as well as the front of her hand to discipline them even when there was no need to, insisting that she was their mother.

She never struck her children no matter how poorly they behaved. All she needed to do was look at Frances and the girl understood that she should not take the course of action that she had chosen. She would shake her little blond head and say: *No, no, Frances Ann Boyle,* saying her own name in self-admonishment. *Okay, Mommy?* she'd ask. *Yes, dear. Okay. I'm a good girl, Mommy. Yes, you are.* She would take a chair from the dinette table, place it against the sink and wash the dishes when she was five years old, cutting herself once between thumb and index finger, a scar which still showed and which required eight stitches to close and a long time to heal. And now Fran didn't know what had happened to Kenny and she wasn't sure who was going to tell her. Jerry said that he would call her. Tommy was away.

*K*enny had gone into the barn, placed the rifle on a bale of hay and opened the stall where his favorite horse stood, one leg cocked as it slept. He patted the big chestnut horse, Sendero, awake and led him out into the middle of the barn, holding him by the mane. He then retrieved the bridle, harnessed the horse's head and laid the reins on the floor of the barn. Kenny placed the large flashlight on top of the bale of hay next to the gun and retrieved the blanket and saddle from the enclosure where the equipment was kept. When he was done cinching up the horse, he grabbed the flashlight and rifle, swung himself up on the saddle and led the horse out of the barn. He leaned over the saddle and unlatched the gate, and after they'd gone through he leaned down to latch it shut.

*W*hen she first met Tomás Eduardo Romero she did not like the boy. He seemed dumb, smiling stupidly and his yellow eyes like a hawk's, watching everything, his nose sharp and curved like her own, beakish and birdlike. That and her prejudices against Spanish people had soured her against him. She hated getting off the subway on 138th Street and Brook Avenue with the Puerto Rico Theater and all the shops with their Spanish signs in the 1950s when she brought the children to see their grandmother in the old neighborhood. They were loud and spoke quickly in their silly tongue and fast music blared everywhere. Even though the neighborhood was still Irish further in, around St. Mary's Park, they were moving in on them and now this Spanish boy had come into their lives and the way he looked at Frances was like a wolf licking his chops at the sight of a newborn lamb. She imagined him enormous, like Martin, tearing into her little gentle girl.

They dated for a short while and then one day he came dressed in a suit and asked to speak to Martin. Martin got a strange look on his face and ushered him into the parlor. She had spoken to Martin about the fact that she did not want Frances marrying anyone except a nice Irish Catholic boy who had gone to college and wanted to be an accountant or a lawyer, or perhaps a civil servant with the government. *Mary, please come in here. Frances, please wait in your room,* he'd said. *Yes, Daddy,* she replied and went into her bedroom. She'd gone into the parlor, sat on the sofa and Martin had pointed to one of the stuffed chairs before taking the other across from Tommy. There was a long silence and then Martin said: *Well?* Tommy had nodded and said: *Mr. Boyle, sir, I know I've only known Frances, your daughter, six months, but I would like to have your permission to marry her.* Oh, my God, she'd said as if she'd heard the Devil make the request. *No,* she'd said. Martin had said: *Quiet, woman!* And then he called Frances's name loudly and Frances came into the parlor. He ordered her to sit next to her mother.

Thomas here has informed your mother and I that he wishes to enter into holy matrimony with you. What do you have to say to that? She began to say no again, but Martin looked at her and she tightened her lips against the rage. *I love him, Daddy,* Frances's words had come out of her as honestly as any she had ever uttered. *Do you, now?* Martin had said. *Yes, I do, with all my heart. He's a very good person, Daddy. And he's gone to college and he and Jerry are good friends and partners and I know we'll be good for each other. It doesn't matter that he's Spanish, does it?* Martin had shaken his head and said it didn't matter to him and that he had spoken to Jerry and everything that she said was true. *Is that how you feel, Thomas? Yes, sir. That's exactly how I feel. Your daughter is a treasure and I will always honor your trust in me,* talking like he was a knight, she guessed, figuring it all came from being Spanish like he was Tyrone Power in *Captain from Castille* or some movie like that. *When?* Martin had asked. *Well,* Tommy said. *It's now November. We figure Valentine's Day would be fine, if it's all right with you.* Fran nodded happily, and she knew they had agreed on the date beforehand. *That sounds fine but I don't want her marching up the aisle with her belly a foot out and three months later we're grandparents. You have my word, sir,* Tommy said and that had been it. She figured Martin had given his assent to the wedding simply to vex her, to contradict her, to show his power against her.

She hadn't spoken to Martin for nearly a month, grunting when he asked her questions and turning her back on him when he spoke. Everything had gone well and they had a beautiful wedding and reception and all their Irish relatives were more curious than glad at this union. His family was even more Catholic and austere than they were except for the mother, who was a hell-raiser like herself, from all appearances. After they cut the cake and Rosa Romero had eaten a piece, she took out a big Havana cigar, prepared it, and gave it to her husband. She lit it for him with a big lighter from her purse, which seemed fine, but she then went back into her bag and took one for herself, licked it, clipped the end, placed it in her mouth, lit it and in her pink mother-of-the-groom dress sat contentedly smoking the big Havana and drinking from a glass of rum. Not a vulgar woman but certainly a strange one.

Tommy took Fran off on a honeymoon to Puerto Rico and when she returned she came to visit Frances at her new apartment in Brooklyn. *So?* she'd said and all Frances could do was grin and blush and say: *Oh, my God, Mom, he's so wonderful, so tender and he loves me so much. I can't talk about it. It was like Heaven and everything is warm and beautiful and we lay in the water of the sea and I'm a little sunburnt but not too much because we were indoors most of the time,* she giggled. *We went into the mountains and stayed in a small house in the woods. The mountains are green and there are trees with red flowers called flamboyán. There are birds everywhere. Hummingbirds, Mom. They're called picaflores, which means flower pickers.* And then three months later in May 1962 she called up to say that she had morning sickness and had missed her period twice so it was very likely she was pregnant. Kenny was born with a head of dark blond hair and blue eyes later that year.

She never heard a complaint from Frances except to say that in the past three years after little Tommy was born, her husband had stayed away for days at a time but always called to tell her where he was, Michigan or Kansas, somewhere out there in the country, and she missed him so much but when they were together it was like they had just met and she still loved him as much as she did when they first met at her birthday party. *Does he ever yell at you now that you've been married a while? Never, Mom. And he's never raised his hand to you? Not once and he's the same with the children. We're fine, but there's never enough money. We're eight now, Mom.* And probably another one on the way, Mary Boyle thought. She hoped Fran's nerves weren't too affected when she found out about Kenny.

search

*Kenny's father was Tommy Romero, a
Puerto Rican boy born in East Harlem, a
different kind of ghetto that produced some
successes although its myth persists as a
cradle to great accomplishments. Before
he was ten the family took flight to the
Williamsburg section of Brooklyn known
as Los Sures because of the numbered streets,
such as South 6th and South 7th, which
carried their direction.*

K ENNY HAD first searched along the stream where
earlier in the day he'd walked six hundred yards looking for the lost cow. The horse was sure-footed as he
splashed through the stream, climbing naturally back onto
the bank when he felt the water would be too deep. Kenny
stopped at the barbed wire that separated the properties,
came back and crossed the stream to search the small meadow
where perhaps the cow had lain down to calf. He concen-

trated now, trying to figure out where the cow could have gone.

*t*ommy Romero sat at the table looking at his cards, deciding which of the other men had the ten of diamonds, the big casino. He had been playing the game since he was a boy and his father came home from work as a carpenter and sat with them at dinner, all of them with their hands down on their laps and his mother saying grace and Evelyn and Delia with their heads bowed and then when supper was over and their mother was doing the dishes his father would play casino with them. His father was always partners with Evelyn, who was the youngest. His mother was strict and often cursed but only in Spanish, sprinkling what she was saying with *coño, mierda, puñeta* and *carajo* even when she was not angry. But she was loving and respectful of them and sacrificed herself for her children, making sure they were well fed and clean and had attractive clothes for school, helping them with their homework when she could, and when she couldn't, figuring out where she could get the right information, saving and subsequently purchasing an *Encyclopaedia Britannica,* reading the books avidly whenever there was something with which she was unfamiliar or which awakened her own curiosity, not caring much that she mispronounced the English language but wanting to learn the information. She wanted all her children to go to college and they had. He couldn't believe he'd gone to college and was now earning his living as he did. He didn't miss being a cop.

In the winter his mother made hot chocolate and in the summer lemonade and when everyone was set and they began playing she brought a chair from the kitchen and kibitzed the game, blowing cigar smoke up into the air. When spring came his father played catch with him and he eventually played baseball in high school and then traveled back to East Harlem and played baseball for his father's hometown team of Cacimar. When Kenny started growing up they went out and played catch as Tommy had with his father. He hoped that Kenny would return to baseball but he was set on being away and maybe it was all for the best. He had met the girl Claudia when he drove to the farm to bring him back for the beginning of school. Mary Margaret and Rose wanted to see where Kenny had been all summer, so he brought them along. The girl was a beauty, the two of them taller than everyone else, including him, it seemed; their hair was the same length, Kenny's streaked blond from the sun and hers totally blond and thick, not like his mother's but not unlike hers, a bit more of a wave in it, he'd thought. They had stood close to each other and when he placed his gear in the trunk of the car, he returned to the porch and the two of them went off to say their private good-byes and he returned alone because she had remained behind the house weeping, he said. Peggy and Rose were impressed and gaped at their brother, awed that he could have an effect like that on such a beautiful girl.

*h*e had picked up the three men at his father's house. They were like his father, quiet but younger than him, perhaps his own age, early forties, serious men with the same demeanor of the *jíbaros* of the highlands; Moorish looking, the eyes black and unsmiling. His father had introduced them by their last name: Rivas, Martínez and Escobar. Everyone wore gloves, which they would take off should they be stopped by the police. Their names were interchangeable Spanish names and he wasn't sure if they were their real names. He didn't care. One sat up front with him in the truck and the other two rode in a van behind them. They took the

Brooklyn-Queens Expressway ahead of the evening rush hour and drove to Long Island, through Nassau and into Suffolk County until they reached Jerry's house, where they parked the truck, and then he directed the three men and they drove the van to Jerry's beach house in the sand dunes.

The house was two stories and was used mostly in the summer for friends who wanted to get away from the city. It was a place for men who wanted to fish, for others who needed privacy with lovers, or for families of friends or relatives who wanted to come there and stay weekends on the quiet beach. He had come there several times with Fran when Kenny and Mary Margaret were little. And once again a year later when he and Fran needed to get away, the girls and little Tommy staying with the Romeros in Williamsburg.

The house was also a meeting place of intrigue. This is where they made their plans when something big was about to happen. It was rumored that Gerry Adams and Martin McGuinness, later to emerge as leaders of the political wing of the Irish Republican Army, had stayed there. Jerry had squelched those rumors and said the IRA wouldn't be caught dead in such a place. But he knew that Spillane and Finnegan had met with Jerry there many times. Jim Murphy had used the house when he was seeing his own cousin, Adelita Quiles. Another Irish-Rican romance. And now Jerry.

Does Sheila know about the girl, Jerry? he'd asked. *She doesn't know, Tommy. I'll tell her when it's time. Does Patrick know? He knows. And? He's okay with it. He's involved with an Angela Davis type, daughter of a black judge, prelaw radical at St. John's. She's still living out some bullshit civil rights fantasy from the 1960s. It's not going to matter how much they jump up and down and protest. They're always going to be fucked for being from Africa. That's the way it is. And it isn't because they're black. It's a good excuse so that the poor white fucks don't have to look at what the government's doing to them. Fucking blacks over keeps whites thinking they're doing better than the blacks. Do you understand, Tommy? You went to college. Poor people are fucked, no matter what color they are. Anyway, what's Patrick going to bitch to me about? He likes black pussy, I like spic pussy and you like honky pussy. It's all pussy.* That's how Jerry talked. He didn't mean any harm. Fran had once said that talking like that kept him from feeling vulnerable. Maybe she was right.

How long ago had it been since Jerry motored out into the Sound? He looked at his watch. The sun was about to set when he left. It was ten o'clock, so it was now two hours. The house was an eighth of a mile from the Sound, set apart from the small town. The clapboard weather-beaten gray from the wind and the sun, the inside of the house smelling of the sea, the foundation half sunk in the sand dunes and sea grass that grew there. There was no heating system except for an old woodstove with a pipe that vented out to the sheltered side of the house. The night was cool now that August was ending but it was bearable. The closer it came to the return of the trawler the more anxiety Tommy Romero felt. This time it was big and he didn't know if he was up to it. Why couldn't he just purchase the merchandise here and drive it to Chicago? Jerry had shaken his head. He said they didn't want to be involved in this one. *This is from China,* he'd said. *We'll unload the merchandise, they pay the second half and off they go,* Jerry said. *They're my people,* he'd said. *Precisely why you don't want to be involved. You know I don't deal directly with mine. I take my cut and turn the money over to Spillane and Finnegan. That's how it is.*

His father had come to him and explained that his friends needed a favor. He had conveyed the message to Jerry and Jerry shook his head and said he should keep his family out of their business. *And, anyway, how did your father know about them? He's in our own Army, I guess. Like Spillane and Finnegan?*

Jerry had asked. *Yeah, like them except that they speak Spanish and not Gaelic. Irish,* Jerry had corrected him. *Irish,* he'd said. *Are they the ones who did Fraunces Tavern a couple of years back? I guess,* he'd said, although he didn't know for sure. *Probably. They also blinded that one cop,* Jerry said. *What's his name? I don't remember,* he'd said. Jerry had looked at the coded list and shook his head. *That's a lot of merchandise,* Jerry had said. *I guess it is,* he'd said. Jerry thought a moment and said it would cost twenty thousand dollars. *That may be too steep for them. Jesus, Mary and Joseph, they have friggin rocket launchers in the order. What the hell are they planning? I don't know. They're not from here. Where?* Jerry asked. *Chicago, I think,* he'd said.

The previous month he and his father had left his father's house on South Third in Los Sures away from the sanctity of the home as if safeguarding it, not taking any chances that it might be under surveillance, the phone tapped or a listening device, a bug, installed. Silently, they walked slowly west toward Kent Avenue with its factories on the East River, past the Domino Sugar plant and then toward the Brooklyn Navy Yard, where his father had worked during the Second World War, plying his trade as a carpenter but getting transferred to New Jersey and the Bayonne shipyard to help construct wooden PT boats. Later he explained proudly that he had worked on President Kennedy's boat. There was a framed photograph of himself with his coworkers standing on the deck, the big black 109 painted on the gray hull of the brand-new PT boat. The photo was displayed in his den, the inscription in white ink: *Bayonne, NJ 1942.* Next to it, in a gold frame, the ubiquitous photograph of the dead president.

In 1963 Kenny was almost a year old. That November day he'd come home from the precinct after working all night, hanging around Lexington Avenue playing the junkie, hoping to get a lead on the big dealers. He had looked at baby

Kenny sleeping in his cradle in their bedroom. He had fallen asleep next to Fran, loving the curve of her hip as she slept, her nightgown raised to reveal her thighs, her mouth slightly open and her skin smooth and taut on her face, the freckles on her nose making him smile, the lashes long and reddish blond. Toward afternoon she woke him up holding Kenny and weeping to tell him the president had been shot in Dallas.

Friends? he'd asked his father as they approached the Navy Yard, now sixteen years later, all the good intentions of the president: the Peace Corps, VISTA and the rest lessening in importance, leaving only the rhetorical revolution and the clandestine workings of liberation movements. *Mostly from the island,* his father replied, relighting the stub of his cigar, stone-faced, his green eyes serious. *From Cacimar, from my hometown, some of them. Their fathers, anyway. But not from New York. From out of town. They need help. What kind of help, Pop? Your kind of help, son. Like you help the Irish,* he said. *It's for a cause. Pop, you believe in that cause?* And his father explained as he always had that he believed the island was the chattel of the United States and he would do anything to help his friends. *It's not that I don't love the U.S., son,* his father had said. *Are you involved, Pop? I help,* his father had said. *It's dangerous, Pop. You're not getting any younger. I know it is,* his father had said. *Are they the same ones who blew up the restaurant on Wall Street? I can't tell you that, son. I'm sorry. And they have the money, Pop? They have the money, son. All cash? Yes, all cash. Twenty thousand? That's too much money, Tommy. How much? Maybe half. I'll see what I can do, Pop. It's a big order,* he'd said. *It's a big cause, son,* his father had said, the two of them talking like men doing business, and he not quite believing that his father also lived in the shadow world of secrecy.

He came back a week later and told his father that the best

they could do was fifteen thousand. *Half up front and half on delivery,* he'd said. *All cash. We know it's for a cause. Very well,* his father had said and the men had brought the money, all of it in one-hundred-dollar bills that had very likely gone through the cash registers of bodegas, beer distributorships, cigar stores and even travel agencies. Seven hundred and fifty bills in a small black bag with a zipper that he had delivered to Jerry and out of which Jerry had counted out two thousand for him, which he'd put away for the kids' college education. Even if they had scholarships and financial aid there were other costs. He hoped Kenny would do well and get a full scholarship. The coach had said Princeton, Boston University and RPI were interested in him. What an athlete he was. He lamented again Kenny's rejection of baseball.

*W*hen he had finished riding through the small meadow, Kenny once again crossed the stream and headed up the steep incline of the bigger meadow, penned in by barbed wire, so that there was no place the cow could have gone. Kenny checked his watch, shone the flashlight on it and saw that it was ten-thirty. He searched in the small hollows of the meadow but she was nowhere. He checked the perimeter of barbed wire to make certain that there was no breach through which the cow could have gone into another property. When he was done he checked the gate into the bull meadow, let himself through and checked that as well, making sure that he kept himself a good distance from the bulls, which were unpredictable and could charge the horse if they thought it presented a danger.

*A*s he sat waiting for the ten of casino, Tommy thought about Jerry's mother and wondered how much longer she'd live. She hadn't looked well and Fran suspected that she was ill. Her father had gone quickly, a coarsening of his voice, an order from the doctor that he quit smoking, a refusal, and, seemingly from one Christmas to the next, he was skeletal, his voice barely audible, and then he was gone. They'd said they could remove his larynx and put in a voice box. He said he'd think about it, went outside the hospital, lit up another Camel cigarette, coughed violently, spit out a glob of bloody phlegm and told his wife they could all go fuck themselves with their voice boxes. He was always complaining about one thing or another. If it wasn't taxes and the politicians, it was the price of food, and he reminded everyone that he worked in the butcher shop and that is why they had the greatest cuts of meat.

He never understood why Fran's mother put up with such a disagreeable man. Although Martin Boyle had always treated him with respect there was about him an air of dissatisfaction, a bitterness that pervaded everything he did. He talked to his wife like she was worth very little in his life even though she was the one who kept things together. Jerry had sworn him to secrecy about his mother, Mary Katherine Grady, and revealed to him that she had been in a convent but Jerry didn't know why she'd left, or at least Jerry didn't tell him. Jerry was a brilliant detective and he would have gotten better if things hadn't turned out as they did. For himself he couldn't really say that he missed the life of being undercover and pretending that he was a junkie but after a while he might have gotten a transfer to Homicide or even Safes and Lofts and investigated diamond heists and sophisticated white-collar crimes. He might even have gone to John Jay College and finished his degree. The thought of perhaps going to law school had crossed his mind back then.

Jerry had learned that Mary Boyle had spent two years upstate in a convent waiting to become a nun, which he couldn't imagine given his mother-in-law's disposition, her apparent disdain of most rules and her need to treat matters with sarcasm. But then again he could understand it because at St. Cecilia's he'd had a nun who was strict and funny. He couldn't recall her name. After they moved to Brooklyn he went to public school. His father paying for the mortgage on the house didn't allow for Catholic school. Mary Boyle had gone away to be a nun when she was a young woman. He wondered how someone could turn away from a regular existence and become so totally different, silent and withdrawn from life. But Jerry had figured it out.

When Jerry's wife, Sheila, had their second child and Mary Boyle went over to their apartment to help out, she said that she had some baby clothes of Jerry's that she had saved and would bring the next time she came over because she'd put them in a shopping bag and had simply forgotten them. Jerry said he had to run into the city and he'd be glad to bring them back. He went to the apartment while Michael and Frances were in school and his father at the butcher shop. He found the bag and wondered how much more his mother had saved. He went into Frances and Maureen's room and found an old trunk. He opened it and in searching for clothes he found a sweater box of photographs. In it he'd found a notebook into which his mother had written lessons, but also cryptic notes. Above each section there was the inscription St. Ann's and the date and year 1931, and her name Mary Katherine Grady. And he found letters from her sister written to her at the convent. So she had been there from 1931 to 1933. The entries in her diary stopped in April of 1933, but there were letters well into the fall of that year.

What a woman she was. She hadn't liked him very much at first, never disguising that she didn't think he was very good for Fran. But slowly he had won her over and when she came to the hospital and saw Kenny when he was born she smiled at him, put her arm through his and said Kenny looked exactly like Fran when she was born. *Would you look at him,* she said. *He's so delicate, so beautiful. Do you think he'll remain that white?* she had said irrepressibly, honestly, without malice. He had nodded and said that he and Fran would keep him out of the sun as much as possible. And not feed him rice and beans. Did she know that it was rice and beans that made Puerto Ricans dark? *The more rice and beans they eat the darker they get,* he'd said. *We'll make sure to go easy on the rice and beans, Ma.* Catching on immediately that he was putting her on, she smacked his arm and said that a good sense of humor was rubbing off on him from being around the Irish.

Those first few months she'd made the trek daily from her apartment on the Grand Concourse, riding the subway trains and making three changes to come to Brooklyn early in the morning to help Fran with the baby, staying until she had to make the trip back to the Bronx to begin cooking supper, she was so enthralled with Kenny. When Mary Margaret was born she came over twice a week and commented on the fact that the little girl looked so Spanish but loving her as well. After Rose was born the novelty wore off and she'd come over once a week, stay a few hours and return to the Bronx. It made no sense. Fran needed more help than ever and her mother came over less with each child.

A couple of times both grandmothers encountered each other and it was like watching two tigresses prowling around in the same cage, measuring each other, ready to roar their displeasure should the other one make the wrong move. But they never did, the two of them replicas of each other, headstrong and impassive in the face of attack. They would sit down and have coffee and pastries at the dinette table and tell stories about their grandchildren. Once in a while they talked about their offspring and the great things each had contributed to this marriage in the middle of which they sat in grandmotherly majesty. His mother always talked about how bad he had been, which some Puerto Rican mothers proclaimed, smiling proudly each time they said their child was bad and adding some humorous story about his trying to hang up wet kittens with clothespins after dropping them in a filled bathtub and getting his face scratched.

He was really so bad, his mother would say and laugh. Mary Boyle laughed politely with her, wondering why she thought that was bad when she had seen Jerry at the age of eleven running and jumping from one roof to the next, six stories up like a crazy person. She'd gone up to the roof to get him so he could run to the store and he had been up there with his friends. She was in shock when she saw him run, leap and disappear. She ran to the edge of the roof and looked down expecting to see his broken body in the yard below. *Hi, Ma,* he said, popping up from the other roof, where he had rolled from the force of the leap. The other boys had run away at the sight of her, scurrying back downstairs. *Jerome Boyle, you get home right this minute,* she screamed, pointing at the stairs of the other roof. *Go right now and tell Mr. Kanavan at the Emerald store to give you a box of sugar. Here's a quarter,* she said and tossed the coin at the other roof. *Okay, Ma,* he said and before she could say another word he had picked up the coin, placed it in a pocket of his corduroy pants, turned and walked toward the stairs of the other roof. Rather than continue walking he suddenly turned around and at lightning speed he began running toward her. Frozen, she stood openmouthed watching her son flying through the air. He landed a few feet beyond the edge of the roof and rolled over before jumping to his feet with a silly grin on his face. When she had recuperated she'd wanted to slap him. Instead, she looked at him narrowly and asked him if it was his intent to cause the premature death of his mother. He shook his head, not quite understanding the connection between his prodigious leap and her health. He couldn't imagine how Fran would take her mother's death. Fran sensed something and she'd told him. It was a sixth sense that he recognized in himself and therefore trusted in her.

*U*ndeterred by his failure to find the cow, Kenny again traversed the larger meadow, thinking that perhaps he had missed the cow, and debating whether he should attempt to go into the woods with the horse. The terrain would be rocky and the woods dense. Although the horse could handle the ground, the vegetation would be too thick in places. He considered whether he should leave the horse to graze overnight and continue into the woods or return it to the barn. There were coyotes around but they wouldn't bother the horse. An occasional bear might come down and spook it but would likely leave the horse alone. He rode along the perimeter of the woods, almost a quarter of a mile above the farm and then another eighth of a mile along the short side of the L of the wooded area that served as the foothills of the higher mountains.

*t*ommy Romero recalled these things years later when things had settled down and a new generation had taken root and he became a grandfather perhaps a little too soon. That night he was out there in the late summer night waiting as he had waited on street corners and awful-smelling tenement halls and darkened roofs where each shadow caused fear to rise up in his stomach. He wished Jerry hadn't done what he did but there was no sense judging him. His own actions had not been anything to admire as a model of ethical behavior. Each time he thought about how their lives had turned out he was sickened that he had been drawn into Jerry's scheme, but he was left no choice.

Kenny was a wonder child. There was nothing that could describe the birth of a first child, he thought. After Kenny was born everything he did had greater importance. As he changed into his junkie clothes his awareness that he shouldn't take as many chances grew. There was a sense now that he had to be more careful and be even more convincing so that he could get back to see his son. He didn't recall ever yelling at Kenny, perhaps a warning if he sensed danger but never in anger. And he had never seen him experience fear. Everything he did had a quiet self-assurance, his movements natural. He was amazed at how easily all athletics came to him. By the time Kenny was nine he was playing ice hockey, baseball, soccer and in the playgrounds, basketball, with great proficiency.

When he got to know Jerry and then he fell in love with his sister he and Jerry found themselves in that tribal space where men got together apart from the company of women. Part of that space was attending ice hockey games at the new Madison Square Garden to watch the teams of Eddie Giacomin, Jean Ratelle, Rod Gilbert and Vic Hadfield. They went there not as cops but as fans and often overlooked the displeasure of people who heaped verbal abuse not only on visiting players when they played well, but on hometown ones when they did not perform up to expectations. Once in a while they took Kenny and Christopher, Jerry's youngest son, in their little Ranger sweaters, the one with the number 19 and the name Ratelle (Christopher) and the other the number 7 for Gilbert (Kenny). By the time Christopher was an adolescent his interest in sports had dwindled and he found a guitar more to his liking. Kenny, however, continued developing, playing All Star hockey through the different age levels, Mosquitoes (7–8), Squirts (9–10), Pee Wees (11–12), Bantams (13–14), Midgets (15–16). By the time he was fifteen he stopped competing in the leagues and was concentrating totally on high school athletics, running, stretching and remaining in the gymnasium's weight room, doing repetitions for hours, which had come into fashion. He hardly ever spoke and when he did he addressed everyone as sir and ma'am as if he had been brought up in the South or the West, but it was his mother who taught him manners and encouraged him to be courteous, explaining that these were the words he should use. No one needed to tell him to protect his sisters. He was watchful whether they were in the playground or at school, making sure they got home safely before he asked permission to join his friends in the playground.

His reverie was interrupted when the man on his left playing the ten of hearts picked up a seven and three. He watched his partner, whom he would never see again, smile, play the ten of spades and announce that he was building tens. The ten of clubs had been played, so his partner, he didn't know whether it was Rivas, Martínez or Escobar, had the ten of diamonds. Even though the upcoming play was obvious, the other two men maintained their composure, revealing nothing. He kept his queen back, watching the queen on the table, knowing the man on his left didn't have a face card. He played his last card, an ace, and then his partner picked up the remaining ten with the ten of diamonds. The other man played a nine and he ended the game by sweeping the remaining cards on the table, picking up the queen with the queen in his hand. They had the most cards—three points, the most spades—one point, an ace—one point, and the ten of diamonds—two points. Seven out of eleven points. His partner wrote down the tally. They'd reached one hundred points first. Out on the channel a boat sounded its foghorn and he wondered how long it would be before the phone rang to let him know that they should pick up the truck and head for the dock.

So there he was, waiting. Not to ship the merchandise to Angola, Mozambique, Sudan, Guatemala or Honduras, dealing with Castro's people or reaching down into South Africa to deal with the African National Congress, but to take part of the shipment itself and turn it over to his own people. There was a special pride in the operation, although he didn't feel the same fervor as his father. This was different. He was not purchasing the merchandise in the Carolinas or Michigan or other states where not too many questions were asked, but he was making available a shipment. He thought of it as a living, he and Jerry in business for bigger bosses, like before. Jerry with his fishing trawler and he with his moving trucks, ferrying people's furniture from one apartment to the other, employing two teams and competing with La Rosa del Monte and Flor de Mayo. They were the major leagues of Hispanic moving companies. He was somewhere in the minors, lost with his dinky *mudanzas* from the Bronx to Brooklyn. He kept track of everything and whenever possible everything was cash and screw the government that had screwed him. And then at night traveling away from his home, armed, carrying thousands of dollars for payment, driving the truck with ROMERO AND SONS, MOVERS, the merchandise, as they called it, hidden from sight.

*k*enny rode back to the farm, unsaddled the horse, returned him to his stall, put some more hay in the stall's feed bin and went back out into the night with the rifle and flashlight, and the knapsack on his back. He headed for the horizontal side of the L that formed the line of the

woods, listening closely for the cow. An owl flew closely over-
head and disappeared into the woods, the flight silent, a ro-
dent likely in its talons, flying to a nest to feed its young. He
wondered again if the cow had birthed the calf. He hadn't yet
worked out what he'd do if she had. She wouldn't want the
calf moved until it was ready to travel and that could take
hours.

*t*he horn sounded again out on the
water, this time closer, and Tommy wondered why the ship
was signaling when the night was clear. Perhaps there was another ship close by in the channel. In the end he figured it
had to be the freighter letting Jerry's trawler know that she
was approaching. Tommy looked at his watch. It was now a little after ten and his casino partner at the table addressed the
other two men. *Otro juego?* The two men shook their heads,
turning down another game. One of them got up and said he
was making coffee and a sandwich and asked them if they
wanted one as well. He nodded along with the other men and
his casino partner got up and went to the bathroom. The
other man looked at him and asked how much longer they
had to wait. *Another hour,* he said. They spoke in Spanish. The
man had unreadable eyes and reminded him of a Cuban FBI
agent he'd known in Manhattan. He wondered if this group
had been infiltrated. If they had been, then he and Jerry
would be implicated. *You were a cop, weren't you?* the man
asked. *The two of you. The Irishman and you.* He used the word
jara, or hara as it was pronounced in English. It meant cop
from the time kids on the beat had encountered a policeman
named O'Hara who was fast and often caught them and
slapped them for stealing fruit or candy bars from the stores
in East Harlem, so went the story. These ties between the
Puerto Ricans and the Irish were improbable but true, the

two people making individual alliances that appeared as abominations, since most of the others on both sides of the divide, be they the San Juan or Dublin tribe, spoke ill of each other and apart from the Jews and Italians, whom they also detested, produced great antipathy in both groups. He said he had been a cop, avoiding including Jerry in the question.

The man asked him why he had left the force and he'd shrugged. *Discrimination?* the man had asked, knowing it was his last question. *Yeah, discrimination,* Tommy had said. The man nodded and shuffled the cards. *Your father said we could trust you,* he said after the third shuffle of the cards. *You can trust me,* Tommy said. *And the Irishman? You can trust the Irishman. He's like my brother,* he said, looking the man in the eyes to let him know that he trusted Jerry more than he would ever trust him. *We're in business together,* he said. *You provide the money and we turn over the merchandise,* he added coldly. *Mercancía* was the word in Spanish. It had a nice ring. Dope had so many words. *Tecata, manteca, estofa.* The Italians called it *babagna.* He never knew why. But this was called merchandise. Domestic merchandise. Russian merchandise, British merchandise. Wherever the merchandise was made, someone there was willing to trade it for good old American dollars or give gold or diamonds in return. He rose, zipped up his jacket and went outside.

The night was clear and the chill of autumn already present even though it was late August, the sky full of stars. The quarter moon was gone. Beyond the dunes, out on the water, a light buoy glimmered green in the water. Farther out, like a fallen firmament, the lights of the Connecticut coast, its towns distinct, the diminutive lights of the houses clumped together like a galaxy and then an expanse of dark space and then another galaxy. He'd wanted to study astronomy as a boy. His father bought him a telescope, which he used from inside his room. It had been difficult for him to see very much, so his father, working on weekends, and to his neighbors' consternation not resting on Sunday, constructed above the second floor a sturdy observation deck, which could be reached from his room through a fixed ladder and a trap-door. It was rare that one could see stars in New York City with the naked eye because of the volume of light generated by the five boroughs. But there, in his observatory, he had traveled and documented his data, drawing what he saw and then checking his constellation book and returning to confirm his findings, sitting on Arctic-like nights when the skies were clear, bundled up and shivering more from the excitement than the cold.

Later he couldn't understand, once he knew what Kenny had done, how Gabriel had let it happen. But that night, as he stood waiting, he was not aware that while he waited for Jerry Boyle to return so they could complete this transaction, Kenny was out attempting being noble while he was out making money for the boy's college education. Thus he rationalized his efforts. Revolution money, he called it. Gabriel was a mystery. Fran said that he was now forty-four and had never gotten married. No children. She said her mother heard that there had been a girl while he was in Peru in the Peace Corps but that it hadn't worked out. He came back and got involved in the farm and that was it. *How did your mother know this?* he asked Fran. Fran had shrugged her shoulders. The farm had to be backbreaking. Seven days a week, just he and Gabriel's father and hired help working the big farm day in and day out from four in the morning until ten at night, sometimes later if a cow was having a calf or a storm came and they had to make sure the animals were safe.

He concentrated again on the dark water and then way out he saw the lights of the ship's superstructure. How could Gabriel do without a woman? He was now forty-two and he still couldn't help the desire that rose up in him whenever he saw Fran. Gabriel was two years older and he wondered where all of his desire could have gone. Jerry said the girl in Peru had been forbidden by her parents to marry him because he was an American, but he said there were other factors. They had run away together and it had caused a minor international incident because she was the daughter of a high-ranking Peruvian official.

When Kenny said he didn't want to play baseball the previous summer and wished he could go away and work, Fran sat down and tried to help him make a decision but truly to mediate between himself and Kenny. It didn't matter, Kenny was firm about it. All he told Kenny was that he was disappointed. He stopped short of saying that in his opinion he was a more gifted baseball player than he was an ice hockey player and God knew he was spectacular in ice hockey. Fran called up her mother about Kenny working away from the city. Mary Boyle said she'd ask around. A week later his mother-in-law called back and said they ought to contact Gabriel Brunet upstate. *Who is he, Ma?* Fran asked. *I asked Father Crespo at St. Ignatius and he knew a priest up in Utica and he knows a dairy farmer,* his mother said. *Where is it? Up past Albany. It's pretty nice country. Quiet and plenty of fresh air. Ma, you know about this place? No, but I trust Father Crespo. He said he has visited his friend and says that it's quiet and healthy. It's a dairy farm. He said the farmer takes in boys from the City to work up there. Like summer camp, Ma? Yes, but they have to work hard. From early in the morning into the evening.*

Fran had told her mother that she'd talk to Kenny and if

Kenny decided on it she'd like to call the farmer. Kenny was immediately excited and Fran called and arranged for Kenny to come up during the Easter break. He and Kenny and Jerry and Christopher drove up, Jerry thinking that maybe life on a farm would do Christopher good and it would get him away from rock and roll and his disrespectful friends, half of them with fathers on the job and the sons drinking and smoking weed. They started out early in the morning as they did when they'd driven to hockey tournaments in the Syracuse, Rome, Utica area in years prior. They stopped off at a rest stop on the Thruway and ate a second breakfast at McDonald's until they reached their destination, where they met the old man, Henri Brunet, who owned the farm, and Gabriel, his son, who ran it.

Christopher was unimpressed by the pastoral surroundings and hung back stroking his long tresses and his thin facial hair as if he were urging his sparse beard to make a better showing. For Kenny, however, it was like he'd come home. Ever polite, he asked Gabriel and the old man questions and wanted to know if he could learn to ride the horses and how much a calf weighed when it was born and if after they milked the cows was there any left for the newborn calves to get nourishment, all of this between bites of the big lunch that Gabriel served them: steak and baked potatoes and salad and big wedges of pie and cold milk. Gabriel asked Tommy if Kenny was like this in school and he'd said that Kenny was a straight-A student and read novels and biographies. Gabriel had nodded approvingly and said the job was his if he wanted it.

Another boy from the city was coming up, a Puerto Rican boy from the Bronx, Gabriel had said. *We're Puerto Rican,* Kenny had said, pointing at his father and then at himself. *You're a mick,* Jerry had said, touching him on the chest and saying he'd spilled gravy on himself. When Kenny looked down Jerry brushed his chin, lips and nose with his index finger. *Look at him,* he said. *He's got the map of Ireland written all over his face. Who are you kidding? Your old man lost that match. Ireland one, Puerto Rico nil.* The old man and Gabriel had been a bit embarrassed and then Kenny said: *My mother is Irish. My uncle's sister,* he added, smiling at Jerry, cool and understanding of his uncle's poor taste.

It was set. At the end of the school year they would return and bring Kenny back up to start work. Room and board and seventy-five dollars a week. He couldn't believe it. Tommy had never seen him happier. Before they left to drive back to Brooklyn, the old man gave them a large cured ham and ten mason jars filled with fruits and vegetables: pickled beets, tomatoes, marmalade, strawberry preserves and even pickled watermelon rind.

The following week when he'd driven out to see Jerry on the Island about a trip to pick up merchandise in South Carolina, Jerry said in passing that Gabriel looked Irish. He said Jerry was crazy. *They're French Canadians,* he said. He shook his head and laughed and Jerry said that he didn't know what the hell he was laughing about and wasn't he able to tell Dominicans or Colombians from Puerto Ricans. *Mostly from the way they speak English or Spanish, or how they dress,* he said. *And never from the way they look? Sometimes from the way they look,* he admitted. *Well? Well, what? Well, so can I,* Jerry said, insisting that Gabriel looked Irish. They sat at a table in the house in the dunes eating tomato soup and grilled cheese sandwiches until he admitted that Jerry might be right. *Black Irish,* Jerry said.

The phone rang as he was looking out at the dark water and he returned inside. The three men were eating. There was a plate with a sandwich and a cup of coffee for him. The man handed him the phone. It was Jerry to tell him they should be at the dock in a half hour.

*W*hen Kenny was finished with the vertical side of the L he walked the horizontal again, listening for sounds. He heard small animals scurrying about in the undergrowth and thought he heard a fox yip. He stood still for several seconds but all he heard was the silence of the night and then once again there came the flapping of wings of perhaps a different owl as it emerged from the woods and dove behind the hill, its wings spread as it glided in its search for prey along the ground. Kenny finished, and at the top of the L, he thought he heard something back where he had come from. He listened and waited for the sound to repeat itself. Nothing came. He listened to the night, mesmerized by the silence.

*t*ommy ate the sandwich and drank the strong, milky coffee that the man had prepared and sweetened collectively. He didn't realize he was so hungry. When he was done, he went into the bathroom, removed the Beretta from the holster under his left arm, checked it, and reassured himself that he had another clip in his jacket. Putting his foot up on the toilet bowl he did the same with his ankle gun, a snub-nosed .32 caliber. Finally, he felt the right pocket of his pants to make sure he had his switchblade. It was a knife similar to the one he'd carried during his time undercover and the one weapon over which he felt the most regret even though what he did had been necessary. When he was done he became aware that he felt queasy and took a deep breath, knowing the sensation would pass and he'd be alert. Maybe it was the sugar in the coffee. He came out of the bathroom. The men were waiting for him. *Listos?* he said, asking if they were ready. They nodded. They once again were wearing their gloves. He knew they'd be coming back to the house but he turned out the lights and locked the front door. When he was outside and moving toward the van he donned his own gloves. No prints anywhere. The gloves were thin and they were expensive.

His partner in the casino game was driving. They urged him to sit in front. He didn't give it a thought and instead began elaborating a plan should anything go wrong. He was certain that if something happened, the Beretta could take care of the two men in the back through the seat unless the projectile hit a spring and started acting erratically. His casino partner would be easy. He didn't think it would come to that but he planned it out. They drove along the darkened highway, the hour now late. On the right the potato fields were like long carpets. The plants laid out in neat rows were like the exact weave of a rug. On the left was the sound. At ten minutes after eleven they were at Jerry's house. The house was completely dark, except for the intermittent flickering of a TV on the second floor. If he and Fran ever had a house he would have wall-to-wall carpeting. He got out of the van, opened the driver's side of the truck and stepped up. He opened the passenger's side and one of the three men got in.

Ten minutes later they were at the pier and in another five minutes they saw the lights of the trawler coming closer, running almost silently with hardly any wake. He told the man that the boat was coming and he and the others should help unload. *And you?* his casino partner had asked. *I'll stand guard,* he'd said coldly. *No funny business,* one of the others said in perfect English. *No funny business,* he said. *I'm my father's son. I may not believe as strongly as he does, but I have the same amount of respect. Good,* his partner said in equally perfect English. He learned later that the man was a graduate in chemistry from Northwestern University.

He stood apart from them cradling the sawed-off shotgun from the truck and thinking about Fran, wanting to be with her. The moving business kept them afloat but everything was getting more and more expensive. They should've gotten a house long ago but saving for the children's education was more important. Lately, he knew that he could've done both. They shouldn't have had so many children. She was too Catholic, he'd thought. And then he smiled and although he wasn't much for religion he thanked God for Catholic girls and their supposed sexual repression, especially good Catholic girls like Fran. He had been with other girls before Fran, but he couldn't imagine that there would be anyone else as passionate as she was. In the past five or six years she had become fierce, and more often than not it was she who initiated their lovemaking. It took him longer these days and she was more pleased than ever.

They'd driven up in the middle of the summer, all the children excited by the trip, the younger girls, Katherine and Diana, arguing that they were going to Kenny's farm and Rose, who had been up before with Peggy, correcting them that it was not Kenny's farm but the farm where he worked. They got there at noon, everyone trooping out of the station wagon and descending on their big brother. Kenny greeted them with kisses and hugs. The girls draped themselves over him as if he were their personal teen star. Tommy Jr. stayed back with his mother, clinging to her dress. Kenny introduced Gabriel and Mr. Brunet to them, naming each one and saying something complimentary about each. *This is Katherine, she's ten years old and is learning to play the violin. Fiddle,* Rose had corrected. Gabriel introduced Carlos, a very shy boy who couldn't speak English. Kenny showed them the farm and the rabbits and the big sow with the baby pigs that had been born two weeks into the summer, fifteen of them. Diana was frightened by the peacock which, excited by the children's commotion, took the opportunity to flare his majestic tail, making the eyes of each feather sparkle in the sunlight. Kenny then took each of the girls, one at a time, for a ride on the horse, first sitting them on the saddle and walking them around the corral and then sitting them behind him on the saddle and galloping with the little ones screaming their delight. Peggy wanted to ride on her own and she did fine. Katherine and Diana wanted to ride the donkey but Kenny told them the animal was too old so they petted and stroked his long ears and Rose said he was going to die like Grandpa Martin.

In the afternoon Claudia drove up and Kenny introduced her to them. Diana, who was seven, said that Claudia was very tall, to which Katherine piped up and said she was supposed to be tall since she was Kenny's girlfriend. *Do you think he's going to want a shrimpy girl like you?* Katherine said. This made Diana cry and say she was not a shrimpy girl. Rose was appalled and walked away to the other end of the porch, *totally embarrassed that she was part of this family who had such impolite girls,* she later said. Peggy placed Diana on her lap and moving back and forth on a rocker whispered something to her younger sister that made her smile first and then make a face and *ewwww.* Peggy later told Fran that she'd said maybe Diana would grow up to be as tall and have a handsome boyfriend like Kenny. *Boys, yucky,* Diana had said.

Tommy had spoken briefly with Claudia and learned that her last name was Bachlichtner and that her mother was German. *From Germany? Yes, from Germany. She came to the United States after the war,* she said. *What was her last name?* he asked, always curious about others' ethnicity. *I forget,* the girl said.

Some weird last name worse than Bachlichtner, Claudia said, pronouncing it "backlightner." *We have a weird name,* Tommy had said. *Oh, no, you have a beautiful name,* Claudia had said. *Romero's a beautiful name. What does it mean?* she'd asked, engaging him, trying out her girlish charm on him. *Do you know what mine means? Bach means stream and Licht means light,* she said. *Like a shining stream?* he'd said. *I don't know what Romero means.* Gabriel had overheard the conversation, came over and said that Romero meant *peregrino. Like a hawk, a peregrine hawk?* she'd said. *No, romero means pilgrim,* Gabriel said. He added that it also meant rosemary. Rosmarinus officinalis, *from the mint family. It's used for cooking. See, I told you,* she said, flirting openly with him. He knew Claudia was enjoying the entire family because she was totally lost in her love for Kenny.

He laughed and she called out: *Hey, Kenny Romero.* Kenny was wrestling with Tommy Jr. on the lawn in front of the house, Rover, the big dog, barking at their game. Kenny looked up and waved. Claudia bounded off the porch and asked Kenny if they were going to the movies later. *Sure,* Kenny said. Tommy was impressed that Gabriel had taken time to learn Spanish. He spoke the language carefully and very likely better than he did. They'd gone off to the back of the house.

*h*e moved slowly, as if he were stalking prey, recalling his uncle and father hunting. And then he thought he heard a distinctive sound and stood still. He was there nearly five minutes standing very still and then the sound came again. He crept forward, the rifle held loosely and the flashlight off. A few minutes later the sound came and this time he counted one Mississippi, two Mississippi and waited. Thirty seconds and it came again. He counted three times. Thirty, twenty-nine, twenty-eight Mississippis. He moved forward, counting as he went until he seemed to be in a direct line with the sound. Could it be a bear? One by one he placed the six bullets into the rifle, pulled back on the lever and heard the bullet enter the chamber. He took the safety off the rifle and waited for the sound.

*J*erry came down the pier trailed by his son Patrick, who was now twenty, studying finance at St. John's University. Patrick was his eldest. *Enough of this bullshit with poverty,* Jerry had said. *The Boyles are ready to move into Wall Street and young Patrick is going to lead the way. Fucking A,* Patrick had said. He knew Patrick was holding a .45 by the side of his leg. The two men on the boat, Rick Maloney and Teddy Grady, Jerry's cousin from his mother's side, probably had automatic weapons at the ready. Teddy had done a stint for armed robbery and Rick had been Special Forces. Both of them were no nonsense, quiet and deadly. The two of them were blooded and with more than half a dozen bodies between them, like Puerto Rican street kids said about the demise of their enemies. A funny world they lived in now that he had crossed over the line. Was it a line between good and evil or simply a line that separated the lawful from its darker side? Fran knew more about this ethical divide than he did. Gods from Olympus and those of the Underworld, she called them. *Zeus and Hades were brothers,* Fran had said. *Hades is not like Satan,* she'd said. *He doesn't punish anyone but he's ruthless.* Maybe that's all they were, part of the same thing. Supplying merchandise for others. Revolution money there to be made. He no longer thought about the right and wrong of it.

Jerry greeted him with the same seriousness he always displayed when he was working. Patrick nodded as severely, emulating his father. He was a younger replica of Jerry and copied his every move. *It took a while longer than we thought,* Jerry said. *The fuckos wanted more money. They wanted another five grand. We had to turn over two grand to cover the freighting expenses. Thieving bastards. Greek captain. Are they ready to receive the shipment?* Jerry said, pointing with his head toward the three men. *They're ready,* he said. *I'll get the truck ready. Tell them to come ahead.* He waved to the men and two of them came forward, nodded at Jerry and Patrick. Patrick led them to the trawler and they began moving the crates forward. *What's with the other guy?* Jerry asked. *I guess he wants to make sure everything's on the up-and-up. I told him I wasn't going to screw up my old man's deal. Hell, it has nothing to do with your old man,* Jerry said. *Word gets around that we don't keep our word and it's all over. You know that. One day you wake up and you'll be dressed in white and fucking girl angels. You, because you're such a good guy, will end up in Heaven. How's my sister? Still horny? Your mother thinks she's pregnant again, Jerry. Jesus, Mary and Joseph! Give the girl a break. Leave her alone. Get some rhythm in your life, Papi. I asked her about contraception and she says I'm crazy,* he said to Jerry. *Too Catholic.*

They chattered like that for a few moments and then moved down the pier to the truck. Tommy unlocked the back of the truck and opened the doors. When his casino partner saw the furniture he shook his head and asked where they were going to put everything. Jerry laughed. *Jesus, didn't I tell you to take the furniture out before you brought the truck?* he said. *That's what you get when you hire Puerto Ricans,* he said, turning to the man. The man didn't appreciate the remark. *C'mon, give me a hand, and stop being a tight-assed revolutionary,* Jerry said to the man. *Have a little fun.* Between the three of them they removed two easy chairs, a coffee table and an oriental rug. When they were done he pried the floor of the truck open and about a four-foot section lifted up on hinges to reveal a deep compartment beneath the floor. *How far back does it go?* the man asked. *All the way to the front of the truck,* he answered. *Everything's going to fit with room to spare,* Jerry said. *Hell, a couple of you could hide in there for the trip back if you wanted. We'll buy you some rice and beans, cuchifritos and a six-pack of Bud and you guys'll be fine.* The man was again not amused but again didn't reply.

Jerry was a cold bastard when he wanted. He played the hippie, carrying a guitar and wearing a bandanna, his blond hair long. He dressed in garishly colored bell-bottoms and flowered shirts, cutting heroin deals in East Harlem and he fronting for him, explaining to the junkies that he just wanted some coke and smoke and he was cool and the heroin was for people in Greenwich Village. *He's a musician, man. Can't you see that, bro?* Coming back the next day and accusing the dealer of giving him bad shit and asking to see his boss and going higher until he drew enough attention so that he had a big dealer lined up and once he had the dealer hooked, he made small buys, delivering the cash a few times until they were ready for the big time. A big bust would have developed but it didn't because Jerry was being set up and he went down with him even though he hadn't wanted to be part of it. Jerry hadn't suspected the setup and they were caught off guard and that was the beginning of the end. Eventually they were kicked off the job.

When the last of the twenty-five long crates and the ten smaller metal boxes that contained the ammunition, all of them with Chinese characters on them, were in the compartment, the three men spoke among themselves, the two reassuring his casino partner that they had opened every crate and everything was as it should be. Casino nodded and Tommy closed the compartment. The furniture was once again placed in the truck. *Now comes the good part,* Jerry said. *The envelope, please.* At this point Rick Maloney and Teddy Grady appeared. Patrick and the two came forward. Patrick placed himself beside his father and Grady and Maloney on either side of them. Maloney wore a long black raincoat, his right hand in his pocket, the pocket removed to permit easy access to a weapon, likely a shotgun or a machine pistol, cocked and ready.

Four Irishmen facing four Puerto Ricans. For a second Tommy sensed a slight fear and some misgivings that something had gone wrong. Jerry repeated the phrase: *The envelope, please. El zipper,* Casino said. Tommy moved slowly, turned his back to Jerry, trusting him once more for the umpteenth time, and brought the zipper of the man's jacket down almost to the bottom. He opened the jacket, reached in and removed the satchel. When he was done he zipped up the jacket, turned and held out the satchel until Patrick came to him, took it and brought it to his father. *Is it all here?* Jerry asked. *It's all there,* Casino said. *Can I keep the pouch? As a token of our esteem,* the man said. Jerry came forward and shook hands with the man and smiled at him. *Good luck,* Jerry said. *Thanks,* the man said. *Hopefully, it'll take us less time. Less time?* Jerry asked, puzzled. *Yeah, less time,* Casino said. *We've been at it eighty-two years. You've been at it, what? Been at what?* Jerry said. *When was the Battle of the Boyne?* 1690? *William of Orange. What is that? Two hundred and ninety years?* Jerry burst out laughing. *You son of a bitch,* he said. *What the hell is your name? Sean Rivas,* the man said. *Sean? Yeah, we borrow from everybody. Jerry Boyle,* he said and once again extended his hand. The two men embraced stiffly and Jerry asked Patrick if the boat was secure. Patrick nodded. He took Grady and Maloney aside, paid them from the pouch and they drove off. It was likely that what they had loaded in the truck was only one quarter of the merchandise and the rest was in the hull of the trawler. Later in the week there would be another exchange with a freighter, perhaps one sailing to Latin America or Africa.

He and the three Puerto Ricans parked the moving truck down the street from the pier, got into the van and drove back to the house on the dunes. It was a little after midnight. They would sleep four hours and be up before dawn. After breakfast they'd begin the drive to Chicago and final delivery of the merchandise. He was happy everything had gone well. Sean Rivas congratulated him. *Your father was right when he told us we were in good hands,* he said. *How long have you known your partner?* he asked. The use of the phrase amused Tommy. He thought about the time. *Almost twenty years,* he said. *I'm married to his sister. Irlandesa? Yes, Irish. Kids? Six and maybe another on the way.* Rivas held up three fingers. *I married a Polish girl,* he said. *It's funny seeing kielbasa and morcillas side by side,* he said and they both laughed.

What a laugh life was. He had lied only once to Fran. What he had done still bothered him, but he had no choice. You started out with so many choices and after a while there were less and less to be made. They had suggested that he cut a deal because they knew he wasn't involved. Kelly said that they could arrange it so that he didn't lose his job. He turned and walked away from them outside the Chinatown restaurant where they'd eaten dim sum. They were fucks and were asking him to turn against Jerry. He wasn't going that way even though he'd warned Jerry that he shouldn't have been involved with Patterson and Kelly.

He had watched the dealer for months, knowing his routine. It was like clockwork. When he got dressed up he was going to make a delivery. He was due. He staked him out and then waited over a period of a week until he finally showed up, dressed in his suit and carrying a briefcase. He carried the drugs to the big guys in the projects by the East River. The heroin would be brought there and possibly transferred someplace else where it would be cut and mixed with lactose or something else to dilute its strength. It was then placed in small glassine envelopes for street distribution. This was how the street value was reckoned. That night he waited for the guy to get out of the car and walk across First Avenue with his guard, also dressed in a suit. They looked like two young Puerto Rican salesmen or junior executives still living at home, returning to their mothers' apartments in the projects. He pulled back on the thin black gloves, took a deep breath and removed the .22 with the silencer on it. When they were in the dark between two buildings he came out of the shadows, and demanded the briefcase.

The guard went for his gun and he shot the kid twice in the head and put the gun back in his pocket, hitting the safety, automatically. The courier took off running toward the last building of the projects. He ran after him thinking that they wouldn't be able to trace the gun to him, since he'd taken it from a junkie. He reminded himself to dispose of it as soon as possible anyway. He caught up to the young guy quickly and knocked him down just as a group of girls were coming out of the building. They didn't notice the scuffle on the grass. As he rolled with him he saw the guy pull out a gun. His own gun was pinned against the briefcase. He reached into his pants, pulled out a button switchblade, grabbed the dealer's hair and pushed the button. The knife clicked and he stabbed the kid through the neck three times in quick succession.

The body went weak and blood pumped out with remarkable force from one wound. He wiped the knife on the guy's jacket, grabbed the briefcase and was gone, racing through the yellow and green haze created by the trees and the light from the housing project's lampposts. He hurtled the low fence to the highway, and as he and his friends had done as kids, timed the traffic downtown and crossed over to the island in the middle of the highway. The traffic uptown was even less and he was on the other side of the East River Drive no more than two minutes after the courier had expired. He was over the iron fence and between the saplings that lined the walk and he was free, walking along the dark river, beside which for a few years he'd run and played before they moved to Brooklyn. He recalled stopping to watch the old men lowering their crab traps with whitened pieces of chicken, or raising the blue crabs and placing them in a bucket to be sold. He couldn't believe it had been so easy to rob the courier. When he was at 100th Street he stopped briefly and looked out over the dark water. The city was beautiful, the lights of the buildings like sparkling diamonds lying on a piece of black velvet, he thought. Like the stones they laid out in the diamond district. He wouldn't be getting a transfer to Safes and Lofts, he thought. The walkway was deserted, the bridge to Ward Island raised. He stopped, looked around, took the pistol out, released the clip, unscrewed the silencer and flung the gun out into the river. He walked a little farther and in quick succession threw the silencer out into the water, threw each bullet out into the current and then floated the clip out. Let them dredge the river. It would cost them a couple of hundred thousand dollars. His salary for about six years. He then took the knife out of his jacket pocket and threw it into the river as well. He removed his gloves and put them in his pocket.

EDGARDO VEGA YUNQUÉ

Five minutes later he emerged at 96th Street, took a cab to the West Side and then the subway home. Tomorrow he would get rid of his shoes, wrapping them and leaving them in a trashcan. Fran and the kids were asleep when he got home. He took the briefcase into the bathroom, locked the door and opened it. Four half-kilo packages. He fought the urge to keep the extra two, closing his eyes as he reckoned how much he could get. A hundred thousand, easily. But he couldn't. And then he thought that he had transgressed in killing the two men, so why not continue. He finally went into the medicine cabinet, got the scissors, cut the first plastic bag and poured its contents into the toilet bowl, flushed it and repeated the action. He cut the two empty bags into small pieces and flushed them as well. He then closed the briefcase and shook his head at the two bags, despising what it did to so many people. He retrieved a sponge and the cleanser and scrubbed the toilet furiously, wanting the presence of the illness to be away from his children. He brushed his teeth, urinated, flushed the toilet again and showered, letting the hot water relax his muscles. He came out, dried himself, put on a bathrobe, checked his clothes to make sure there was no blood on them and placed them in the hamper. He came out and put the briefcase with the two remaining bags on the shelf of the closet, placed a box with phonograph records on top of it and closed the door. In the bedroom, he removed his bathrobe and slid into bed with Fran. He was awake a long time listening to the night, numbed and his mind refusing to see again what he had done. Two Ricans to save the life of one mick. Finally, around two in the morning he fell asleep.

In the morning, he had coffee and toast with Fran, kissed Kenny and Peggy and said he had to go into Manhattan. He placed his sneakers in a paper bag, rode the subway and deposited the shoes into a trash bin on a subway platform. At eleven o'clock that morning he turned the two missing "bags" over to Internal Affairs, signed some papers waiving a jury trial, and another agreeing to his dismissal from the job. No badge, no guns, no uniform, no benefits and no pride about his work. And then he was gone, no longer protected by the cloak of blue that had bonded him to the thousands of good cops. He was now alone, out into the uncertainty of the day, just as he would be tomorrow as he traveled the highways of the land. There were so many roads, some big and some small. They were like the circulatory system of a person. Arteries, veins and capillaries. All of them carrying blood to each part of the body. He thought of the truck as a pill that a great being had ingested, traveling in the bloodstream. He couldn't figure out whether the pill contained poison or a medicine that could cure an ill. He decided that this one shipment was medicine. His father had initiated this one transaction and his father, if nothing else, could be trusted and he was blood. *Carne de mi carne y sangre de mi sangre,* the saying went. Flesh of my flesh and blood of my blood. The blood had been traveling for thousands of years through the ages from Africa and Spain, from the Taino Indians who had come from South America through the islands of the Caribbean, from Moors who invented algebra and constructed buildings of unequaled beauty and reckoned the orbits of planets, and blacks who had been brought to the Island and enslaved. And his children who now, besides his own blood, carried blood from Vikings, Normans, Angles, Saxons, Britons, Gaels over and over, duplicating itself through bloodstreams, through semen and ova, round and round, traveling from one generation to the next, repeating itself in screams of joy and in cries of sorrow. *Carne de mi carne y sangre de mi sangre.* He knew there was some similar saying in English but he couldn't remember it.

*K*enny stepped into the woods and before he had taken three steps he had to turn on the flashlight. He stopped again and listened, the grunting growing louder. He turned, took out the compass and shone the light on it. The farm was below to the northeast. He noted the direction, put the compass back in his pocket and went on, turning left for a while and then altering his ascent until he could now hear the faint lowing and knew he'd found the cow. The knowledge that he'd found her made him content, but he was immediately on guard as he yawned and knew instinctively that he was beginning to relax and shouldn't. He was certain that once he found her he could urge her back down where she'd be safe. He reprimanded himself at once for forgetting to bring a rope. He again tried to imagine what he'd do if she had already had her calf. He decided he'd stay with the cow and her calf and wait until Gabriel and Carlos came looking for him when they found out that he was missing.

*B*ack at the house Tommy showed the men the bedrooms downstairs and said he'd be upstairs if they needed anything. The men nodded and went off to sleep, telling him they would be starting out before sunrise. Once upstairs he unstrapped his guns and placed the Beretta in a drawer and the ankle gun on the floor next to the bed. He'd bought new guns, but they were the same as the ones he had on the job. If anything happened he didn't want the bullets traced. He stretched several times, the tension in his body leaving him after the day of constant tension. He removed his clothes, showered quickly, dried himself and put on clean underwear from his small traveling bag. On the dresser there was a picture of Jerry's girlfriend, a Puerto Rican girl from Central Islip. She looked like a poor man's Rita Moreno. She was a dental hygienist and only four years older than his son Patrick, and almost half Jerry's age. *I'm getting even with the Puerto Ricans for you marrying my sister,* Jerry joked, but it was apparent that he loved the girl, Gloria Pujols, still living at home.

He dialed his number in Brooklyn and Fran answered on the second ring. *Everything's okay, honey,* he said. *Good,* she said. *How are the kids? They're good. Rose said that maybe when she got older she'd become a lesbian. Was she kidding?* he asked. *I don't know but Mary Margaret crossed herself and closed her eyes. I think in spite of her temperament maybe Peggy'll become a nun. Would you object? No to the lesbian and yes to the nun,* he said and they both laughed. *I miss you,* she said. *And I you,* he said. *When will you be back? Three days,* he said. As usual they didn't discuss his destination on the phone. *Be careful driving,* she said, but meant much more than that. *I will,* he said and asked her if she'd make a ham with lima beans and blueberry cobbler when he got back. She said she would and then said she loved him, and he said he loved her and they said good night.

Tommy got under the sheets and blankets of the wide bed and was asleep a few minutes later. During the night he dreamt about making love to Fran. It was a slow type of lovemaking that went on forever and their bodies became smoke figures undulating and sensuous but retained their form and the pleasure persisted. When the alarm clock went off at five he felt completely refreshed. The other men were up already making coffee and cooking breakfast. *Buenos días,* they each said, now having gone back to talking solely in Spanish.

By the time the sun came up they were on the road and

heading west, ahead of the morning commute. By noon they were on the Pennsylvania Turnpike. Sean Rivas was driving the truck, taking over at a rest stop after they'd crossed the George Washington Bridge. Tommy sat back and relaxed once they'd settled into the monotonous rhythm of turnpike traffic. He recalled being flattered that Jerry Boyle was inviting him to his sister's birthday party. He'd gotten the address, ridden to the station, and walked two blocks along the Grand Concourse. The building was large and well kept. He entered the lobby and went up on the elevator. When he got to the Boyles' apartment he could hear the party in full swing, and the door open. It was a large, high-ceilinged apartment. He arrived purposely late to appear inconspicuous. Maureen, Fran's older sister, already married, opened the door and shouted that Tommy had arrived. Sheila, Jerry's wife, ruddy faced and pregnant, greeted him a bit coldly and stood by as Maureen brought him into the living room, explaining that Jerry was in the bathroom. She introduced him all around to different relatives and friends as Jerry's partner, the relationship permissible in canceling out his obvious Spanishness. Jerry came out rubbing his hands dry and threw his arms around him. *Dad, this is my partner, Tommy Romero,* he said. Martin Boyle came forward and shook his hand a little suspiciously, eyeing his mustache with an apparent frown. *It's part of his natural disguise,* Jerry had said and laughed. And then Jerry asked where Fran was. *She's in the kitchen helping Mom and Aunt Liz,* Sheila said. *It's her party and she's in there helping out. Same old Frances.*

They laughed and Jerry went into the kitchen and dragged his sister out. She had her head down as she wiped her hands on an apron. As Jerry began introducing them her jaw dropped at the sight of him. He had the same unmistakable reaction of being dumbstruck by her. All at once, as if the room had emptied and the only ones who existed were Frances Boyle and Tomás Romero, they took each other in and accepted their lives as if they had belonged together forever. The introductions were unnecessary and she came forward and said: *Hi, Tommy, you made it. I wouldn't have missed it for the world,* he said. He reached into his pocket and extended a little square gift to her. *Thank you,* she said and immediately unwrapped the present, opened the box and let out a small squeal of delight. *Earrings,* she said, looking at the delicate gold earrings with two diminutive red stones in each, picked out from his uncle's jewelry store in El Barrio. *Oh, but you don't have pierced ears,* he said. *I'm sorry. I can get you regular ones. No, no. I'll get them pierced this week,* she said and Sheila arched her eyebrows. *Well, I'll leave the two of you alone to get acquainted. Come on,* she said, grabbing Jerry's arm.

And that had been it. When he picked her up the following weekend to go to the movies her ears had been pierced, and she was wearing the earrings, her thick blond hair in a French twist and her thin-shelled ears delicate. She was more beautiful than he remembered her at the party. Inside the movie theater she took his hand and held it throughout. They saw *Breakfast at Tiffany's* and then later when they were eating sundaes at a restaurant on the Upper East Side she said she'd read Truman Capote's *The Grass Harp* and did he like reading? He said he liked adventure stories. *Like what?* she asked. *For Whom the Bell Tolls* and *To Have and Have Not,* he said. *Hemingway,* he added, *but I like John Steinbeck. He's funny sometimes and sometimes he's sad. Really?* she smiled. *Yes, have you read* Cannery Row? *Yes,* she said excitedly. *It's sad and funny. What about* The Pearl? He said he hadn't read that one yet. *I also like James Michener,* he said. *He's more historical. I like spy stories too.* On the way out of the restaurant she placed her arm through his. On the subway she rested her head on his shoulder. It was like they had known each other for years and nothing the other did was strange. When he saw her to the door she held his hand and pursed her lips for him to kiss. He kissed her lightly and she smiled broadly and asked him to please call her. All the way to his parents' house in Brooklyn he couldn't stop thinking about Frances Boyle and wondered if his parents would like her because she had totally erased the memory of any girl he'd known and she was a *blanquita*, a white girl.

discovery

*His mother was Frances Ann Boyle, an
Irish girl from the Bronx, whose family
was unable or unwilling to escape to
the suburban tranquility of two-family
houses and front yards in the outer boroughs
of New York City.*

K ENNY HAD gone slowly into the woods, not quite knowing what to expect. He had never been in the woods
at night except that one year when he was a Boy Scout
and they had camped out. The fear that he might encounter
a large animal, a bear or a coyote, even a deer produced a
sliver of fear in him. Higher and higher he went. He listened
with each step, stopping at the slightest sound. And then he
heard the cow moan loudly as if she sensed his presence and
was issuing a call for help. He stepped through a thicket,
shone the flashlight in a slow wide arc and there, in a small
clearing, he saw the cow lying on her side breathing with difficulty, the ground half moss and half gravel, an outcropping

of rocks, perhaps eight feet high, creating a natural wall a few feet behind her. He heard a scurrying in the undergrowth, stepped forward, knelt and stroked the cow's face. She looked up at him with her huge, lashed eyes, dumb and unknowing.

*f*ran wanted Tommy to let it go and stop insisting on being Puerto Rican. They were Americans. There were no arguments about it but the subject and the things he talked about lately frightened her. She was born in the United States and so was he. And her brother was no better and he ought to also forget about his pride in being Irish and try to be a good American. Back before the trouble they had good jobs but couldn't wait for the St. Patrick's Day parade to come around to put on their uniforms and wear little green shamrocks and when the Puerto Rican Day parade came they marched in that as well. Her brother even wore the Puerto Rican flag on his uniform and became Jerry Boylgado just as Tommy became O'Romer for St. Patty's. They were so crazy, the two of them, and they had lost good jobs and now they ought to stop tempting fate because sooner or later they'd get caught. They didn't think she knew but she did and had put it all together from things Sheila, Jerry's wife, said. It was useless talking to them. What was she going to do with six children to raise and him in jail? They were like the ones who had blown up Fraunces Tavern and were constantly blowing up buildings in England and Ireland, killing innocent people. What did it matter? Most of the people wanted to remain as they were. Only these small groups on these two islands kept making trouble and she had to be connected to both of them. It was like a sickness that had followed her here from the Ireland of her grandparents. The Troubles, they called it there. What about her troubles?

She tried praying but it was no use. And what a sweet man

Tommy was apart from everything. How considerate he was even when they were young and had met after she graduated from college, wondering what was going to happen to her life but looking forward to teaching. One year she'd taught, before she was pregnant. She had looked at him, he'd smiled at her and she had blushed from head to toe, her pale skin turning red, Virginia McQuinlan, standing across the room, said. And then when he had given her the gift her sister Maureen said she knew she was love-stricken and would never be the same. And Maureen was right.

And now she was pregnant again and God help her but she had gone to the abortion clinic and had inquired about the possibility. Something didn't feel right and she couldn't figure out what it was but something was wrong. She couldn't tell if it had to do with Tommy being gone longer and longer each time, the stress of the children growing up, or her getting older. She was still young and healthy but something was definitely amiss. She had just turned thirty-nine and this one was different from the others. The doctor had suggested an amnio to detect irregularities but she wanted to wait and discuss it with Tommy. She should have been more careful. Rose talking about being a lesbian worried her more and more each day. She was sure she needed attention and that was all. Mary Margaret wasn't taking it very well. She wished the summer were over and Kenny would come home. He was such a steadying influence on the girls.

*k*enny shone the light on the cow and saw the muzzle of the calf emerging from the distended vagina, the black of the nostrils odd against the redness so that he thought of playing checkers with his grandpa Romero in the backyard of his house and smelling his grandmother's cigar drifting out of the kitchen window as she cooked. She'd brought them tamarind juice. *Refresco de tamarindo,* he thought, recalling the tartness. He knew he was thinking of other things because he was afraid. He made himself concentrate. He shone the light on the cow again and now saw the pool of blood beneath the cow's neck where she had lain her head.

She thought again of what it would be like to lie down and have a child that was growing inside of her ripped out, vacuumed out of her as if it were a dust mote or lint. She liked the word "mote" and wished she had fine oriental rugs on the floors of her apartment instead of linoleum and cheap five-and-ten throw rugs. Even when she was in college, girls were going away and having abortions. Deirdre Duggan had gotten pregnant but she wouldn't tell anyone who the father was and eventually went down south and got an abortion and came back and it was like nothing to her and then she saw Deirdre in Central Park with a very black student from the college and she knew that the baby had been his. Her family moved to Yonkers and then two years later she came back to the neighborhood and she was Deirdre Cannizzaro and had a baby boy with black hair and that was it. She was lucky. Megan Flaherty wasn't so lucky. They found her dead over by the docks in Manhattan. She had bled to death and people said she had a wire hanger sticking out of her. Her boyfriend, Nicky McCarthy, had tried giving her an abortion. He took off, held up a bank in New Jersey and got killed by the cops trying to get away. Megan was seventeen and Nicky was nineteen.

But it didn't make sense. Not with Tommy's baby. In spite of her Catholic beliefs she was confused. Seven years after the case she was still digesting what *Roe v. Wade* meant in real terms. Was she a feminist? She didn't know. Did women have the right to choose what happened with their bodies? She didn't know. God had made men and women, so He should have a say-so in what happened with women's bodies, and men's. But God didn't speak. Not really. The pope spoke for Him and that's what she had always followed. And now this.

Each of their children had been so precious, like a gift from God, she thought as she was bathing Tommy Jr. He loved the water and continued splashing in his attempt to sink his boat. With each splash he made a booming sound. *Please, Tommy,* she said. *Mommy is soaked. Please stop, sweetheart. Look at me. I'm dripping. Give me the boat, please. No, I'm the submarine,* he said and once again slapped at the water. In desperation she took the plug out of the bathtub, stood up and pulled a fresh towel down from the shelf. *Time to get dried,* she said. Tommy was making sure he didn't miss any of the fun of the receding water.

She was stunned by how one minute she was a young girl just graduated from college and eighteen years later she had three teenagers and three others. Everything had happened so quickly. There were highlights but most of her life was like a slide projector shooting out images at a rapid pace: births, diaper changes, feedings, baths, dressing them, putting them to bed, their first steps, their first words, baptismals, birthday parties, day camp, first communion, homework, pimples, picnics, the beach, amusement parks, school, dance, music, fighting over the telephone. And through it all he was there telling her not to worry, that things would work out okay. He'd come home and she'd be waiting for him, timing his entrance with the warming of his food because he was punctual, racing to be with her. He'd come in and kiss her deeply, holding her body to him desperately and sighing as if he'd held himself in all day and immediately feeling his hardness against her making her want him. *Come on,* she'd say.

I made meat loaf. Fresh string beans. And blueberry cobbler. Sit down before it gets cold. And he'd say such fresh things. *I want to eat you before you get cold,* and she would still blush because it felt so good when he did it. She loved his body on her. She had to stop thinking about it. He wouldn't be returning for a while.

He'd tell her he wanted to see the children first and they'd go into the bedroom and look at Kenny, sleeping peacefully in his youth bed, and Mary Margaret in her crib in her foot pajamas, sleeping on her tummy with her little butt sticking up. And then he'd sit down to eat and tell her about his day, how he just stood out there with the rest of the junkies, trying to get more information about where he could cop heroin, making the small buys and getting to know everything. He didn't want to talk about it but she made him, convincing him that it was good to be debriefed, she'd said, hoping he understood that. She knew he didn't tell her about the horror of being out there in the desperate blackness of that world, but he told her about the times when it rained and he sat in coffee shops with the junkies, guys like himself, Puerto Ricans who had been damaged and had turned to drugs to quiet the pain. Once in a while he would tell her about a beautiful Puerto Rican girl who was barely in her twenties and looked as if she were in her forties.

And while he ate she'd fill the bathtub and when he was done she'd take him into the bathroom, lock the door and undress him while he kissed her and touched her breasts and then he'd get in the tub and she would wash him like he was one of her babies and shampoo his hair and rinse him and then she'd lather his chest with all the hair and then she'd wash him below and make him hard and stroke him as he kissed her. And sometimes he would whisper that she should undress and she would, watching his eyes as he took in her body that she knew was not perfect and now had stretch marks from childbirth and maybe was a little too fat, but he loved her and it didn't matter, reminding her that she was beautiful and she didn't want to do it yet and she'd kneel on the floor of the bathroom as if she were in church and imagined Mary Mother of Christ washing her dead son but he wouldn't stop kissing her, biting her lips and her ears and eventually he'd coax her into the bathtub with him and she'd lie on top of him, placing herself so that he was within her, moving slowly until his pleasure came and she washed him again and rinsed him and let the water out. And then she'd dry him and they put on their bathrobes and they'd check the babies and then go to the bedroom and now it was her turn because now it took him longer and it was wonderful. She remembered doing it in the water standing up on that deserted beach in Puerto Rico, until he came. And he loved her so much and she loved him like her life, God help her, almost more than the children, which no mother should permit herself to even think.

And then one night when Rose was just a toddler, when the temperature had reached one hundred during the day and the children had been cranky even though she'd taken them to the playground and they had played in the sprinklers, he came in and was devastated and mute and when he saw the children he burst out crying and couldn't eat and collapsed in the hall so that she had to hold him for an hour before the tension left his body.

What is it, baby? she'd asked after a while and he just shook his head. And then the phone rang and it was Jerry asking how Tommy was. She told him he was in pretty bad shape and asked what had happened. *We had to waste a couple of guys. Black fucks,* he said. *Nigger cocksuckers. Please don't talk that way, Jerry. Sorry, sorry, Fran. It was bad. Tommy didn't do either of them,* Jerry said, but she knew he was lying and it was likely that

Tommy had finally killed someone. *He'll be all right,* he said. *What about you?* she asked. *How are you doing? I'm okay,* he said. *It was them or us, you know. I'll sleep like a baby. Take care of him,* Jerry had said. *He's a good man, Frankie,* he'd said, using his pet nickname for her, which no one else but him used.

They said good night and when she came back to the hall Tommy had gone into the children's room. He had changed Rose and was holding her as he sat on the floor, soothing her and singing the baby a *nana,* a lullaby in Spanish: *Duérmete nena, duérmete y no llores, que tu papito bueno siempre te adora.* It was so tender that she sat next to him and they both wept quietly until Rose was asleep. *Sleep, little girl, sleep and don't cry, because your good daddy will always love you.* They put Rose back in the crib and went into the bedroom, and without turning on the light took off their shoes, lay down and held each other with their clothes on and eventually fell asleep. In the night the heat wave lifted and the skies opened up and it poured and poured and they woke up with the rain coming in through the open window misting them. She'd gotten up quickly, climbing over him and closed the window next to their bed. He was awake next to her, holding himself to her, clinging really. After a while they got up and went out into the storm and sat on the fire escape nearly an hour, watching the lightning and listening to the thunder, holding each other as the heavy rain pelted them. Eventually, they came back inside and took off their wet clothes and made love, licking the rainwater from their bodies. He was violent and then tender and he cried and then fell asleep.

*k*enny touched the cow's neck and knew she had been bitten badly and didn't know whether a bear or a coyote had wounded her. Gabriel said that the eastern coyotes were bigger than the western ones and had mated with wolves from the north and drifted south, expanding their territory. His mother had said that it was called hybrid vigor when similar breeding species mated and produced healthier and stronger individuals. He had seen the animals loping through a field, chasing a rabbit, and they looked like large German shepherds. He touched the cow's throat where the bite was made. His hand came away covered by the blood. The smell made him slightly nauseous. It was likely that the wound had cracked the voice box and now the cow could hardly make much of a sound. He wiped his hand on his jeans and shone the light on the one eye facing him. After the first recognition the eye was now dim and he knew that the cow was either in shock or dying. The previous summer he had seen the old plow horse that the old man had had for twenty years collapse and die. Gabriel had wanted to go in and put him out of his misery but the old man held the horse's head and spoke to him in French, telling him to fall asleep, calling him *mon cheval, mon cher cheval*. He was certain that the cow had begun birthing and had been surprised by a coyote, which had run away when he heard him approaching.

*f*rances wondered whether she should confide in her mother that she was pregnant again and was thinking of having an abortion. She wouldn't understand. In spite of her gruff manner and her jokes, her mother was firm in her Catholic beliefs and whether she liked it or not things would not go over well with her. She didn't want to hurt her. Her life had not been the easiest and she had done her best with few resources. She was sure she loved her father but Martin Boyle had been a man who lacked ambition, blustered about injustices and never did anything to remedy them. She had listened to his advice and loved him but it was her mother whom she trusted and feared at the same time. She dreaded her disapproval more than anything else in the world. She loved sitting with her listening to the radio and learning to darn socks, or holding the yarn as she wound it around her fingers. She taught her how to knit and embroider although she could do little of either these days. Her mother knew so many things and surprisingly she was bright and read even though she had only attended high school. And she loved hearing the stories she told about growing up. The family had come from Ireland and she was the first one born in the States. Her father and mother and her brother Michael, eight years old, Terrence six, Rosemary five, Elizabeth four, all of them dead now, and she, Mary Katherine. There had been three more children born after her but they had moved away and lived in far-off places. One had even gone to Australia and lived there and they'd lost touch with them. Sean, Patrick and Fiona, gone into the mist of memory. Sean lived in Australia and raised sheep, she'd heard.

Her mother told about living in Hell's Kitchen and her father driving a wagon with an old horse and collecting rags and walking with her brothers and sisters around the neighborhood and drunks coming out of the saloons trying to grab her breasts, which were quite prominent by the time she was twelve. James Anthony Grady and Frances Patricia Riordan. Her mother rarely spoke about Grandma Frances, after whom she had been named. And they saw her even less. *She's a horrible woman,* her mother would say. They'd go and see her and she would be fine and kind for about a half hour and then something would trigger her anger and she'd begin complaining and before long there was a fight and her mother was being threatened with going to Hell by her grandma.

And don't think because you're now a big, grown-up woman with children that you won't see the back of me hand, she'd say. *It's a mir-*

acle that you haven't been stricken dead yet by God for going back on your word, she said once. And her mother, Mary Boyle, responded by saying: *It's a miracle the Devil hasn't come around to take you dancing because you'd make a fine partner for him.* Her grandmother would close her fists and her eyes would narrow and she looked like she was about to take a step forward and come at her daughter and let fly with her fists. *That's okay, Frances Riordan,* we're leaving. *Your grandchildren will be forever grateful that I didn't lie to them about witches. And remember, Halloween comes once a year, but a witch is forever,* or something smart and original like that. When she died her mother got roaring drunk and howled at the moon and her grandpa Grady had to hold her head as she vomited into the toilet bowl. She refused to go to the wake or the funeral.

Fran forgot about other times when her mother and grandmother had gotten into disputes, but that one time stuck in her mind maybe because of the witches or her dancing with the Devil, which she could see clearly, the Devil dressed in his red outfit with the horns and tail and her skinny grandmother in her apron, the two of them stepdancing, but it wasn't about that, so it had to be about her mother going back on her promise. So, when she was about eleven after they'd gone to a mass that was said for her cousin Eddie Grady, her uncle Michael's son, who was a soldier and had died in Korea, she asked her mother. When they came out of St. Luke's on 138th Street and were walking on Cypress Avenue and she was holding her older sister Rosemary's hand and her brother Michael was lagging behind talking to friends and spinning his yo-yo, which his mother had told him he shouldn't bring to church, she asked: *What did Grandma mean about you not keeping your promise to God? Oh, more of her nonsense,* she'd said. *The woman manufactures these things. But what did she mean, Mom? I'll tell you later.* When they'd gone upstairs and she was cooking supper she hung around, as always, helping her mother. She peeled potatoes and cut string beans and made Kool-Aid or mixed Jell-O and put it in molds. *What did she mean, Mom? You didn't keep your promise.* Her mother turned from the stove and smiled at her. *Oh, that,* she said. *Tattletale Nora Gilhooley saw me on a Friday eating a hamburger and told her mother and her mother told Mrs. Mahoney and Mrs. Mahoney told Mrs. Neely and Mrs. Neely, who is the biggest gossip around St. Mary's Park, told everyone that Mary Katherine Grady had eaten meat on Friday and who knew how long that had been going on and how long it would continue. That's it?* she'd asked. *Yes, that was it. Did you? Yes, I did and I got a big stomachache, which should be a lesson to you not to do such things. Did you go to confession, Ma? Yes, I dutifully went to confession and was assigned severe penance. What are you reading these days? I'm reading* Wuthering Heights, *Ma. Good, good. Watch yourself with men like that. They will talk sweetly to you and frisk your drawers. My drawers, Ma? Never mind. Set the table and then call your father and your brothers and sister. Yes, Ma,* and she took the silverware out of the cupboard drawer and began setting the table.

But then when she was fourteen and was entering Cathedral High School at the new building on Lexington Avenue, she again asked her mother about not keeping her promise. She now had a different story and she laughed and said that there was a boy by the name of James Fitzpatrick, a suitor. *A suitor? Yes, a young man who had practically no jaw and at the age of twenty-four still had a pimply forehead and a very large red nose— like this Rudolph in the song—who asked me to marry him. And you said yes, Ma? Yes, I said, yes. A terrible mistake and it got around the neighborhood that I was going to marry this very ugly boy with dirty fingernails and my mother was appalled. Why did you do that? I was kidding but he took it as a serious promise. Mary Katherine, my mother said, did you promise to marry James Fitzpatrick? Yes, I did but I was only joking, and I'm sorry. I'll give you sorry, she said and smacked my face six or seven times before I could raise my hands to protect myself. She was very fast and my father said she could have probably given Jack Dempsey a go at it in the ring but couldn't make the weight requirement she was so skinny.*

So she had changed her story and Frances didn't want to ask again, certain that she would have another story to tell. She was a wonderful storyteller and it had never mattered much that she wasn't very truthful.

*K*enny urged the cow to push but the animal was fading quickly and all she had managed was for the head of the calf to emerge, its eyes closed so that he feared that the calf had died. He touched the animal and it was warm and moist. He felt the pulse as Gabriel had done when one of the cows had experienced difficulties last year. He couldn't tell clearly whether there was a pulse. He had seen that one birth and had been awed as the cow made an effort to expel the calf and it finally emerged and she reached back and licked the calf's face and bit off the umbilical cord as the small animal lay on the barn floor. He had no idea what he should do and began to say an Our Father and then the Rosary, his heart beating as if he'd just finished a shift and was on the bench trying to recover his breath. He touched the cow's neck and there was still a pulse. He looked at his watch. It was now midnight. There was a growl in the woods to his left. He reached for his rifle, his own pulse quickening. He shone the flashlight at the sound, but there was nothing there. Whatever it was scurried away at the sight of the light. He was certain that the animal would return.

*S*he thought about Kenny and wondered where he could be at that moment. Was he with the girl?

A small tugging in her heart made her wonder whether it was from Tommy or Kenny. She missed them both. She truly didn't have any favorites, unlike other parents who claimed that they didn't. She knew that Jerry was her mother's favorite. She didn't have any favorites except perhaps Katherine, who was quiet and thoughtful in the same way she liked thinking of herself. But Kenny was special and he was her first, so that had a different status. But he was his father's boy, his favorite even though he loved the others. Kenny was fortunate that other boys hadn't followed him because she was sure Tommy would have lavished as much attention on them as he did on Kenny. She loved seeing them together and happy. His whole name wasn't truly Kenny. His real name was Kenneth Paul Romero, named Paul after Tommy's father, Pablo Romero. His father began calling him Kenny right away and all his documents in school said Kenny Romero, even though he was registered as Kenneth Paul Romero. Why Kenny? They wanted him to have a special name. Also they both liked Kenny Rankin, the singer. He had been a wonderful baby to care for and she was so lucky. He was always healthy and active but always thoughtful. He'd wanted a puppy and always made her stop when they went by the pet shop. His father explained that they couldn't afford a puppy just then because he was too young to take care of it and his mother couldn't because she had to take care of Mary Margaret and Rose. *Okay,* he'd said. *When I grow up I'll have a puppy,* he'd say and he'd go back to play and content himself with looking at the puppies in the pet shop and once in a while going in and petting them and laughing when they tried biting him. And he was so athletic, which made everyone happy. She didn't know much about sports but loved watching him play, telling her friends that he just looked cute in his uniform and that he was very good, although she couldn't tell the difference between the quality of one or the other players. She was sure that all the mothers felt as she did about their sons.

He had called her late one afternoon about two weeks after he'd gone to the farm the second year, telling her that he couldn't talk long. She asked if he was all right and he said he was. Even talking in half whispers she could tell that he was particularly happy. *You sound like the cat that swallowed the canary,* she said. He asked her if she could keep a secret. *Not even Daddy,* he said. *What's going on? Mom, Claudia and I did it and we've been doing it a lot.* Her heart skipped a beat and she wanted to blame the tall, beanpole girl for taking her baby's innocence. She was stunned and he whispered *Mom* several times before she was able to answer that she was still on the phone. *Are you using protection?* she asked. *Of course,* he'd said. *How old is she? Sixteen, Mom. She's very pretty,* she'd said. *She's beautiful, Mom. She's so wonderful.* And then he said he had to go and they said good-bye and she was left alone and as if something had been ripped out of her heart.

She began weeping softly and went into the bathroom and closed the door and wept openly into a towel, the sobs coming uncontrollably as if something of uncommon value had been lost forever. Diana and Tommy Jr. were knocking on the door and after a while Mary Margaret came and got them and they asked if she was all right. *I'm all right, darling. I've got something in my eye and I'm trying to flush it out. I'll be out in a minute. Check the roast, honey. See if the potatoes are done.*

When Tommy came back from meeting with Jerry out at his house they ate together and he asked her about possibly going out to the beach house in mid-August, but she was abstracted and feeling as if nothing of importance was happening. All she felt was a sense of loss. The children watched television until ten and then the younger children were sent to bed. She kissed and hugged each one with uncommon disinterest. Mary Margaret and Rose wanted to watch a movie. Tommy said that was a good idea and reached for her hand. She sat next to him, holding his hand until he fell asleep, his hand limp on her lap. She gathered the hand gently and placed it on his own lap. She then rose and kissed the girls good night, went to the bathroom, brushed her teeth, urinated, wiped herself, washed her hands and face, brushed her hair vigorously, searching for gray within her thick blond hair and found not a trace. She removed her sleeveless blouse and then her bra and examined her breasts for lumps, carefully cursing herself for wishing that there appeared some trace of the dreaded C, so she would not ever again have sex. She put her blouse back on, dropped her bra into the hamper and went to their bedroom. She undressed, put on a nightgown, turned down the bed and lay there staring at the ceiling and listening to the night sounds.

She figured she'd lain rigid on the bed for an hour and then far away she heard the door to their bedroom lock and Tommy came to bed naked and kissed her and called her baby but she couldn't respond and he said he needed her. She could feel him hard against her thigh and felt his hands against her breasts and she urged him to her, parting her legs until he was in her and she placed her arms around him but felt nothing except the tears escaping her eyes silently and then she saw them together, her Kenny and the tall girl whose name she could not now recall, the two of them naked, two blond children but sexually mature and in her mind she saw her Kenny entering her; Claudia, she now recalled, a truly beautiful girl in the pictures he'd shown her at the end of last summer. He was going into her, in and out and then she screamed, the bellowing half pain and half pleasure; clutching at Tommy, her pelvis arching against him, and his hand coming up to silence her. She opened her mouth hungrily and sucked at his fingers and again the shuddering came until she was done and was laughing and he was telling her that he loved her and she couldn't stop laughing until he asked her what was the matter. *Nothing,* she said, *I missed you. I missed you too, Irish,* he'd said and they slept in each other's arms. Before she fell asleep she decided that if the girl loved Kenny as much as she loved his father, then it was okay. She was at peace then.

*K*enny had to make a choice soon. He tried to consider everything before him. It felt like being behind in a game and only a minute or so left to play, and skating over to the bench with the other players and the coach telling the goalie that as soon as the puck was dumped over the blue line into the other end he was to come to the bench so he could send another skater on the ice and maybe tie the score. That's how it felt. The cow was breathing hard, the large chest rasping and the sound deep in its throat. He always gave it his best and they had managed to tie the score three times in all the time he'd been playing since he was seven. Fifty games a year, maybe more, not counting tournaments and playoffs. Times ten years. Maybe five hundred fifty or six hundred games and three times they had manage to tie the score. One time he was able to prevent the other team from scoring into an empty net when he skated back over his own blue line and dove headlong and with his stick outstretched he kept the puck from going in just as it entered the crease. They didn't win that one. He wondered if he should try straddling the cow and pushing down on its belly while he pulled at the calf's head to urge it out of its mother.

*S*he woke up refreshed and every time she looked at Tommy she couldn't help smiling. A couple of times when the children had gone downstairs to play he came over to her while she was reading a cookbook and she touched him through his pants and they went into the bedroom and made love. She didn't reach an orgasm but he was incredibly passionate and she urged him on until he was done and lay against her, heavy and sleepy. She squeezed him down there as if she were hugging his thing and placed little kisses on his neck and ears and they napped. She'd wanted to imagine Kenny and Claudia together again but didn't dare and wondered if she should confess such a thing to a priest. She decided she didn't have to and instead decided to call and talk with Gabriel.

He was an odd man and she didn't know who to believe. Her mother said Gabriel's father was a friend of an old priest at her parish. But Mary Boyle told stories and could entangle anyone in her tales, much as she had done to her all of her life. Her mother wasn't content with the little people and nursery rhymes. She had to create this other world of myth, of family intrigue, of fabrications and lies. It appeared quite innocent but too often confusing. Her mother wasn't quite a pathological liar but close to it, she thought. Jerry had said that Gabriel was in the Peace Corps and had gone to Peru. While there he got mixed up with Communist guerrillas. *Communist?* she'd asked? *Yes, Shining Path. Maoists,* he said. *What do you mean? That's what they're called. In Ireland it's the IRA. Over there it's the Shining Path, but they follow Mao. Mao Tse-Tung? Yeah, him, but not in Ireland.* Evidently, Gabriel had a connection to the Shining Path people. *What does it mean?* she asked Jerry. *I don't know, but they're pretty strong in the area. Upstate New York?* she asked, feeling stupid. *No, Peru, Frankie. Peru. In South America. What do they want?* she asked. *I don't know,* he said. *The same thing people want all over the world, I guess. What?* she asked. *To get the rich bastards off their back,* he said. *I guess,* she said. She was silent a moment and then asked him why Gabriel was involved with them. *I don't know, Frankie. Maybe you should ask him. How am I going to do that, Jerry? I don't know, Frankie. Maybe you could get Tommy to take you and the kids on a trip to visit Kenny.*

She called Gabriel Brunet and asked if they could come up and visit. He said it was a great idea. She called up her mother but she said for them to go ahead, that she had a little cold and wanted to rest. They had driven up on the following Saturday after Tommy got back from a trip down south. He rested two days, sleeping long into the afternoon and taking the kids out to play. They left early in the morning after she and Peggy made sandwiches and snacks. She was over the business with Kenny and Claudia and she truly wanted to see them together. When they got there it was incredible watching Kenny moving around the farm so confidently as he always seemed. He and Claudia didn't display any behavior that indicated anything other than the fact that they were friends. She didn't know whether they were avoiding each other, or if they were being distant for Tommy's sake and that of the children. She didn't care. They ate a big lunch and the kids were given big slices of watermelon. At four in the afternoon Kenny announced that he had to bring the cows in. He left, went into the barn and emerged riding on the big horse and the other children ran and climbed up on the big wooden fence or stood looking between the slats. Minutes later, way up in the meadow they saw Kenny herding the cows toward the corral. Claudia explained what Kenny was doing.

When all the cows were in they watched the milking, the children amazed that milk getting to their table involved all this work. Tommy Jr. wanted to know how the milk got into the containers and Rose said there were milk elves and Katherine and Diana said: *Really?* Everyone laughed and

Gabriel explained what happened and pointed to the large refrigerating containers that held the milk.

A half hour later Tommy announced that they should be getting back but Gabriel and his father shook their heads and begged them to stay and eat supper. The old man said he'd cooked a couple of hams and yams with honey and had plenty of fresh corn on the cob and more watermelon. The children cheered. Tommy protested that they would get back to the city too late, but Gabriel said there were plenty of bedrooms and beds and they were welcome to stay. The old man said that the people who had owned the farm before them had seven children. *Three boys and four girls,* he said. Hearing about the seven children reminded her that she had already missed her period and suspected that she might be pregnant. Tommy looked at her and she nodded and everyone clapped. She helped Mary Margaret and Claudia in getting the table set and the food to the table. She enjoyed Claudia's company and industriousness around the kitchen. The girl had the same confidence of women who dedicate themselves to service. Claudia seemed comfortable and she fought the urge to think about Kenny and the girl together. It was obvious that Mary Margaret was totally taken with Claudia, smiling at everything she said. A year younger, she'd found the perfect girlfriend, she hoped.

After supper with the sun still up, Claudia pulled Kenny aside and then Kenny came over to his father and, out of earshot of the others, asked if it was okay to take Mary Margaret and Rose to the movies with them because he and Claudia and Carlos were going. It was fine with him but he should check with his mother. She said it was fine and they got into Claudia's car, she and Kenny in front, and Carlos, seated very uncomfortably between Mary Margaret and Rose, who were both very serious about this new development. Mary Margaret reassured Rose that this was not an actual date. When they were traveling down the dirt road and away from the farm she worried about the girl driving. Gabriel said she was a good driver, very safe. *She drives to Utica a couple of times a week to volunteer at the hospital,* he said. Fran was impressed when Gabriel added that she wanted to become a nurse. The children asked where they were going and before either she or Tommy answered, Gabriel said that they were going to look at the town. And that it was very boring and he was sure they would have a better time and what did they think about a campfire? *A campfire?* Tommy Jr. said. The word excited him. *Yes, a campfire,* Gabriel said. *Will you help me?* Tommy Jr. said he would help and took Gabriel's hand as they went inside the house.

When the sun finally went down and the air was cold, Gabriel brought the children sweaters and a jacket for her. They'd gone outside beyond the silo and into an open area with a little grove of apple trees in the background. There, in a pit with several stones around it, the old man had built a small pyre. The old man explained about kindling, and small pieces of wood and then the logs. With a big box of matches he lit the fire, and as they watched the flames rise, he handed each of the children long, very thin sticks, which he had whittled. He gave Tommy and her sticks as well. Gabriel brought out blankets and she had helped to spread them around the campfire. *In case anyone gets cold,* he said. He returned to the house and came back with a guitar and a concertina, which he gave to his father. When the fire was going, Gabriel sang a few songs and taught the children the verses as he went until they were singing "Green Grow the Rushes," "Go Tell Aunt Rhodie" and "The Fox" with the old man playing his concertina. Gabriel then introduced his father, who spoke in French, and said he would now sing "Alouette" and off he went and Gabriel also taught the children the song: *Alouette, gentille Alouette, Alouette, je te plumerai.* He was such a gentle man, Gabriel, she thought. And he seemed so alone. She cried for him and when Tommy and the old man were helping the children with roasting marshmallows she went and sat next to him, her knees drawn up, and watched him in the light of the fire. There was a plainness to him, his features common. Not unattractive but asexual. His eyes were sad. She recognized them but couldn't place the resemblance. *You speak French,* she said. *You and your father. He's from Quebec,* he said. *Were you born there as well? No, I was born around here. I'm from right here,* he said, sweeping the darkness beyond the fire. *Did you speak French as a child? My father taught me and we'd go back to Quebec and see my father's mother and his sister, my aunt Simone. And your mother? I never knew her. My father says she left. He raised you?* she asked, her voice tremulous and filled with an uncommon sorrow. *On this farm,* Gabriel said.

He explained that he'd gone into the Peace Corps after college. *The year after Kennedy was assassinated. Where did you go? Peru,* he said. *So you speak Spanish. Yes.* And then she addressed him in Spanish and he answered and there they were two Americans talking Spanish around a campfire. Amazing, she thought and said so and they both laughed. *And you've never met your mother?* she asked again and when he'd nodded she said it was sad. *Did you feel abandoned?* He shook his head and said that his father worked at the farm and he was raised as one of the woman's children. She was a great big kind Dutch woman and that's how he grew up. *Mrs. Vanderveer,* he said. *Did you call her Mom?* she asked. *Yes, exactly.* When he came out of the Peace Corps his father told him that the Vanderveers were selling the farm and going to Florida, where one of their sons was working in the space program, and how did he feel about buying the farm and helping him run it? He thought about it, contacted people in the Peace Corps and they directed him to a farm loan program. They bought the farm and began running it. *It's the only home I've known,* he said. *And you have no family other than your father? A grandmother outside of Montreal who died two years ago. Her name was Gabrielle. Like you,* she said. *Yes, but spelled differently,* he replied. *Cousins?* she asked. *Yes, three. My aunt's children. And don't you get lonely by yourself?* she asked. He didn't reply for a long time, perhaps not wanting to answer. *Yes, I get lonely,* he finally said and then he announced that Kenny and Claudia were coming back. She saw the lights of the car as they pulled into the front yard of the house.

She stood up and ran shouting at Kenny and the rest, that they were back here at the campfire and they all came and Gabriel went back to get more marshmallows and they sang some more songs. She asked them what they'd seen and Rose said they'd seen *Alien* and it was very scary and Kenny said all three of them were screaming along with all the girls in the movie theater. Claudia said they were not. Carlos said: *muy cobardes. What did he say, what did he say?* Diana, who refused to learn Spanish, demanded. *He said we were chicken,* Rose said. *Cowards, cobardes, cement head. Rosa!* she admonished the girl. Undeterred, Rose said: *Carlos tried to kiss Peggy. He did not,* Mary Margaret said. *But you were holding hands,* Rose insisted. *No, we weren't. You are such a crazy.* Everyone was laughing and then they sang "Good Night Irene" as the fire was dying down. Kenny and Claudia stayed behind to make sure the fire was out. She saw them kissing and was again aroused, her face feeling hot.

They went to bed and Sunday morning they had breakfast and an hour later they were heading back to the city, loaded down with hams and sausages and preserves and a bushel of corn on the cob and one of peaches. When they were saying good-bye she went to Gabriel and hugged herself to him and kissed his cheek and said that they were his family now. *Thank you,* he said and patted her hand. He was a sweet, kind man, she thought.

*K*enny did as he had planned. He straddled the cow's belly, pressed down and pulled on the calf's head. Very little happened. He pushed down harder on the belly again without much result. He did manage to pull a bit of the head out so that the calf's ears were now visible. He again tried to push down on the belly but little happened other than a long rasping sound from the cow and then a violent shudder. He got off immediately to see if the cow was still alive. Her breathing was shallow, and she was emitting little sounds but definitely weaker. The pool of blood under her neck was larger and he heard scurrying again in the undergrowth. He shone the flashlight but whatever it was had moved away. The thought that he'd lose the cow and the calf troubled him and he knew he would have to do something drastic and at least save the calf. He tried recalling the dissecting of a frog in Biology but doubted he could do the same with such a large animal.

*t*he following week Rose went downstairs to get the mail. She had a pen pal in England and couldn't wait to get another letter from the girl. *Nothing for me,* she said and handed her the mail. Mostly bills, some catalogues, but there among the monotony was a square rose-colored envelope. It was from Claudia Bachlichtner and addressed to Mrs. Frances Ann Romero, the handwriting elegant and confident. She opened the envelope carefully, working the long fingernail of her right index finger along the glued triangle until she could lift the flap. She extracted the letter, folded once.

As she pulled it out a photo fell on her lap. She lifted it and there was Kenny standing holding hands with Claudia in front of a hospital. She was wearing her candy-stripe volunteer uniform, her body tapered, narrow hipped, her legs long. They were both smiling. She turned the photo over and in Kenny's handwriting was the inscription: *To Mom from Kenny and Claudia with Love.* She returned the photo to the envelope and read the letter, carefully phrased but informing her that it had been a pleasure to meet Kenny's family, but especially her because she was exactly as Kenny had described her: *thoughtful and cheerful, loving and respectful.* She read on and was reassured by Claudia that she and Kenny were very serious but would not do anything foolish because she realized that Kenny had to attend college and so did she. At the end she reiterated how much she respected her and she hoped she would grow up to be the kind of woman she was. Not girl, or wife, but woman. A little women's lib message, thank you very much, she thought. She signed the letter *With Love, Claudia.* Definitely, getting it together at the age of sixteen was young Ms. Claudia Bachlichtner, facing the future with poise and tact and well-oiled loins. Well-read lower-middle-class girl with aspirations to a better life. She had probably read the same novels she had and had learned the same things she had learned that no Irish mother except maybe Rose Kennedy could teach her girls.

For the next two days she thought about whether she should respond to the girl, vacillating between thinking she was pretty cheeky to write her such a letter and admiring Kenny for choosing such a smart and thoughtful girl. In the end she called Gabriel and asked about the girl. He had nothing but praise for her and explained that she would probably be her class valedictorian, played on the girl's volleyball and basketball teams, had been offered a scholarship to play basketball and volleyball at Syracuse University, where he'd gone to school and to which he'd written a letter of recommendation, since she would be graduating the following year, a year ahead, having skipped a grade in grammar school. He added that people were encouraging her to take a more rigorous premed program at Syracuse and go to medical school but she wanted to be a nurse. *Quite a stubborn girl, very determined,* he'd said. *She plays the piano and even plays golf. She's a natural athlete like Kenny,* he'd added. *He even rides a horse easily,* she'd said. *Yes, he does, Frances,* he'd said. She liked the way he said her name.

And she and Kenny? she asked. Gabriel was silent for a moment. She wanted to reveal Kenny's secret but she didn't. If she hadn't told Tommy she wasn't going to tell Gabriel. As if he had divined her thoughts he said that he thought they were being intimate. The words took her by surprise. *It's a new age,* he'd said. *Yes, I know. Are they using precautions?* she'd said, feeling her face redden. She chastised herself for being such a prude. *I've talked to him and have provided him prophylactics,* Gabriel said matter-of-factly. *I don't think they're being promiscuous. No, I can't imagine,* she'd said. *But I meant other things, you know. Oh, I see,* he said. *No, I think there's too much at stake for both of them. They're smart kids. Okay,* she'd said. *How's your father? He's fine. Well, thank you again for having us. Our pleasure, Frances. Maybe you and your family can come up again at the end of the summer, before Kenny has to go back to school. That would be nice,* she said. *We can press apples and make cider,* he said. *I'm sure the kids would like that. I'm sure they would,* she said and they said good-bye.

She hung up the phone and stood listening to her life. That evening on her own light blue stationery with the monogrammed *FAR* she wrote Claudia a thoughtful and loving letter and praised her for being considerate and said: *you and*

Kenny looked lovely together and I am very proud that Kenny could choose such a fine friend. She thought a long time and finally said that she hoped she'd see her at the end of the summer, since Gabriel had invited them to come and visit again. She added that were that not possible she hoped that she could come and visit and stay with them during Thanksgiving or even Christmas. *It'll be crowded in our apartment but it will be warm and fun and maybe you and Mary Margaret can help me and we can bring the children to Radio City Music Hall for the Christmas special,* she wrote. She again vacillated between signing the letter with warm affection or simply love. In the end she wrote: *Love, Fran.* She addressed the envelope, placed a stamp on it, and wrote their return address on the back flap. She sent Mary Margaret down to mail the letter and again felt the weight of her upcoming decision. She started to cry but steeled herself and shook her head.

*K*enny saw no other choice now. He stood up and then knelt at the cow's head, listening. She was barely breathing now. He patted the pockets of his mackinaw, searching for his work gloves. Not there. He checked his back pocket and went to the backpack. They weren't there and he remembered leaving them on the workbench where the old man repaired saddles and harnesses. He cursed himself for being forgetful and careless. The night was quiet and he unsheathed the knife, the scratching sound of the blade against the leather breaking the silence. The knife had an eight-inch blade, sharpened repeatedly. He had used it in helping to skin animals the old man had trapped—beaver, raccoon, mink. He prayed silently for a moment asking God to help him and guide his hand so he wouldn't make the animal suffer. When he was finished he straddled the cow's neck, placed his arm under the large head and plunged the knife with all the force capable into the left side of the neck and with the hilt next to the skin ran the blade across so that the cow shuddered and died instantly, the esophagus and windpipe torn and with them the aorta, the blood gushing out, gurgling in the quiet of the cold night. He stood up and vomited and then looked at the calf, its eyes still closed. He glanced at his watch. No more than five minutes had passed since he first examined the cow and made the decision to kill it. He thought that it had been a mistake because in effect he was cutting off the flow of blood to the calf. No blood, no oxygen, he thought. That was one part done and now the more difficult part awaited him. He had to work fast and as he knelt again next to the dead cow he tried to remember the little understanding of anatomy he had. His cut had to be accurate so that he did not harm the calf.

She had put the three young children to bed, given Katherine and Diana a half hour to read while she read *Winnie the Pooh* to Tommy Jr. When she was done, she prayed with Tommy Jr., kissed him and turned off the light. She checked in on the girls. Diana was already asleep. She kissed her on the forehead, Diana's hair already damp from her deep sleep. Katherine begged for another five minutes and she said she was on her honor and she should turn off the light when the five minutes were up. She tried watching television with Mary Margaret and Rose but couldn't concentrate and went into the bedroom and tried reading *Centennial* by James Michener. She dozed off and at midnight Mary Margaret and Rose came and said good night. She kissed them and hugged them as they lay on either side of her on the wide bed. When they were gone her thoughts returned again to the feeling of unrest that continued to plague her.

A few minutes later the phone rang and it was Tommy calling to say that things had gone well. She was so happy to hear from him and knew it was missing him that was causing her so much unrest. When he said good night she stood up, undressed and put on her nightgown. She fell asleep immediately and it seemed like she had slept only a few hours when the phone rang again but the sky was beginning to lighten. She looked at the clock on the night table and it was a few minutes before six. It was Jerry. He said that something had happened. *Tommy,* she said desperately, fearing that he had been arrested. *No,* Jerry said. *Kenny. Up at the farm. Is it serious? Pretty serious,* he said. *Is he dead?* she asked, the words choking her. *No, he'll be all right. Patrick and I are going to the Islip airport. Charlie Doherty's meeting us at there and he'll fly us to Albany. We'll rent a car and drive to the farm. It's six o'clock. We should be there by eight o'clock. Tonight? No, this morning, Frankie. Don't worry. He'll be all right.* She asked what happened but all Jerry said was that Kenny tried to save a cow and got injured. She asked him how he'd found out and he said that their mother had called him. *Who called her? I guess Gabriel,* Jerry said. She wanted to get more details but heard Patrick calling his father in the background and Jerry said he had to go.

When she hung up she felt betrayed. Why hadn't Gabriel called *her?* Why had he called her mother? What was going on? She went into the kitchen and started making coffee. Her heart was beating too quickly and she was shaking. While the coffee brewed she dialed her mother and asked her what'd happened, wanting to know whether it was bad. Her mother said he'd been attacked by wolves. Possibly rabies but otherwise all right. She was relieved and then realized that you could die from rabies. *Why did Gabriel call you?* she asked. *He didn't,* her mother said. *Who, then?* she asked. Her mother was silent for a moment and then said the priest had called. *Was Kenny given last rites, Mom?* she cried into the phone. *No, no last rites. It isn't that serious. Don't worry. Take care of the children. Don't panic, Fran.* She hung up and took a deep breath. A sob escaped her chest and she prayed. Her mind was crazed and she knew she had to get herself together and not worry the children. When the coffee was done she turned off the burner, ran into the bedroom for fresh clothes and put the clothes in the bathroom. She returned to the kitchen, poured herself a cup of coffee, added cream and sugar, swallowed a quarter cup, went into the bathroom and closed the door. She took another two gulps of the coffee, placed the cup on the windowsill and turned on the water, almost burning herself before she stripped off her nightgown and stepped into the shower, letting the water help her relax. She wanted to scream and tear at her hair and couldn't imagine what could have happened. Had the wolves bitten his throat? Was he dying? Oh, God! And Tommy didn't know. He was on the way to Chicago. Where would he be right now? They were going to drive all day without stopping.

She stayed under the shower for a long time until all she could hear was the inside of the rush of water as if she were a little girl and Jerry were lifting her and holding her up under the arcing torrent of the fire hydrant, the stream of water hitting her from above like hard rain. She could never put together the fact that Jerry was so tender with his family and at the same time was a killer. He never spoke about it but other people said he had been a terror in Korea, reckless and ruthless. And she knew that as a cop he had killed those two black drug dealers. And for a time he'd worked for the people in Hell's Kitchen. Nobody talked about it. Tommy wouldn't talk about it but she'd ask him questions and he'd answer no and when he didn't answer she knew that it was true. *Did he kill those two men to defend you? Yes, he did. Has he killed for money, Tommy?* No answer. *Has he killed people in the Mafia?* No answer. *Has he killed innocent people?* No, never, Tommy would say.

Have you? she'd asked him. *What?* he'd said. *Innocent people? Yes, innocent people. Have you harmed innocent people? Probably. Killed them? No, I haven't. Have you done so for money? No, I have not.* And then he had shaken his head and said that he wasn't being truthful and she went totally cold and he explained without going into detail that it was a thin line and that the man had not been a good man but hadn't deserved to die. *Why, then?* she'd asked. Tommy had explained that it was for us and she'd asked if he meant them and the kids and he'd said that it was *for the bigger family because we're blood,* he'd said. *Because of Jerry?* she asked. *Yes,* he said, and said he didn't want to talk about it anymore and she held him, his body tense and unyielding.

She thought again about good and evil. She tried to fathom *eros* and *thanatos.* Love and death. Creation and Destruction. Light and darkness. Heaven and Hell. She wondered if she would be killing an innocent when she had an abortion. She decided she would have the amniocentesis exam and determine afterward if she would go through with the abortion. The doctor said that if there were any genetic abnormalities with the fetus she could terminate the pregnancy relatively easily. Spina bifida. Down's syndrome. Terminate the pregnancy. It sounded so official, so sterile. Jerry terminated people. Tommy had terminated someone but he wouldn't say why or who it was. She wished Jerry had wanted her to fly up there with him and see Kenny but his was a world of men and women were of little importance in it.

What a horrible thought to believe that all she was good for was to have babies and spend a lifetime taking care of them. From the time Kenny was born seventeen years ago, until Tommy Jr. was shipped off to college it would be twenty-nine years. She would be fifty-two, graying and wrinkled and the way Tommy was going probably widowed. Assuming the baby was healthy and she had it she could add another eighteen years and she'd be fifty-eight. In another two years she'd be sixty. She couldn't imagine the year 2000. A new century. She wouldn't last. She would die of grief, of boredom. They should come home. *Tommy, come home,* her mind screamed. *Come home, Kenny. Jerry, make them come home,* she cried in the little girl's voice she used when she called on Jerry to protect her. *I'm scared, Jerry.*

She put on a pretty dress, combed her hair, wore her little gold earrings that Tommy had given her on her twenty-first birthday, put lipstick on, slipped on a pair of flats, had another cup of coffee and waited for the children to wake up and come in to eat breakfast. *Oh, Mommy, you look so pretty. Thank you, darling,* she'd smile, like the mothers on TV. *I'm dying inside,* she'd said to herself. *How are you?* she'd inquire happily of the child. *I'm fine, Mommy. Are you going to a party? No, no party. Should I make pancakes? Yes, pancakes, pancakes, pancakes.*

Oh, God help her. She didn't have the strength anymore. Had she dressed for Kenny's wake? She should change into a black dress. How could she mourn in a pretty summer dress? It wasn't right. She prayed. *Hail Mary full of grace, the Lord is with thee, Blessed art thou among women and blessed is the fruit of thy womb, Jesus. Holy Mary, Mother of God, pray for us sinners now and at the hour of our death, Amen.* They would have a Puerto Rican boy and they'd name him *Jesús.* That was it. God would forgive her for thinking about an abortion. If it was a girl they'd name her *Jesusa* and then she wouldn't be punished. *Haysoosah* it was pronounced in Spanish. *Jesusa Rosa Maureen Virginia Fiona Romero Boyle Grady Alcántara McGillicuddy Ryan Rodríguez. She would have one of those long comic television Span-*

ish monikers but mixed in, Hibernian names. Another Mickorican. Another Harpospican. Another Paddyrican. She wished she were not a woman as she was with all the burdens. She wished she were simply a myth, a deep Irish myth—Aine, the daughter of the Irish Neptune. Aine represented sun worship and she recalled her honeymoon when everything was so dreamy. She wanted to travel to the sea and go into the water again and taste the salt and feel the sun warming her skin and Tommy within her, relentless, passionate, loving, wanting her as if she were nourishment, his lips sucking at her body and beckoning to her heart and she lost in him. *Kenny, don't die. Please don't die,* she cried.

birth

*After a few beers of celebration with
others from the squad at a saloon in
Upper Manhattan, they were hugging
each other and horsing around and
Jerry Boyle looked at Tommy Romero and
admitted what he'd known for a while.
This Spanish kid was special and much
more than a partner. It was one of those
things that happens between men when
they recognize love for one another.*

K ENNY STEELED himself and made a shallow incision
on the outer epidermis of the cow's carcass, the skin of
which when removed and treated could be tanned and
cut, shaped and made into shoes and bags or, complete from
neck to tailbone, with the quarters splayed and head, tail
and hooves removed, made into a rug, its black or brown and
white patterns natural and abstract at the same time, individual as each bovine was. The cut ran about four inches from
the backbone along the side from the shoulder to the hip and

then in a half moon that ran to the lower half of the cow's belly and returned to the original incision, his hand steady now that he had begun. He pulled on the skin but nothing happened. It wasn't like skinning a small animal and he pulled harder until the hide began to give. When he had removed the flap, he threw it over the outcropping of rocks in front of him. He knew immediately that it had been a mistake. With the flashlight in hand he went quickly behind the rocks, retrieved the large piece of hide, returned to the carcass and the calf, and brushing dead leaves from the skin with his knife, placed it face up beneath the calf's head. He stroked the face and rested for a moment on the eyes, wishing that the calf would open them. He noted that the calf had a skewed diamond on its forehead, one corner pointing downward at its right eye.

He heard a noise, turned rapidly around, shining the flashlight and locating his rifle. Nothing. The calf was stirring. The small animal was moving around uncomfortably as if it had been asleep and had suddenly awakened. Kenny wondered if the flow of blood had ended and the calf would die before he could pull it out from his mother. He returned to the carcass and now cut deeply into the lower epidermis, exposing ribs above and below on the half moon, feeling the skin give and the blood come trickling out. This revealed the internal organs: the lungs and liver, the kidneys and heart exposed. The nausea attacked him again as the thick, sickeningly sweet aroma of fresh death invaded his nostrils.

*W*hen Jerry Boyle and his son Patrick got to Islip's MacArthur Airport, Charlie Doherty was already there. He had filed a flight plan, refueled the plane and was going through the exterior checklist of the twin engine Piper Apache. Five minutes later they were aboard the plane and buckled in. Patrick sat in the back and he in front with Doherty, who was going through an onboard check. Doherty had flown reconnaissance in Vietnam in single-engine planes, had been shot down twice and still went back up, logging about one hundred missions and getting wounded only once, through a thigh. No bone damage. He now taught flying to rich kids and their mothers, and to wealthy business executives for whom a BMW, a motorized golf cart and a speedboat weren't enough toys. When Doherty was done he called the tower for clearance and began taxiing from the apron to the queue area. Doherty received final clearance for takeoff and increased the revolutions on the engines. The sound of the motors grew in intensity, a cargo plane took off ahead of them and sixty seconds later he turned the corner onto the runway and they were moving rapidly, the speed increasing as the plane hurtled forward, seemingly eager to take flight.

Doherty's first wife was an Italian girl who looked and behaved like a movie star, demanding a life Doherty couldn't afford. Eventually, she ran away with some Mafia playboy while Doherty was on his second tour in Vietnam. He had divorced the movie star and married his second cousin, Moira Rafferty, Mary Boyle's sister's eldest daughter, an almost catatonic redhead who had incredible patience and worshipped Doherty. They had four kids. Like all tough guys he was a pushover for his kids. Doherty was about Fran's age, thirty-nine or forty years old.

He asked Doherty how soon they'd be in Albany. No more than forty minutes, Doherty said once they were aloft. Before the plane was a thousand feet off the ground, rising steadily against the dawn, Doherty banked steeply. The water below was brilliant with the rising sun. Jerry thought he saw the shadow of a whale about to surface. Maybe it was a shallow. He loved the sea. At this distance it was sterile, abstract, devoid of its fury. They circled out over the Atlantic, the whitecaps forming on the blue as the surf rolled against the white sand. They climbed rapidly and headed inland, moving steadily through the haze and cloud cover. When they were at cruising altitude Doherty fixed the heading and placed the aircraft on automatic. His eyes, behind the sunglasses, remained fixed on the horizon, ever on the lookout for other planes as he swept the air for danger. Above them, twenty thousand feet into the blue, a large jet was heading north, its contrail white against the deep blue.

After a while Doherty asked what had happened to Kenny. He explained that he'd been in the woods, ran into wolves and was bitten pretty badly. Patrick said there were no wolves left in the Northeast. *Probably coyotes or wild dogs crossed with coyotes,* he said. *There's a possibility of rabies,* he said, politely ignoring Patrick. *They don't know.* Doherty asked if that was it and was the farm the one that belonged to the guy he'd had checked out with his boys in D.C. He nodded and said that was the one, Gabriel Brunet, and that his nephew's left wrist or hand or maybe both were pretty much mangled. *No more ice hockey, I guess,* Doherty said. *Who knows,* he said. *Where's the old man? Your partner?* Doherty asked, avoiding mentioning names. *On the way to Chicago to make a delivery,* Boyle replied. *Furniture? Yeah, Chinese furniture,* he said and added that Patrick had been along on the boat when they picked up the merchandise, the previous evening. *He's in the family business, then,* Doherty said. *Summer job,* Boyle said and told him that Patrick was still studying finance. *St. John's.* Doherty looked back approvingly. *Jimmy's talking about going to law school,* Doherty said, mentioning his eldest son. *He's in his first year at Georgetown.* They fell silent as if talking about their sons would jinx their chances, the superstitions of their parents surfacing. He had never asked Doherty to help him transfer merchandise but was certain Doherty would turn him down. From time to time Doherty did small jobs for Washington, secret stuff in Latin America and the Caribbean. He thought again about the previous night and recalled how the whole thing could have blown up.

The trawler lay at anchor on the Sound, the water calm and its running lights blinking in the moonless night of late summer. Jerry Boyle stood at the wheel looking into the night, waiting for the freighter to appear on the horizon. He thought about his son Patrick sleeping below and wondered if he should be involved in this part of his life. But he was a natural. He enjoyed the danger and he had nerves of steel. Before he was twelve, Patrick had pretty much figured everything out about him and his business with Spillane and his connection to John Finnegan. He figured out that his old man wasn't just a fisherman. It wasn't the same with Tommy's boy Kenny, still unaware of what his father did. Kenny was just like his sister, Frances, he thought. The light was in their eyes and they were both honest and brave. They both would've made good cops, one brave and the other cunning, Patrick like him, and Kenny like Tommy, pure and idealistic about the job.

When the freighter had finally come and lay at anchor, they had motored out to it, anchored and tied up next to it, the smaller boat bobbing against the iron plates. They had gone on board. He and Grady and Maloney with Patrick staying on the boat, standing guard. If there was shooting he was to pull up anchor, take the trawler a distance from the freighter and wait for a radio call from him. Patrick should then come back, sit at a distance until he could get a visual okay from him. If nothing came and the freighter moved away he should leave and explain to his mother that there had been an accident and he was lost at sea. She was not to report anything. He explained to him that Sheila would understand what had happened and where to find the keys to the safe deposit boxes. He was to contact Spillane and tell him what took place. Spillane would take care of letting Maloney's wife and Grady's girlfriend know what happened. After that he should have a good stiff drink, finish college, get rich and marry a nice Irish Catholic girl. Nothing ever happened but those were his instructions to Patrick.

The Greek had almost bought it with his demand for more money. He couldn't admit that he had to pay five thousand dollars more for the shipment. It was worth it but it pissed him off to have to pay the money. At one point he debated greasing the whole crew, seventeen of them, removing all the merchandise on board, taking the boat out and setting it adrift out on the Atlantic. He'd paid the money and the Greek, now a bit scared, had thrown in fifty Czech pistols. They'd sell for a hundred apiece so he'd make the money back. He couldn't understand the Greeks and their fascination with anal sex. He'd never fucked anyone in the ass, not even a woman, even though he came close with the taunting guinea broad that had married Doherty. Jesus she was a pig, cheating on him with his friends. Vaseline her butt and he'd give her a toilet job like Masterson used to say. Fucking Masterson and the merchant marine. The stories he had. What a mistake that fucking Gina had been. She actually changed her name to Heather. Some women were so easygoing and some were a fucking terror.

Sheila was a sweetheart but it was over with them. He'd have to figure out what he was going to do with Gloria. She was talking about wanting to have a family and him almost fifty years of age. He'd have to maintain two homes. Hell, Vinnie Rattigan had done it all his life and he was a colonel or some high muckamuck in the Pennsylvania Highway Patrol. He was smart to leave New York. He wondered whether the two women knew about each other. He went back and forth from Bucks County in Pennsylvania to Westchester County in New York. Two zip codes, two sets of hunting buddies, two PTAs, two Little Leagues. Amazing. He'd have to go see Rattigan next time he came to see Nancy in White Plains. She was Italian and had turned out okay and Rattigan hadn't even married her although she wore a wedding ring and the kids had Rattigan's name. She had her own beauty parlor and did well. He even put the kids in private school, which she helped pay for.

He closed his eyes and listened to the steady droning of the engines. What the hell got into men? Women couldn't understand men, and men couldn't understand women. But hell, sometimes he didn't understand men. What could the kid have been thinking? Going into the woods like that. He wondered if Kenny had brought a rifle with him. He'd taught him to shoot and he and Tommy had taken the boy and Patrick hunting a few times when he was thirteen. Kenny was an excellent shot and enjoyed target practice, his aim accurate and his hand steady. He didn't like seeing the dead buck and turned away from it. Maybe he wouldn't make a good cop. If you couldn't face death, then you had no business on the job. One false step and you'd be dead. Frankie must be going crazy thinking about Kenny. Suppose it was worse than Gabriel had explained.

*k*enny placed the flashlight in a crevice in the rock so that the light illuminated the carcass and the woods in front of him. From behind the carcass he now dipped his hands in and cut each part, throwing everything into the undergrowth, knowing with certainty that it would attract animals, foxes and coyotes. He wondered if they would come in a pack or singly. Maybe a bear. And then he saw the uterine sack and touched it gingerly and then more forcefully until he could feel the calf's legs. The calf was encased in a gray-white sac, seemingly pinned by other organs. He didn't dare slice the sac. He pushed at the calf until he felt it stir involuntarily. He either had to force the calf out or pull it back in. Before doing anything else he slapped the lower body of the calf repeatedly until the small animal's lungs filled with air and it cried out, his head out and lowing mournfully, babylike even before it was fully born from its mother, now dead. He wondered how he would feed the poor thing if the milk had not started coming in. Would it starve before he got it back to the farm?

She was a saint, he thought as he imagined his sister. He was glad that he had introduced Tommy to her. They were perfect for each other even if Tommy was Spanish. It was his instincts, he thought. He met people and knew after a couple of times if they were good people or, like himself, they lived in a world of shadows in which the only thing that counted was staying alive and getting as much out of the situation as they could. He had been ruthless as a kid and still recalled smashing a Coke bottle against cross-eyed Jimmy O'Brien's forehead because he was cheating at cards when they were eleven and O'Brien had cursed him out and called him a mick fuck. Like what the fuck was O'Brien if he wasn't a mick!

He often wished he hadn't gotten Tommy involved in everything. First on the job and now the business with the guns. But he owed him. Tommy had deserved better. He didn't want to see his nephews and nieces doing without.

Christ, if things hadn't gotten fucked Tommy'd be coming up on twenty years on the job. Retirement, pension, still young enough to hook up with some security outfit. He was a good cop, clean and a straight shooter until he got involved with Crazy Jerry Boyle. Hell, he wasn't going to let Patterson and Kelly get all the spoils from working undercover. Jesus, Mary and Joseph, they were taking in a hundred grand each a year. And that was beyond their salary. Clear cash. No taxes. Every time they made a bust they managed to keep back a little and sell it, traveling to Philadelphia or Boston, where they had hooked up with other crooked cops. Fuck them.

He'd gone up to Boston to watch the Rangers play the Bruins with some of the guys from the police department hockey team. Devlin, Martino, Russo and the old Polish guy who skated for New Hyde Park when they used to play before the Rover games at the old Garden on 50th Street. Some unpronounceable Polack name. Everybody called him Ski. In the third period, with the Bruins pasting the Rangers 6–1, he'd gone to the bathroom. Too much brewski. On the way back four high school kids with too much beer in them as well had surrounded this little redheaded guy with the map of Ireland written all over his face. He'd gone over and put his arm around the little guy and ignoring the four guys said: *What's the problem, Jimmy? These fellas giving you a hard time? Nothing that I can't handle, Mike,* the little guy said. *You guys weren't thinking of fighting me and my little brother, were you?* he said, grabbing the bigger one's cheek and twisting it between his fingers. The guy went pale, a roar went up from the crowd and the other three kids said the Bruins had scored again and they'd missed it. He released the pressure on the teen and patted his face where a welt was already rising. The kid glared at him but was thankful his friends were pulling him away.

Thanks, the redheaded guy said, sticking out his hand.

Kevin Riley. Hell, I thought your name was gonna be José Rivera, Jerry'd said. They both laughed and the redheaded guy said he was just about to tell them that he was a cop. He told Riley that he was also on the job in New York. Matter of fact, Riley had said, his partner from Somerset had an uncle on the job that knew some cops from New York. *They come up once in a while,* Riley said. *We had a beer a couple of times. Patterson and Kelly. Do you know them? Jimmy Patterson and Vinnie Kelly. Patterson's a tough, stocky nigger and Kelly's a tall mick, with black hair and dark eyes. Mean-looking bastard. Looks like a wop. I don't think I know them,* he said. *They got family up here?* The little guy shrugged his shoulders. *Sports fans? I don't know, to tell you the truth, but I've seen them a few times,* the little guy said. *They seemed like nice guys, though. Well, I better get back,* he said, extending his hand to the little guy. *I'm Matt Scanlon. I'm here with guys from New York. They're three sheets to the wind and with the Bruins beating the shit out of the Rangers I don't think they're in a good mood. Thanks again, Matt,* Riley said patting his arm and going off. Patterson and Kelly. Fuck. They were coming up to Boston often and they were in narcotics. Plainclothes, but investigation and backup, no direct undercover work. What the hell was the deal? It smelled and he'd find out what it was about.

Frankie went to pieces when she found out that they had been dismissed from the job. Nine years ago it was. Kenny was eight and little Peggy, Mary Margaret, was six. He, looking like a little mick kid and she like a little *señorita* with all that black hair and black eyes, pretty like her mother. She'd cried and cried and asked him why over and over. There had been an investigation and both of them had been guilty of dereliction of duty and unnecessary use of force. Two dead nigger cocksuckers. Big deal. They dealt smack. Fucked-up motherfuckers who didn't give a fuck who they hurt. Let the fucking worms eat dark meat. And civilians were making noises about police brutality. Fuck them. They could have covered things up but by this time he had figured out Patterson and Kelly's scheme, was taking a cut from the profits and the bastards had screwed them. Not only him, but Tommy, who'd done nothing. They had let him walk into a trap. He'd walk in, they'd shoot him and Patterson and Kelly would waste the two spooks as they left, keep the drugs and return the buy money.

He'd told Tommy that he'd gotten in with Patterson and Kelly and if he wanted in he had no problem if he took half of his cut. Tommy'd said that they ought to stay away from all that and just do their job. *What we ought to do is report this to Internal Affairs,* Tommy said. *Forget it,* he said. *These guys are protected all the way up.* Tommy had told Frankie nothing and he was right not to. His sister Frances lived in a world that was as Catholic as it was dopey, a fantasy world of good deeds and abnegation. She believed that if one did good, good things happened, and Tommy, although not as naive, protected her in her belief and denied part of the reality along with her. Who the hell could tell good from evil anyway? Was it good what England had done to Ireland all this time? Fuck no. Was it good that kids starved in a country as rich as the United States? Was it right that cocksuckers who deal drugs went free because of some bullshit technicality?

They were four of them. Himself, then Maureen and Michael, and then Frances, who was five years younger. Really five of them, but he wasn't going to get into that. That was his mother's business. They'd have to work that out themselves, but he'd find out what the hell went on. She was a sweetheart, Frankie, always smiling and hopeful, and when things didn't go well with anyone in the family or with friends she was always encouraging them and urging them not to give up. God, she had even gone to visit Father Ambrose at the hospital and sat and held his old, thinning hand and prayed with him, telling him that God would never abandon him and he must have hope in his heart. She was twelve years old and when the priest died the following week, she cried a little and then said that Father Ambrose had arrived safely in Heaven and a choir of angels had welcomed him with bright and happy songs. It was understandable, since Father Ambrose had been such a good priest, she said.

But she was like that and when Tommy told her he'd been suspended she was devastated. When Tommy informed her six months later that they were both off the job, she wanted to know what they had done. *What happened, Jerry?* she cried to him. He told her they had been set up and she immediately said they ought to find a lawyer and call for an investigation. *Go to the newspapers and tell them your story,* she'd pleaded. He explained that it wasn't quite that easy. He finally calmed her down by convincing her that if they squealed it would create problems anyway. *What kind of problems? Oh, hell, some assignment and they'd send Tommy up to investigate some apartment knowing that he was walking into a trap. Oh, my God,* she said. *They'd do that?* He nodded gravely and said that she shouldn't worry, that he'd make sure Tommy and their family were taken care of. She had wept and he'd held her and consoled her as he always did when she hurt herself or someone was mean to her. She was a lovely girl who had always deserved better. But he didn't regret introducing Tommy to her.

*k*enny recalled his grandfather Martin Boyle at the butcher shop, slicing meat and with a cleaver chopping ribs, and couldn't figure out how he was to lift the large rib cage, which might block access to the calf. He thought of the ax but didn't want to take a chance of possibly injuring the calf. After a while he hit on breaking the ribs to lift them out of the way. He slid the knife into the cartilage near the shoulder and sliced down. He repeated the same at the end near the hindquarters. With all the strength he could muster he folded the ribs upward, bending them closer and closer to the spine until he heard them cracking and he pushed farther until the rib cage lay hanging like a bony harp on the other side of the cow. He found the windpipe and cut away the lungs and flung them beyond the clearing. The front of his sweater was now bloody and nausea attacked him periodically. He worked rapidly, cutting away the liver and then the kidneys, the strong smell of urine making him gag. He tried to cut the entire stomach intact but he couldn't and the contents, green and bilious, the stench unbearable, spilled out and his own stomach, now empty, convulsed violently and he dry-heaved several times. He again brought everything to the edge of the small clearing and threw the organs into the woods as best as he could. He next worked on the intestines, dragging the lengths away until all that was left was the calf. Finally, he cut the large heart, leaving it for last in the hope that it could keep the calf alive. He held it for a second, marveling at its size before tossing it underhand beyond the clearing. He could sense animals in the undergrowth feeding on the organs. Carefully, he returned to the amniotic sac, grabbed a fold, inserted the knife and sliced. With his hands he tore away at the gelatinous skin until he saw the calf, perfectly formed and delicate, breathing now but still stuck inside of its mother. It was a female and he patted it and watched the helplessness of the small animal, its eyes opened and pleading, its head outside and its body encased in the mess inside his mother. It let out a small bleating moan, likely announcing its hunger. He saw its thick pink tongue.

$\mathcal{W}$hen he was introduced to Tommy Romero he greeted the younger man with a coldly professional handshake, dreading having to work with a Puerto Rican, since they were so cliquish, much like the Irish. It was a good thing there weren't too many of them on the police force but he figured there would be more coming with drugs spreading as they were. Tommy was just out of the academy but had attended Brooklyn College for two years and was thinking of going back and getting his degree. He seemed like a good guy, a nice average cop that would keep his nose clean. *Jerry, this is Tommy Romero. Tommy, Jerry Boyle,* the squad commander had said. Terrific, he'd thought. Tom and Jerry. Big fucking joke. Cat and mouse time. And that's what they became. The old guys talked about Mutt and Jeff, a notorious team at the Two-Three. And now Tom and Jerry. Big fucking joke. But they worked well together. Bruce and Tito, their street names. Tommy had been assigned to undercover right away because he spoke Spanish. They did well that first year. Good arrests and some convictions in Brooklyn and the Bronx and then they were assigned to work East Harlem, where there was a gang of small dealers being run by big operators in the East River projects.

Tommy and Fran started going out right away and then they got married, which shocked the extended family. After a year of preliminary work, he and Tommy stepped up their efforts to get to the big guys. Tommy was totally into it. He felt no pity for the Puerto Rican junkies or dealers. If he did, he didn't show it. It was like their presence was tarnishing the image of all the good Puerto Ricans who worked hard and obeyed the law, like his parents and aunts and uncles. He felt the same way, the Irish kids who started using heroin made him feel like that. But Tommy was on a mission. He was as harsh on Puerto Ricans as he was on everyone else who broke the law. If you fucked up, Tommy Romero would get you. One time in Brooklyn he had chased a small-time dealer for two blocks, up the stairs of a tenement, over two roofs, down a fire escape, into an apartment where he finally made the collar, cuffed the guy and called it in. When the rest of the backup got there the guy was crying that he had trusted Tommy because he was P.R., that he thought he was a righteous brother. Tommy Romero was unmoved.

They went along like that until he made the trip to Boston and found out about Patterson and Kelly. He told Tommy about it but Tommy wouldn't buy it. *They're good cops,* he said. He couldn't convince Tommy that Patterson and Kelly were crooked, so he kept looking into their operation on his own. On his time off he trailed them and asked questions in the street, collected on favors from other cops, picking up bits and pieces of information in saloons. When the break came he moved in. Patterson and Kelly made a bust and when they came back to the precinct they vouchered the drugs. He noted the amount and over the next two weeks, through his street contacts someone was able to talk to a prisoner awaiting sentencing on Rikers Island. The dealer sent back word on how much heroin had been in the bag that Patterson and Kelly had busted him with. As he suspected, at least one plastic bag was missing. He even spent a week in Boston and developed enough contacts to track down the cops that Patterson and Kelly were dealing with. Just like in the movies, using a telephoto lens, he took photos of them with their contacts. When the pictures came back they weren't great but they were clear enough so that in a court of law there would be no problem identifying that it was Patterson and Kelly. All it would take was the district attorney's people catching them in the act. He didn't trust Internal Affairs. This went too high. But what the hell was the value in that? The kids of a bunch of cops paying for the sins of their fathers. Hell, if truth be told, cops didn't earn enough to provide for their families.

He again went to Tommy with the information, showed him the photos, but Tommy wanted no part of it. He said he was going to ask in but Tommy shook his head. *A half a kilo, Tommy. Uncut. We could do the same thing. Do you know what that's worth in the street? I don't want any part of it,* Tommy said. *You could get out of that apartment in Brooklyn and put a down payment on a house in Queens where I am. Think about it. What you're paying in rent you could be investing in a house that you'd own. No way, Jerry,* he'd said. *I want to stay clean. Once you go down that road, you'll want more.* He was right, once he got a taste of it he wouldn't let it go. He'd be addicted to the easy money. *Well, think about it,* he'd said. *I have a kid coming, Jerry,* Tommy had said. *I can't take any chances.*

He and Frankie had come over to their house in Queens and they'd had a cookout in the backyard. Sheila said they looked like they were still nuts about each other. *We are,* they both said. Frankie was as big as a house and a bit bloated, the freckled skin on her face a little blotchy. It didn't matter to Tommy. They grinned constantly and held hands and you could tell that Tommy worshipped his sister.

Without a partner there was no way that he'd attempt anything. If anything went wrong he would at least have someone who would testify that things hadn't quite happened as the dealers claimed. Who was going to believe drug dealers when a cop who risked his life was testifying? So he went to Patterson and Kelly and told them he wanted in. They were old fucks with almost twenty years in. Patterson had a forty-foot cabin cruiser at the City Island Marina. Kelly had a sailboat in Long Island and lived in a beautiful house in Nassau County. Patterson laughed at him. He was sitting across from them at a diner near Canal Street. He nodded, smiled and dropped an 8-by-10 black-and-white photograph on the table. *Say cheese, fuckos,* he said. Kelly went totally pale under the gray pallor that was beginning to appear on him as he aged. After a while Kelly said that he could come in but there was no assurance that one day a stray bullet wouldn't find him.

Things get hairy out there, Boyle, Patterson said. He ignored Patterson's threat, looked at Kelly and shook his head. *You're one dumb mick, Vincent Kelly. What the fuck were you thinking hooking up with this dumb spook.* Turning back to Patterson, he said: *Listen, Martin Luther, let me see if I can help you understand the deal. If anything happens to me certain people are going to become very chummy with the district attorney downtown. With all the information I've collected on you two clowns you could have your first heart attack up in Attica, if you last that long with all the people you've fucked. The guys in Boston are not going to like what you guys are going to have to give up. Fuck you,* Patterson said. *Fuck me? I don't think so. What you need to do, you African fuck, is wake the fuck up, become generous and let a youngster in on the riches of the trade. Tell me something, you spear-chucking cocksucker. I can tell you're a dumb nigger, but are you also stupid?* Patterson laughed and said he and Kelly would think about it. He knew he'd won and they needed time to save face.

A week later he went to Tommy again and told him it was all set and still Tommy turned him down. *I don't want to know anything about it,* Tommy said. He asked him if he wanted to stay partners with him. Tommy said it was up to him but it was obvious that he was disappointed. *If you're not in, then I don't want any part of Patterson and Kelly,* he'd lied. The relief in Tommy's face was obvious. He reassured him that he was on the level and that Patterson and Kelly would be relieved. He felt no compunctions about lying. To this day he was still amazed by Tommy's innocence and trust. He was just like his sister. Their son Kenny was no different. He felt no contempt for them. In fact he loved them and felt protective of them.

He opened his eyes when Doherty tapped his arm and said

they were starting to make their approach into the Albany airport. In the distance he could make out the capitol's dome. He liked the idea of floating out there in space and the airplane moving through the air and heading for land like a bird. Maybe he'd ask Doherty to give him lessons. Gloria Pujols made him feel young. Jesus, all he had to do was look at her face and he was ready to throw a fuck into her. He should have more respect about her given how he felt. Christ, after all this time, he was learning Spanish and behaving like a gentleman like she wanted. She made him grin. Patrick knew about Gloria and was totally unconcerned. He reminded himself he had to call his sister and mother as soon as he got to the farm.

*K*enny tried pulling the calf back through the vaginal canal but it was no use. The opening had dried and contracted in the cold air with the cow's death and he was now once again at a juncture for which he'd had little preparation in his young life. He hadn't thought of anything except making sure the cow and its calf were okay. The cow was now gone and the calf was stuck, partially out but trapped in its mother. The light in the flashlight had grown yellow and he now worried that they would soon be plunged into darkness. His mouth was completely dry. He rose and patted the calf, which was now dozing. The animal stirred, let out a weak low and fell back asleep, dumb as to its fate. He reached inside his backpack, took out the bottle of water, drank carefully from it and recapped it, aware that he would need water again later. He thought of washing the caked blood from his hands but changed his mind. He looked at the wrapped ham and biscuits but didn't feel hungry. He wasn't sure that he'd ever eat again. He took the flashlight and began gathering wood and kindling with the thought of building a fire. There was stirring where he had discarded the inner organs and he knew that animals were there, feeding, hopefully small ones. Woodchucks and raccoons. Maybe a fox or two. Fortunately his presence would make them drag everything away. Beyond the discarded organs he heard growling and knew it was the coyotes approaching. For the next ten minutes he continued gathering wood. He found a medium-sized trunk from a fallen tree and dragged it inside the clearing. He now found five stones, dug them up and brought them one at a time to the clearing. He had to make sure that when he built the fire he wouldn't cause the surrounding woods to catch fire.

*h*e had no idea why he had turned out as he had. His old man was an idiot and he often shook his head at the crap his mother had to put up with. He could understand it a little better now that he had figured out what the hell went on with her before she married Martin Boyle. Frankie had turned out to be without malice and Maureen was just like their father, scared of the world with little ambition, always making excuses for his failures. Mike was just slow. Where had he gotten his courage from? He was more careful now that he was getting older, but back then, growing up, as a paratrooper in Korea, and later as a cop it was like nothing could touch him. It had to be from Mary Katherine Grady, a tough Irish broad from the South Bronx who was a notorious liar and manipulator. She was always inventing some scheme for cutting corners and convincing other people that things were better for them when in effect she was the one who would benefit. He wasn't any different except that she helped others, but hell, so did he. What did it matter how things got accomplished? The fucking church wanted you to behave so they could control you and take your money.

The way they had moved from their apartment on 141st Street to the big apartment up from Yankee Stadium was classic. She told his father that she'd found an apartment on the Grand Concourse that was much bigger and cheaper and had a nicer class of people. When she told him the address he said: *All Jews.* She pointed up the street to Beekman Avenue and said there was a synagogue right there and he never complained. *They only come on Saturday and never bother anybody.* She laughed and he asked what the hell was she laughing about. She asked him if he thought up on the Grand Concourse they had services every day and the Jews would be running around in gangs like the crazy micks in their neighborhood, drinking and fighting and yelling obscenities day and night. *How much?* he'd said. *Fifty dollars,* she'd said confidently. *We pay fifty right now,* he'd said. *Exactly,* she'd said, and his father scratched his head and said he wanted to see the apartment.

So they rode the trolley car up St. Ann's Avenue and changed at 149th Street and went across to the Grand Concourse and she showed him the new place. He was impressed with the big clean lobby, the elevator and upstairs the parquet floors and big rooms. In the meantime she'd worked out a deal with the owner to manage four buildings, keep them clean, collect the rent and make sure that the tenants were safe and comfortable. Rent for the Boyle family? Free. And the owner gave her a hundred dollars a month for the maintenance of the buildings. She went to the precinct, found out who was on the beat, donated to the policemen's fund and asked that her buildings be kept safe. That's how he'd gotten involved in becoming a cop. Bill Conlon encouraged him. He didn't want to think what the hell had gone on between those two, but they were pretty chummy when they were around each other, joking like they were old pals. He wouldn't have doubted if Conlon had thrown a leg over his old lady from time to time. She was fearless and from the looks of it enjoyed a man between her legs.

She had managed to move her family away from the craziness and misery of the tenements and into a free apartment. At the end of each month she went to his father, collected the fifty dollars and used it to pay for nicer clothes for her children and to buy books and gifts for their birthdays. What was left over, which was considerable, she banked with the hope that they could go to college. Only Frankie had gone to college and she was proud of that. The old man never found out. If he did he wouldn't have admitted it, anyway.

Each day after he went to work and she'd taken Frankie, Maureen, and Mikey to school, she came back and took the elevator to the basement. She got broom, mop, bucket with water and disinfectant and worked rapidly, sweeping and mopping the floors. First the lobby and each subsequent floor starting from the top until she was once more in the basement. She put out the garbage, hired a Negro man to shovel coal in the furnace and take out the ashes in winter, and whenever repairs were needed she contacted the owners, gave them an estimate for the job and hired plumbers, masons and carpenters, always haggling with them and making a profit. She repeated her cleaning routine in the other three buildings, taking a break only to eat a nice pastrami sandwich from the delicatessen or an Italian sandwich of sausage and peppers from the restaurants on Arthur Avenue, where she liked walking in nice weather, her full figure causing the old Italian men to say: *Hey, blondie, you enjoying that sachiche? because I got plenty more where that came from.* She asked the sandwich man how to say *sausage* in Italian and then she heard people saying *bafangoo* and she'd say this to the old men and prop up her breasts and they'd roar and comment on how she was carrying bocce balls under her blouse. *Madonna mia,* they would say and laugh. She was done around two in the afternoon. On weekends she was on call as a *shabbos goy,* ready to perform tasks that Jews were not permitted on the Sabbath, such as unplugging some appliance that had been left on or turning on the air conditioner in summer. They were generous and paid her a quarter each. She took the money and used it for the kids' allowances.

He had offered to get his mother a house out in the suburbs but she had chosen to remain in her apartment, jabbering away with the Jewish ladies who had become her friends, listening to their stories about the Nazis and nodding at the misery, her speech at times inflected with their same sadness and resignation. *What are we going to do, Mrs. Liebowitz?* she'd say, turning her head slightly, nodding and throwing up her hands in supplication to God as if to say: will these persecutions ever end? and stopping short of issuing an *oy vey* of lamentation.

He'd struck a deal with Patterson and Kelly. Part of it was turning over the photographs and negatives of them with the Boston guys. He had laughed at them and said it was going to cost them. *A hundred grand,* he'd said, knowing it was an outrageous demand, but smiling at Patterson, who was ready to kill him. *We'll give you ten thousand dollars,* Patterson said. *You better think again, fucko,* he said. *I'd tell you to read the handwriting on the wall but I know you're not one of those intellectual shines like James Baldwin.* He had nothing against colored people, but he knew shit like that pissed Patterson off. They finally settled on twelve thousand dollars. At Christmastime he gave Frankie five brand-new one-thousand-dollar bills in an envelope. *Oh, Jerry,* she'd said and kissed him. *I had a couple of ponies come in at Aqueduct. Don't tell Tommy,* he'd said and made her promise. *Put it in the bank, honey.* It was like the games they'd played when they were kids to get around their mother and her tricks. He knew that she'd told Tommy, but Tommy hadn't mentioned it. It made sense that he wouldn't. He went on like that over the next two years. He and Patterson and Kelly made seven scores. Not big ones, so that his cut from the deals averaged about twenty thousand. He and Tommy continued to work together and he put money away to buy a fishing boat after he retired.

Doherty was getting instructions for his final descent. He rogered the tower and the plane banked once more, the earth below seemingly tilted. Another circling and there was the runway straight ahead, the ground seeming to be coming at them and everything growing larger again. It was beautiful, he thought. A few minutes later the tires were squealing against the runway and the engines were throttling back. Doherty looked at his watch and announced that the trip had taken forty-two minutes. When they came to a rest he told Doherty that he could find a motel room and wait for him or he could go back and he'd charter another plane. *It'll cost you more if I stay,* Doherty said. He explained that he wanted him around in case he'd have to bring Kenny back to get better treatment in New York City. Doherty said he'd stay.

*W*hen Kenny was done gathering wood he sat for a moment, aware now that he was perspiring heavily. He looked at his watch and took a sip of water. A little before one o'clock. In a few hours he would have been rising and getting the dairy ready for milking but he was here, in the middle of the woods, not knowing what to do. For the first time since he had risen, unable to sleep, he thought about Claudia and how much he enjoyed being with her and how sweet it was to be naked, kissing and touching her and being inside of her. The sexual questions he'd had about women had been answered. It was nothing like the locker room talk of the other boys. And then the idea came to him suddenly. He put the bottle back into the knapsack and unsheathing his knife went to the calf. He reached under the calf's throat, resting against the lower end of the distended vagina, now dry and beginning to stiffen. He inserted the four fingers of his left hand below the throat and pulled down. When he had managed to create enough room he slid the knife next to his index finger and replaced his hand with the blade of his knife up to the hilt in the opening. Carefully, he pulled downward and slowly cut until the blade struck the left side of the pubic symphysis, the area already widened by the upcoming birth, and slid through, slashing against the udder to create a superficial cut that bled slightly.

*A*fter they were in the terminal Jerry peeled off a couple of hundreds and asked Patrick if he had his driver's license. When Patrick nodded he gave him instructions to rent a car. He gave Doherty a thousand dollars and a piece of paper and told him to stand by. *Here's the phone number at the farm,* he said. *Call me as soon as you get a room and give me your phone number. Get some sleep. You look like hell.* Doherty laughed and went off to refuel his airplane and find a hangar where he could keep it until it was time to go.

Five minutes later Patrick had returned with the keys and a map of the area. He told his son to drive. On the way out of the airport he looked at the map, gave Patrick instructions and off they went. *It's halfway between here and Utica but north past Saratoga,* he said. As they drove he thought about Kenny and hoped things weren't so bad that the kid wouldn't survive. The wrist and hand sounded bad enough but if he had contracted rabies that was the end of the road. From what he knew there was no coming back from that. The brain was affected and that was it. In a matter of days he'd be dead. Father Mahoney, the athletic director at St. Mark's, wasn't going to take this very well and his coach would be furious. This coming season was going to be an even more successful one. The Catholic high school championship wasn't out of the question. He would be helping Kenny make up his mind which Division One school he would attend. The person who would take it the hardest and who would blame himself most would be Tommy. If he had been more understanding, more intelligent, more he didn't know what, he would have convinced Kenny to play baseball and not come up to the farm and then this wouldn't have happened. He suspected the girl had as much to do with Kenny's decision as anything else. You can't predict things. Maybe he would have broken a leg playing baseball.

He recalled Kenny as a calm boy who appeared immune to the pressures of athletic situations. It was like he was always beyond the moment, above the circumstances, confident and totally convinced that victory was his if he concentrated. And his father was right. Kenny was brilliant at ice hockey but much more so in baseball. There was no use praying. He didn't believe in it but he hoped Kenny was all right. Patrick was coming off the highway and heading onto another road that went into the edge of the town by the bus depot. The road veered left and a few minutes later they were on a dirt road that led them to Gabriel Brunet's farm.

He had shot the one spook through the mouth. The autopsy said that the bullet had shattered the left mandible and sent fragments through the palate and nasal cavity and into the brain, killing the bastard instantly. The other spook had knocked the gun out of his hand and was about to shoot him when Tommy came down the fire escape, dove into the kitchen and with his ankle gun shot the spook three times in the chest. Fucking Tommy. He loved those fire escape entrances. While Tommy was looking at the second dead spook he'd gone into the bedroom. He took the large leather woman's bag, opened it, placed two bags of the heroin into another woman's bag, pulled the drawstrings, knotted them and flung it out the window and into the garbage-strewn bricked well that was formed by the two tenement buildings. Later, when things calmed down, he'd lower himself into the well and retrieve the drugs. He came back into the kitchen, asked if the spook was dead and with a great show of disgust dropped the bag with the heroin on the kitchen table. Two minutes later he was calling desperately on his radio and within minutes Patterson and Kelly came in with other cops. Kelly was saying fuck over and over again. This is going to get in the papers for sure, Kelly said.

Another mile and Patrick was pulling into the farm. There was a police car, an ambulance and several other vehicles. Patrick parked the car and they went bounding onto the porch and into the parlor. Gabriel Brunet came forward and he asked him if the ambulance was for Kenny. Gabriel shook his head and said his father had suffered a heart attack. *They're working on him,* he said. *And Kenny?* he asked. Gabriel motioned him forward and into the bedroom. Kenny was sleeping. He had a bandage around his head and one covering his cheek. His lower lip was swollen on one side and his left wrist had been bandaged. *He seems okay,* Boyle said. *No damage to the hand. I thought you said his hand had been damaged.* Gabriel explained that they thought it was the hand because of the blood, but it was the wrist that had been damaged and was in pretty bad shape, ligaments and tendons. *A couple of bones crushed, it looks like.* He asked if there was any other damage. Gabriel shook his head and said that the thing the doctor was worried about was rabies. He added that Kenny had been given shots. He said he and other people had gone back and chopped off the coyote heads. The doctor said that he'd take them back and have all of them tested for rabies. *Coyotes, plural?* he'd asked. *How many? Eight of them,* Gabriel said. *And Kenny killed them?* he asked. *Apparently,* Gabriel said. *And he was out there on his own?* Jerry asked. *Yes, I should have been stricter. We cut the eight heads and they're being tested for rabies.* Jerry shook his head and looked at Patrick, who was nodding and said Kenny was one tough kid. *Fuck, I wish I'd had him with me in Korea.*

*K*enny raised the cow's leg and gingerly began lifting the calf, now fully awake. Frightened, it cried desperately for comfort. Kenny didn't know what he should do. The animal was no bigger than Rover, the old dog. It was moist and sticky, its smell not unpleasant but strange. He had seen the cows lick their newborns so he stroked it and placed it on the cowhide and dragged it away from the carcass. He remembered Gabriel saying that calves weigh from sixty to seventy pounds depending on the size of the cow. Male calves weighed more. This one was small, perhaps forty to forty-five pounds, as Gabriel had said. He thought of cutting the cow's large tongue and swabbing the calf with it but he was sure the cow had stiffened and it would be impossible to open its mouth. He tried and it was useless. He thought of cutting through the facial skin of the cow but knew there would be too much blood and he was tired of the blood. His jeans were stiff with it. The calf had dozed off again and he now attempted to drag the cow away from the clearing and into the wood, certain that the animals would grow bolder and try to get at the dead animal. Before he attempted to drag the carcass off, he once again unsheathed the long knife and now functioning automatically, his feral life sending messages to his brain and his hands executing the commands, he sliced through one of the teats at the base of the udder. The spongy flesh came back white and he knew the milk had come in. He took the teat and held it to the calf's mouth. The calf woke up and hungrily suckled on the teat, its eyes long lashed and semiclosed.

*h*e thanked Gabriel Brunet for taking care of Kenny and asked him if he could use the phone. Gabriel brought him to the room he used for an office, pointed at the desk and said he'd be back later after he made sure his father was all right. Gabriel spoke Spanish to the boy. Jerry listened as he dialed but he could pick up only a few words. Something about the ambulance and hospital, which were practically the same in English. *Vacas* was cows. He wished he could remember what *tu abuelo* meant but it wouldn't come to him. He'd heard Kenny use it and Gloria had said it once in a while but he couldn't figure then that it meant grandfather.

But he had figured Gabriel out. Everybody had a damn secret but this one was a biggie. He laughed inwardly as he dialed his sister's number in New York. The priest at his mother's parish had a friend at a church up here and that's how she knew Henri Brunet and his son, Gabriel. That's how Kenny had ended up at the farm. Bullshit. Very funny, Mom. He loved his mother but she was one devious Irish broad. No wonder he didn't trust anyone. He had been suckled, weaned and trained by an expert. Doherty's people in Washington had checked on Gabriel and had come up with a couple of interesting facts.

Gabriel Brunet had been sent to Peru with the Peace Corps. He'd gotten mixed up with a rich girl. At the same time he was involved with the girl he was also in the country-side fucking around with guerrillas. Shining Path guerrillas, Doherty's people had said, adding that they were not yet organized as what would in the late 1960s become the actual guerrilla group. He didn't know what the fuck they were but they sounded nasty. Terrorists and crazies like the Viet Cong. No different than the patriots fighting the *feckin' brits,* as they said. They ended up kidnapping the girl, collected a ransom from her father and then she disappeared. They were ruthless. They let Gabriel go and he came back to the States. Other than being a Commie sympathizer he was a good guy.

Patterson and Kelly had opened the bag greedily and looked at each other and then at him. They asked if that was it. *That's what was on the table,* he said. He looked at Tommy for corroboration. Tommy nodded. He pointed at the window and explained that he'd heard shots and knew things hadn't gone well. *I knew the door would be locked and came down the fire escape one flight and the perp was about to shoot Boyle.* Kelly said he understood but Patterson wasn't convinced. He wanted to know if he had already paid him. He told Patterson that the guys demanded the money before they turned over the drugs. *It wasn't supposed to go down like that. Why were they asking for the money first?* he said. Boyle said he didn't know. He placed the money on the table next to the bag and then explained what went down. The first perp went for a gun and he pulled his out and shot the perp point-blank in the face. The other guy charged him and banged the gun out of his hand. *He was going to waste me and that's when Romero came in,* he said.

Patterson and Kelly were slick, they were. They had everyone bought off. The *Daily News* ran a small story but everything was pretty much kept out of the newspapers. The investigation said that the two spooks had been unarmed at the time of the shooting even though there were enough arms in the apartment to supply a banana republic. They'd asked him to voucher the heroin. He did so and turned in the one kilo, the two bags inside the lady's bag on the table. A month went by and they were called in. Pretty soon Internal Affairs was looking into the whole thing. *What had happened to the rest of the drugs?* they asked. *That's all there was,* he insisted. There was enough money for a two-kilo buy. He knew that Patterson and Kelly had set him up. He had sensed it as soon as he walked in and the two spooks began moving around like they were surrounding him. Up to that time they had been cool, joking with him and calling him a hippie and a honky. They were nervous and were ordering him around. He'd seen through it and Tommy had come in just in time. It hadn't worked and now they were going to try and fuck him by claiming that he'd stolen the rest of the drugs, which he had. Tough titty.

Patterson and Kelly told IA that they had seen twice the amount of heroin in the bag. *How much? Four bags,* they'd said. *Are you saying that Detectives Boyle and Romero caused part of the evidence to disappear? I'm not making any such accusations,* Kelly testified. *I'm simply stating what I observed.* Patterson corroborated what Kelly had said. He and Tommy were fucked. How the hell his lawyer had found this out, he didn't know.

The Brunet phone rang a couple of times and Frankie was saying his name, her voice shaking. He told her that Kenny was all right, that he was resting and he would be okay. She asked if he was sure. He again reassured her that it wasn't as serious as they had thought. Kenny had to rest and he wasn't sure whether he'd be ready to come back to New York right away. She said that school was due to start in three weeks. He told her Kenny would be ready to go to school by then. Had

Tommy called? No, he hadn't. He should be in Chicago later in the day and he'd call then. What should she tell him? Tell him that Kenny had a small accident and that he's all right. The kids could come out to stay in Long Island and she and Tommy could drive up and see Kenny when Tommy got back. She thanked him and asked about Sheila and his kids. He said they were fine. She then asked if Claudia had come to see Kenny. He told her that the girl was there and cooking them breakfast. Yes, Patrick had come up with him.

*K*enny cut away the entire udder, but the area became a bloody mess and he settled for slicing each of the teats and feeding the calf the little milk that was there. When he was done he kept the teats and flung the udder into the woods, where it landed and made a fox yip and another one growl. He now began to push and drag the carcass, first one side and then another until he had managed to push it beyond the clearing and down a small embankment, where it became lodged between two saplings. When he turned back he saw a pair of eyes reflecting back the fading light of the flashlight. The animal had been approaching the calf. He picked up a piece of rotten wood and flung it at the animal, making it retreat. Rapidly, he spread as much gravel as he could with his feet where the blood had soaked the ground. When he was done there was hardly a trace of the blood. The smell remained but it would disappear once he got the fire going. For the next half hour he worked at making a fire pit. With the ax he dug a shallow hole four feet across, placed the stones around it and began to place the wood across the stones until he had a good pile of kindling and small branches. He went to his jacket, put it on and reached for the matches. For a moment he thought the matches had gotten wet from the blood but it was only his own hand moist from the sweat running down his arm. He took the matches out and transferred them to the right pocket of the mackinaw. He found some dry leaves, placed them on the kindling, struck a match and dropped it among them. He lit several matches and repeated the process. Pretty soon the fire was going. While the kindling burned against the small branches, he used the small ax and chopped the log, working quickly until he had six good pieces. Five minutes later he had a fairly good fire. He placed two of the logs on the fire and dragged the hide with the calf closer and rested his back against the out-cropping of rock behind him. He would wait until it was light and then head back to the farmhouse. He would have started back but the batteries in the flashlight had ceased working and he didn't trust himself to make the trek through the woods in the dark while he was carrying the calf. A bear or a pack of coyotes could attack him and all his effort would have been wasted.

*H*e couldn't believe what his lawyer told him the following week. He hadn't wanted to talk on the phone for fear that neither his phone nor Tommy's was safe. He drove to his lawyer's down in Greenwich Village watching the real hippies, not the phony hippie he played undercover. The only thing he liked about the scene was smoking grass and drinking wine. Some of the girls were okay but they were constantly talking about love and the Vietnam war and they were too boring for his taste. He'd screwed a couple of them with condoms and they were like cold fish.

He sat down in his lawyer's office and asked him why he'd wanted him to come down. Mickey Gold said that what he was about to tell him was pretty bizarre. He sat there dazed as Gold said that Tommy Romero had been asked if he was aware that his partner had vouchered less than had been in the bag. Tommy said he had been aware of the discrepancy. When asked what happened to the rest of the drugs he said that he had hidden the drugs and hoped to sell them. Was this the first time he and Boyle had done this? The very first time and that he was very sorry that they had taken such a step. He said he was ready to return the drugs if that would help. *You and Detective Boyle haven't disposed of the drugs? No, we haven't,* Tommy had replied. *Give me a week and I'll have whatever is missing back. Why a week? Why not right now? A week,* he'd said. *You and Boyle are facing hard time, Romero. We can do hard time. But the department can't stand what's coming if you screw this up,* Tommy said. *One week. That's the deal. No surveillance, no tails, no nothing. One slip-up and the DA gets what I know. What do you want?* they asked. *We want out. No departmental trial. We walk and you get the drugs. Bring the drugs,* they said. Boyle asked Gold how he'd gotten the information out of Internal Affairs. *You don't want to know, Boyle,* Gold had said. *Everything's got a price down there.* Gold showed him the Internal Affairs transcript.

Gold asked him if he knew anything about the disappearance of the drugs. He told Gold that his information was pretty accurate but that the drugs were no longer available. *Sold?* Gold asked. *They've changed hands,* let's say, he'd replied. *Then what's your partner talking about? I don't know. I'll have to talk to him tonight. I'll let you know. He's lying to protect you,* Gold said. *I'll let you know,* he repeated. All these years and they'd never spoken about it. He didn't ask, and Tommy never told him. He asked around in the street and he figured it out but he and Tommy never talked about it. He knew the two dead kids in the projects. What a tough bastard Tommy was. What a heart he had. They would've done hard time if Tommy hadn't cut the deal with Internal Affairs. He was tougher than he had imagined and evidently his kid was too.

$t$he ambulance had taken old man Brunet away. He looked in pretty bad shape. The girl was pretty and dopey but there was something about her that he liked. She had an edge of toughness that would surface later. She was attractive and smart and it was good that Kenny had hooked up with her. Patrick appeared totally taken with Claudia's girlfriend, the little guinea spitfire. Maybe he'd gotten tired of his safari honey. It was obvious that Kenny and the girl were doing it. He'd only seen pictures of her from the previous summer but the virgin shyness was gone from her eyes and she looked like a woman. He could tell those things. But she was a good kid. He'd checked her out through Pete Garrity, who'd been a fireman in New York and was Sheila's cousin. He'd moved his family up here and hooked up with the Utica fire department. He had friends on the job and they gave Garrity the lowdown. The girl's old man was a kraut bastard who'd knocked up the mother and then left her. The mother did the books for a factory in Utica. To work in the morning and back home at night. To the Lutheran church once in a while. She rented an apartment for the girl and herself. Eventually, she bought the little house where they lived. Eva Bachlichtner never went out except to shop after the old man left. No dates, no men. People said that she talked with an accent. That made sense, since she'd come from Germany at the end of the war.

She came over where he and Patrick were sitting on the porch and asked them if they'd eaten breakfast. They said they hadn't and she said she'd be glad to cook them ham and eggs and there was coffee in the kitchen. He waved Patrick on, said that he'd be in after he made a phone call. Patrick followed the two girls and he dialed his mother. He gave her the news and told her the old man had a heart attack. There was a slight pause and he sensed his mother struggling before she said she was sorry to hear that. She changed the subject and said that he'd gotten up there pretty quickly. He explained about Doherty and his plane. Was he bringing Kenny back down to New York? He didn't know yet but he'd let her know. She was a cool one, his mother.

battle

*Because she had gotten to know Kenny,
some girls in the town often questioned
Claudia Bachlichtner, a tall Lutheran
girl who wanted to become a nurse. To the
consternation of her peers, she was closemouthed about her relationship to Kenny.*

WHEN THE FIRE had taken and there was no chance
that it would go out, Kenny became aware that it had
grown colder and a slight wind was blowing through
the trees. His mind was confused and he thought that maybe
he had been in the woods a longer time and it would soon
begin snowing. He put on his mackinaw and placed the rifle
within reach of his right hand. He brought the calf close to
him, rested its head against his thigh, cradling it and covering
part of the animal with its mother's hide, which he imagined
comforted the newborn. The calf slept soundly now. He had
saved the small animal and that was the important thing. His
body felt sore and his mind, although tired, was still alert

enough to sense the danger around the clearing. The fire would keep the wild animals at a distance, but he didn't know how bold they would become. He leaned his back against a part of the rock and within seconds his head dropped onto his chest and he was asleep.

He was asleep no more than fifteen minutes when the calf was stirring and lowing softly. He reached for one of the teats and let her suck on it. And then he heard grunting and knew that a bear had come to investigate the smell and commotion of the other animals. He peered into the darkness beyond the fire and saw not one but two ursine figures, one larger than the other but unmistakably bears. Instinctively, he reached down for the rifle, began to pull the lever quietly but recalled that he had already chambered a bullet and simply released the safety, took a deep breath and waited, the muzzle of the rifle trained on the bigger bear's chest. If he aimed behind the front leg he'd miss the shoulder blade and shoot him in the lungs. If he was lucky he might hit the heart and the single bullet would stop the larger of the animals. If the bear skirted the fire and began coming at him and the calf he'd have to turn and then he'd have to shoot him in the head as he came. That would be more difficult but he was certain the .30 caliber shot would stop the bear if his aim was good. He again took a deep breath and tried to relax. He knew he could get two shots off before the bear was on him. He imagined the two bears coming at him from the left and the right and having to drop one and then the other.

He could feel himself tensing up, his neck and shoulders aching from the strain. He tried relaxing again, breathing deeply and emptying his mind the same way he did when he played hockey. He was on automatic then. *Skate, skate, skate,* the coach yelled from the bench. Forty seconds a shift. Sometimes sixty. Sometimes he was able to go ninety and a new set of wings hit the ice. He'd dump the puck in and head for the bench. A couple of times up and down the ice and that was it. Stop and start. Stop and start. The swish of the skates an accent within the game. Fifty seconds a shift. A very short time that expanded because of the speed at which the game was played. All he could hear were the blades on the ice, scratching, stopping and spraying ice, the sticks receiving or shooting the puck and the voices. *Dump it in, Kenny, dump it in,* from the coach. *Change, change.* He was flying through center ice and he'd make like he was going to slap the puck into the corner while his wingers were heading for the bench. He was in over the blue line now, his head up and the puck dancing on his stick, the ice in front of him clear and the puck there half through touch and half because of his vertical peripheral vision. He'd deke the defenseman and he was around him and there was nothing but the goalie coming out to meet him, the red pipes obscured for a moment. His head would turn slightly and his right shoulder would drop severely as if he were going to bring the puck to his backhand. The goalie would freeze and in stride he'd snap a shot that traveled no more than a few inches off the ice on the goalie's gloved hand, or he'd bring the stick back in an arc so that the blade was poised near his helmet and he'd let go with a slapshot, the puck rising, and before the goalie could react as he crouched it would be over his shoulder and he had tucked the puck in under the crossbar and was raising his stick and a fresh line had come on the ice and they raised their sticks and were now banging their sticks on the ice and on the bench his teammates were banging their sticks on the dasher boards. Other times he continued with the deke, and when the goalie had sprawled on the ice, he'd lift the puck over his body or at the last minute slide it under the goalie's pads. He remembered the first time he'd talked to Claudia asking her if she skated but he'd never asked her if she liked ice hockey.

        She came awake quickly, the ringing of the phone seemingly too insistent for this time of night. She was confused when she heard Henri Brunet on the other end, the old man's voice shaking considerably. She asked what time it was and the old man said it was four in the morning and Kenny was missing. She asked if there had been an accident. The old man said he wasn't sure and that she should hurry because they needed help in looking for him. He was going to call people from nearby farms to see if they'd come and help but that she should come as soon as she could.

    She rose and dressed quickly, putting on thick socks, jeans and a Syracuse University sweatshirt. She slipped into wooden clogs, and sitting on the bed with her pink Princess phone, she called Angie DiBenedetto, her best friend, and told her what happened. Angie said she'd come out to the Brunet farm with her. Claudia said she'd pick her up in five minutes. Her mother came into her room and asked what was the matter. She said she had to go out the Brunet farm because there had been an accident with Kenny. Her mother stared dumbly at her, not knowing what she should say.

    Claudia grabbed the keys to the car from the top of her dresser, slipped into her down jacket, and going past her mother, she pulled out the big metal first aid kit from the pantry. She kissed her mother good-bye, rushed out of the house, threw the first aid kit into the back of the Volkswagen bug, and sped away. She drove quickly through the town until she was at the other end. Angie was waiting for her and got into the car. Claudia drove back through the town, followed the tar-covered road before turning off onto the dirt one that led to the farm. Angie asked what had happened and she explained. Angie said *Oh, my God* and then the two were silent as she drove, the headlights cutting the night, the cool of late summer and the fear making them shiver. Her heart was beating much too fast. He had to be all right, she thought. Nothing could have happened to him. Please, God, she thought, let him be safe.

If something terrible had happened she was glad that Angie was along. Angie had been there when she'd met Kenny last year. They had seen him with the Spanish boy and they asked Lynn Gardner who they were. *Oh, just boys working up at that weird Brunet farm,* she said. *I think they're both fags and it's bullshit about them being father and son. They hire weird kids from the city who think they're so cool.* Angie had rolled her eyes and when the other girl was gone she looked at Claudia and said: *With such an imagination it's a shame Lynn Gardner is going to be a cashier the rest of her life.* Claudia said, *She's just angry that her boyfriend dumped her.* Angie shrugged her shoulders and asked her if she wanted to go and introduce themselves to the two boys. *You take the tall one with the long hair,* she said. *He looks like a cold fish, probably some jock from the looks of him. He probably gets all the girls going after him because of his looks. Anyway, I'm a shrimp. I'll take the Latin lover. He looks like fun and he's shorter.* She'd said, *They're both cute. Well, you know me,* Angie said. *I move fast.* She had no problem with letting Angie have her way. She had no interest in dating. Angie was her best friend even though she was two years older and had graduated that year. She acted like she was half dizzy, but she was smart and was going to study mathematics at Syracuse. She wanted to be a professor. The two boys were standing in front of the diner talking. She and Angie walked up to them and Angie said hi and asked them if they'd seen the movie.

They both nodded. The film was *The Deer Hunter* and the

Spanish boy said his uncle had died in Vietnam and his father had been wounded and got addicted to drugs over there, that the whole thing of playing "rushing roulette" was messed up. *Russian,* Angie had corrected. *That's what I said,* the boy said. *Rushing. Russian,* she repeated. *Russian, like the people from Russia, not rushing around. Russian,* the Spanish boy relented. *My name's Angie and this is Claudia,* she said. *Angel,* the Spanish boy said. *Oh, wow. Angie and Angel,* he said and held up four fingers. *What?* Angie said. Angel held up his four fingers again and whispered the words: *Angie and Angel, forever.* Angie replied, *Not so fast, Buster,* and then pointing at the tall boy added, *And you? Kenny,* he said. Everyone said hi and then Angie said: *How about your father, was he in Vietnam?* and looked at Kenny. *No, he was a policeman. How about yours?* he asked. *Navy,* she said. *What about yours?* Angel said, pointing at her. She'd shrugged her shoulders and said her father was in the Army but she didn't know if he was in Vietnam. She didn't say that she only saw him once or twice a year.

Angel asked Angie if she felt like having a milkshake. Angie said sure and motioned Claudia to come with them. She'd shaken her head and said that she should go home. And then Kenny's voice cut through her. *Please, don't go,* he said. She had blushed deep red and said, *Oh, my God,* like an idiot but had gone into the diner with them. Kenny held the door open for everyone. Angel and Angie sat in the middle of the booth, obviously not wishing their company. She and Kenny found another booth in the back and ordered apple pie à la mode and coffee. For the longest time they didn't say anything, both of them uncomfortable. She couldn't believe how much she felt for him so quickly. It was like her heart had opened up and she wanted to just take care of him like he was a little baby except that she knew she was sexually excited by looking at him. She finally asked him if he was an athlete. He nodded and she asked if he played basketball. He said he played ice hockey and soccer and baseball, but had stopped playing baseball this year to concentrate on hockey. He asked her if she could skate and she said she could skate pretty good, but couldn't shoot a puck very well. Her joke removed some of the tension and they were laughing easily. He opened up and told her about his family, explaining about each one and how they were and what they liked. When he was done she couldn't believe that he had four sisters. And then he told her about his parents and his aunts and uncles and his grandparents and then she asked him about his last name. *Romero,* he'd said. *Kenny Romero. I'm Puerto Rican. Well, my father is. My mother's Irish. You know, both born here.* She found all the information interesting, but wanted to know if his parents loved each other. *Oh, very much. They're still like us,* he said. *They're still so in love. Like us?* she'd asked. And then he'd realized what he had implied and explained that they were like teens. And that he hadn't meant anything bad by saying like us. *It's okay,* she said and they were silent again and ate their pie and ice cream and drank their coffee. They didn't know what else to say. She certainly wasn't going to talk about *her* parents. He heard the honking outside and knew Gabriel had come to get them in the pickup. He left three dollars on the table with the bill. All four of them came outside. They said good-bye and Angie and Angel made a date for the following Saturday. Kenny had looked at her and she shrugged her shoulders and said: *Sure, might as well.*

*K*enny watched intently. He was a righty but he sighted on the rifle as if he were a lefty and kept the rifle steady, aimed at the bigger of the bears. They were both grunting and then he saw the larger bear begin breaking the bigger of the saplings that held the carcass wedged in. When he dragged the carcass away, the sound was as if someone were raking leaves. The smaller bear followed. Kenny listened for some fifteen minutes until the grunting was far away. It was now replaced in the distance by howling and barking and much closer by distinctive growls. He rose silently, put another log on the fire and retrieved his backpack. For the first time since he'd left the farm he felt hungry. His hands caked with the cow's blood, he opened the tinfoil, took a large bite from the ham, reached into the bag and tilting it let a whole biscuit fall into his mouth. He chewed and swallowed and bit once again into the chunk of ham before placing another biscuit in his mouth. He folded the tinfoil again, closed the biscuit bag and the ham and placed them back in the backpack. He drank some water and closed the bottle.

He felt sleepy but listened closely for the bears. They had left. He knew they wouldn't return, felt his body relax and once again involuntarily closed his eyes. The calf was between his legs and the rifle rested within the crook of his arm, the stock under his left knee. If anything happened he would reach down, bring the rifle up and be ready to shoot. He wished he'd found more ammunition and hadn't forgotten his work gloves. This time he was asleep nearly a half hour. He looked at his watch. It was now two-thirty. An owl hooted and he heard the wings fluttering through the woods. Beyond the fire there were eyes looking at him, the orbs reflecting the light of the flames. He swept the perimeter of the clearing, nearly two hundred and forty degrees, and tried counting the eyes. Before he had completed the sweep he lost count at twelve. He counted again and this time he knew that they had come in full and were stalking him and the calf. Fourteen of them. It had to be coyotes because they would've chased the foxes away. He didn't know if he was afraid but he wished he had never come out and had listened to Gabriel. He petted the calf's head as it slept, its breathing peaceful.

He got up, and holding the rifle in his left hand, he placed another log in the fire. From the ground he gathered quail-egg-size stones and rocks and made a pile of perhaps fifty rocks near the calf. Holding four or five stones in his left hand he stood behind the fire and began picking off the animals as they crouched. His aim was unerring. It was like going into the hole and hitting the second baseman with his throw as he came to get the force-out at second. He hit several of them, heard them yelp in pain and growl back menacingly. He continued firing, making them back up until the eyes were no longer there. He gathered more stones, brought them closer to the place where the calf was resting and sat down again. Minutes later they were back, not as many of them but enough to worry him. He counted eight this time. He'd wait them out. He reckoned sunrise and knew that now, later in the summer, it wouldn't grow light for another three hours. He tried recalling when the sun had come up yesterday. He had hooked up the third set of cows to the milking machine, so it had to be a little after six in the morning. It was now a quarter to three.

Claudia pulled into the yard, turned off the engine and retrieved the first aid kit. She and Angie jumped out of the car, bounded up the steps to the porch and went inside without knocking. It was still night and Mr. Brunet was on the phone, his face worried and pale in the fluorescent light of the little office. When he hung up the phone she asked him where Gabriel was. *He just left to look for Kenny,* he said. She asked where they'd gone and Mr. Brunet pointed toward the back. He said that his son and grandson were heading for the stream in case Kenny had gone to help the cow give birth. He said she should take the flashlight in the kitchen. She asked Angie if she could stay and help Mr. Brunet make phone calls. Angie nodded, looking frightened. Clutching the first aid kit, Claudia went to retrieve the flashlight.

She went out of the kitchen door shining the flashlight in front of her. She walked quickly, past the barn and the smell of manure and feed, her clogs sinking into the moist earth. The chill of the morning was exhilarating but carried with it dread. She hadn't even combed her hair but she didn't care. Kenny had to be okay. Maybe Mr. Brunet was right and he'd gone to help a cow. Kenny was like that. In many ways he was like a girl. Most girls wanted to be useful and boys just wanted to give orders and feel important. Kenny wasn't like that. He was more like Angie, who was always being helpful. She wasn't too good in chemistry but Angie had helped her. She loved making people feel better and that's why she wanted to be a nurse. She felt insecure about chemistry and that was the reason she didn't want to be premed. She hated being embarrassed and wondered if that had to do with not really having a father, or with her mother and her secret life, which she didn't know about, but it was her secret life as well.

His whole family was like that, she thought. His uncle Jerry sounded like he was the same way, always helping his sister, Kenny's mother. *Not only her,* Kenny had said. He helped other people. He and Kenny's father were friends. They had been in the police department together but now they had their own businesses. Mr. Romero had a moving company and Mr. Boyle had a fishing boat in Long Island. Kenny had shown her on the map where his uncle lived. She had been to the sea only once when she was very little and her father and mother had driven to Massachusetts and they'd gone to the beach.

She had loved sitting in the sand. Kenny said there was a beach house that belonged to his uncle and maybe they'd go there and go swimming and have a cookout. *With your family?* she'd asked. *No, just the two of us,* he'd said. *There's a wood-burning stove and a fireplace and we could cook and hang out.* She had nodded and they had kissed and just held each other. She was having her time of the month and had terrible cramps but he was good with her and made her feel special and rubbed the small of her back and explained that his father often did that to his mother. *Because of her time?* He'd nodded and she asked how he knew it was because of her time of the month. *Because of the smell of blood,* he said. *Is it bad?* she asked, all of a sudden self-conscious. Kenny shook his head and smiled at her. *It always seemed special to me like it was part of her and she took care of me and hugged me and held me when I was sad or something, so it was okay.* She couldn't believe he was so sweet and loved his mother so much. That had been at the beginning of the summer around the time they'd started doing it in the woods and then up in the hayloft and later in the motel.

*K*enny decided he had slept enough but now felt a pain in his bladder and realized he hadn't urinated in a while. He'd read that dogs and other animals marked their territory. He went to the fire, removed a branch that had not yet burnt through and holding the burning branch in front of him to ward off the animals, he walked the perimeter of the small clearing urinating as he stepped sideways with his back to the fire until he was on the other side and retraced his steps, the stream becoming weaker as he neared the place where the calf lay. When he was done he once again zippered his jeans and returned the branch to the fire. The marking of his territory appeared to infuriate the coyotes and they growled and barked menacingly at each other as if the smell of his urine had confused them. They argued like this for a while and then they were once again still.

He sat in front of the calf, holding the rifle, and decided he would sing to keep himself awake. He sang "Go Tell Aunt Rhodie." On about the third chorus the coyotes had joined him and were howling. The notion made him laugh and he wished he could tell Claudia about this. He next sang "John Jacob Jingle Hymer Schmit," each verse lower until it got to the end and then his voice rose into a crescendo, louder and louder in contrast with the nearly whispered verses, except that to him it sounded like John Jacob Hinklehammersmith and that is how he sang it. *John Jacob Hinklehammersmith his name was my name too. Whenever we go out the people always shout: There goes John Jacob Hinklehammersmith.* LALALALALAH. And he'd start again. Each time his voice rose the coyotes barked and howled and pretty soon he was laughing giddily at the irony that he was having a campfire singalong with a bunch of wild animals in the middle of the woods. He sang "The Fox" and "A Hundred Bottles of Beer on the Wall." He looked at his watch and it was now half past three.

He recalled a poem but couldn't remember who wrote it. He tried repeating it but the words wouldn't come to him and he gave up. He wasn't too good at poetry. The woods were dark and deep and he didn't know what the fuck he was doing out there. There was something about a promise. He felt like his mind wasn't functioning correctly, like he was drunk. He'd heard other boys describe smoking pot, but he never had given in. He had been drunk a couple of times when he went to the St. Patrick's Day parade with his friends from school, wearing green and feeling stupid because he had a Spanish name, but his mother said that those things didn't matter because he was American. He thought that just that one day he could be Kenny Boyle. And anyway, she said that a one-time president of Ireland, Eamon de Valera, had a Spanish name. Mr. de Valera had an Irish mother and a Cuban father. His father had died and Mr. de Valera's mother had brought him to New York and eventually they had returned to Ireland. She said that there was a section in the northwest of Spain above Portugal and they had bagpipes called *gaitas* and step dancing they called *jotas*. She said she had learned about this during her senior year when she was able to take conversational Spanish and reading about everything she wanted to visit those places but then she met his father.

Kenny didn't hate the coyotes but knew that he'd have to kill them if they tried to harm the calf. It was his calf now. She had no mother and his father was one of the bulls. He didn't know which. The bull couldn't take care of the calf. The calf was his responsibility. He thought that it was always easy to tell who the mother was but not the father. There was no way to tell. He and Peggy looked so different but it was because they both had Spanish and Irish blood. He had come out light like his mother and Peggy light skinned but black hair and dark eyes like their father. That was all. The other girls had brown hair and didn't look Spanish. Tommy Jr. looked Spanish. He was really sleepy now.

Kenny drank some more water and tried counting the eyes. There were only six now. He figured the others had grown tired or were foxes and had returned, no longer afraid of the coyotes. Maybe they hadn't liked his singing. The thought made him laugh and he wondered if he could hold out until morning or should try sneaking away with the calf. That was pretty crazy. He wanted to go swimming and let the saltwater of the sea sting his eyes. He wanted to be with Claudia at Uncle Jerry's beach house. Just the two of them, cooking lobster and corn on the cob and making love. He loved his mother and father and wished he were small again and they were holding him and he felt safe.

The thought of his mother made tears come into his eyes. She was so good, he thought. She worked so hard to make everyone happy and he never wanted to do anything that hurt her. And his father worked hard as well. He didn't know why he wasn't a policeman anymore but it didn't matter because he was also good. He wanted to be good and not hurt anyone or anything. He didn't like fighting and hurting other people. In hockey he had to check people but it wasn't to hurt them. He had once taken a slapshot and the boy went flat on the ice to block it. He had turned his face and the puck struck him in the ear and cut it. The boy was knocked out and he was bleeding. He thought he had killed him. He was eleven and he cried and stood by the boards until the boy came to and stood up. He skated over to him and said he was sorry. The boy said it was okay. The other coach glared at him.

He peered beyond the fire and wondered if he was hallucinating.

She caught up to Gabriel and Carlos as they were getting to the stream and together they began crisscrossing the meadow, hoping to find Kenny. Gabriel said hello and told her to go along this side of the stream and look under the bushes. He and Carlos would cross the stream and look on the other side. They were both wearing rubber boots. She began walking and calling Kenny. She could hear Gabriel and Carlos calling him as well. She liked the way that Carlos called out his name, *Kaynee*. The sun was coming up now and they could see more clearly. She kept the flashlight on.

She wondered if Kenny's mother knew that Kenny was missing. She was glad she had written to her and that she had asked Angie to take a photograph of the two of them. Frances Ann Boyle. She loved the name and wished she could get to know her. Maybe she would. Frances Ann Boyle was such a cool name and she wished she had a name like that. But she was really Frances Romero. That was cool too. Fran. The name sounded like it could be another girlfriend. Fran, Angie and Claudia. She liked Claudia but didn't like the Sarah stuck in there. Claudia Sarah Bachlichtner seemed so heavy. Maybe Claudia Romero, she thought, and nearly slapped herself for daydreaming like that. His mother was going to be very upset if she found out that they were doing it. She was sure of that. She had to figure out a way to tell her. She had to graduate and go to college and become a nurse. And Kenny had to graduate and go to college as well. She had messed up all of their plans. She called his name and looked under a clump of bushes to see if the cow was there. She knew a lot about his family, but he knew so little about hers and there were things she wasn't ready to tell him yet. She was sure he would be disappointed.

*K*enny Romero once again sat back against the rock and fell asleep. When he next woke up the calf was lowing and struggling to get up, its legs still too weak, especially since it hadn't been properly fed. When he looked beyond the calf, one of the coyotes was no more than fifteen feet away to the right of the fire. He was a big male, darker than any he'd seen, much like the dark coloring of a German shepherd. His muzzle was large and his eyes yellowish. He was like the wolves he'd seen in documentaries on television. Gabriel said that some of the coyotes this far north had bred with wolves. Maybe this one had the strains of that cross-breeding. He thought of himself in the same way. He had been crossbred. Two other coyotes were to the left, circling to come at them from that side. Their eyes were yellow and the one closest bared his teeth, the long snout snarling. *Go away, you fuck,* he yelled. He gathered some stones and threw three of them in rapid fire, hitting the coyote nearest him twice and sending him away yelping.

One of the two coyotes on the left ran quickly and took up a post on his right. These two were a dirty gray and eyed him hungrily. When he looked again two more had joined the first two and now the one he had hit with the rocks was sneaking around on the periphery, ready to get closer. He had roughly a dozen rocks left. He menaced them with his arms and they scampered back but returned, oblivious to the fire, which was not yet dying but would do so soon if he didn't drop another log in. He had no choice. He raised the rifle, and from a sitting position he fired at the nearest coyote on his right. The bullet shattered the animal's skull and it dropped without a yelp. He swung the rifle around and aimed at the dark one in the middle, hitting him in the chest and sending it yelping away. He was sure he would run a hundred feet and drop, its lungs filled with blood.

The other three coyotes had backed off and were crouching in the undergrowth. He stood up, and lowering the rifle to his hip, he picked up the fourth and fifth log and placed them on the fire. Maybe if the fire was bigger they wouldn't be so bold. He backed up, watching the coyotes beyond the fire. And then he saw another big one, blondish and bold. It was running hard on the left around the fire and heading straight at the calf. He dropped to one knee, sighted and fired. He caught the animal in midair as it leapt at the calf. He'd shot it below the left ear. It yelped, began convulsing and died. The calf's eyes were wide open and it was moaning loudly, one cry after the other. He poked at the fallen coyote with the barrel of the rifle to make sure it was dead. He was now in a rage at the coyotes. Why wouldn't they just go away and leave them alone? When he was certain that the animal had expired he set the rifle down and picked up the coyote by the tail, whipping it around as if he were Bobby Consino at school tossing the hammer, which was just a heavy ball on a chain, he flung it beyond the fire. He had tried throwing the javelin just to satisfy the coach of the track and field team but he wasn't into it. The coyote had to weigh fifty pounds but he sent it over the fire into the place where the three other coyotes were crouching. It landed with a thud. The coyotes yelped and growled but wouldn't go away. He was so angry now. He had three bullets left. For a moment he wished he'd found more bullets but he hadn't and there was no sense regretting it. His mind wasn't functioning well because for a split second he thought of going back to get more ammunition. How stupid, he thought.

*g*abriel and Carlos had returned and shook their heads. In the pearly gray air of the predawn Gabriel said they should spread out and cover the large meadow. He could be behind one of the small hills tending to the cow. They spread out and walked, calling Kenny's name. Nothing. When they got to the field where the bulls were grazing she began going in but Gabriel called her back. He came over and said he was sure they weren't there. He explained that there was no way for the cow to enter that area. *What now?* she'd said. Gabriel said that they'd look along the edge of the woods. She looked at the woods and knew that they went on for a long way, rising steadily as they eventually led into the Adirondack Mountains. Bears often came down and roamed around. People said they even came into town sometimes. Maybe a bear had gotten Kenny. The thought frightened her and she wanted to scream, no, no, no. Someone else said that a bear had grabbed a small girl near the old convent that had burned down. They'd found the girl dead and mauled but it turned out that the girl had been raped and whoever did it tried to make it look like it was a bear. Someone said the man had used a bear claw. She wondered what made people do things like that. She continued calling Kenny's name as she walked along the edge of the woods.

She wished more people would come and then when it was light they could go into the woods and look for Kenny. She hoped dozens of people would come to help them. Maybe hundreds. Kenny had told her about his cousins. There were so many. He told her about his grandmother Mary Boyle and her family and all the cousins from that side. And then he told her about his other grandmother, who smoked cigars. He had many aunts and uncles and cousins. She had nobody. Her father had three other children, so she had at least some siblings, but no grandmother or grandfather. Her father had come east from Minnesota. He never talked about how he'd grown up. *German Lutherans*, he'd say. *A lot of heavy food with cream. That says it all,* he'd say, laugh once and clam up. And her mother? Zilch. No mother, no father, no brothers or sisters, no aunts or uncles and she wasn't much help either. All gone. This past year after she got to know Kenny she'd asked her mother what had happened. She'd opened up and told her a little, about living in a place called Schwabach in Germany and the picnics they had before the war. But the memories were too painful and after a few minutes she stopped talking and left the living room to hide in her bedroom.

Her only connection to family was Kenny. She had asked him if he thought his grandmothers would like her. He said he thought so and that Grandma Boyle was pretty easy to get along with. *She tells a lot of stories and after a while you can't tell what's true and what's not, but she's cool. And Grandma Rosa, your father's mother?* He shook his head and laughed and said that she would disapprove of her and say she was too skinny and she'd take it on herself to fatten her up. *She'd try to get you hooked on smoking cigars,* he said. They both laughed and began undressing each other and kissing. They were getting so good at making love in the motel. Angie hadn't done it with anyone yet and was constantly asking her questions. She didn't mind telling Angie but she couldn't tell anyone else.

One Saturday she had driven to the farm in her VW and he'd gone in and told Gabriel that he was going with her to look around Utica and that they'd probably stay there overnight. It was all matter-of-fact and Gabriel didn't mind. He was so cool. They drove all the way to Syracuse and had dinner in an Italian restaurant and then got a motel room and made love over and over. It was beautiful and when she came it went on and on. They went to sleep with their arms around each other. In the night she woke up with the air-conditioning going full blast. She pulled the covers over them and went back to sleep and in the morning they made love again. She shook her head and made herself stop thinking about Kenny that way until she found him and he was safe. She didn't know how she was going to tell him everything when they were together again. She was sure he would be upset.

*h*e was hungry and thirsty and once again opened the bag, ate the last of the ham and not caring about the dry blood on his hands, took another biscuit and ate it. He drank some more water. The calf was looking at him pleadingly. He tried feeding the calf a piece of biscuit but she made no effort to eat it. He tried giving it some moss but that didn't please her either. He finally held the dry teat out to her and she took it greedily and sucked on it until she was once again relaxed and dozing off. When he looked up the coyotes were back, four of them this time. Two on each side. Where the fuck did they come from? They were making him crazy. He shouldn't curse. His mother didn't like it and neither did the brothers at school, even though some of the lay teachers slipped up once in a while and said dammnit.

He looked at his watch. Four-thirty and now two more coyotes had come closer to the fire. One of them had crept up to within ten feet of him. This one looked like a definite cross with a wolf, the snout not as sharp as that of a coyote. The animal eyed him insolently and when he waved the rifle at it he snarled but didn't back up. He raised the rifle, sighted and pulled the trigger. The animal's skull shattered and the face seemed to explode as it rolled over and died. Rather than retreat, the other five were now in a frenzy as if they had finally grown tired of him.

They came at him now filled with a fierceness that the other ones hadn't displayed. He raised up and shot a blondish one, a female, wounding her in the hindquarters and setting her to yelping. This made the others crazier and they began growling and snapping at him as they came closer. One bullet left, he thought. He measured their chaos, took aim and killed another one. Now there were four and he didn't know whether others would come. No more ammunition. He grabbed the rifle by the barrel and made charges at them, hoping that one would be bold enough to come close enough so he could clock it with the stock of the rifle. A small female did just that and he struck her a good enough blow to stun her. She lay motionless and he stomped her with his heavy work boots, crushing the left orbital bone and causing the eye to pop out. Placing his boot under her flank, he lifted his foot quickly so that she landed half into the fire, sending sparks into the air. The singed fur created an awful, sickening smell. She burned like that for a minute, and then stunned awake by the heat she jumped up and yelping she limped into the woods.

Another rushed at him and he swung, striking the animal on the head. The stock of the rifle broke off. Angrily he threw the barrel after the other two. He unsheathed his knife, transferred it to his left hand, extracted the small ax from the backpack and grasped the handle tightly. Crazed by his fear he screamed wildly. It was a feral scream, something which he had never heard. He was alone now and he thought about the Indians of the Iroquois Nation who had walked these woods without firearms. He tried to name the tribes and remarkably he was able to recall the names: the Iroquois, the Mohawks, the Oneidas, Onondagas and the Cayugas. The old man had told him that they roamed the state of New York, extending north to the Great Lakes of Ontario, Huron and Erie to southern Ontario and Quebec. The old man showed him the book with the map and he asked him if perhaps he was himself part Indian. The old man was pleased by the notion and said maybe that was true and told him that his grandfather remembered hearing of the French and Indian wars.

He tested his memory and was able to recall many little-known facts that he had memorized for school: historical dates, formulas for obscure chemicals, as well as irrelevant things such as the names of all the Beatles albums and the Most Valuable Players in both the National and American League for the past ten years. He wondered if like in sports he had reached a state in which the only awareness was that of the game and within that awareness the ultimate task of winning. He continued screaming at the animals, which came closer and closer, eyeing the calf, which was now panicked and lay cowering and moaning, unable to stand and flee, too young to do so, which was good because the coyotes would have knocked it down quickly and killed it within minutes.

He saw one of the coyotes leap at him and with the ax raised he came down on it, catching it above the shoulders and snapping its spinal cord. The animal rolled away and began convulsing. On his follow-through he saw one coming at the calf. He turned and chopped at it with the ax. He struck the animal a glancing blow, which sent both the animal and the ax bouncing away, the coyote six feet away and the ax a dozen or so feet into the undergrowth. Missing made him lose his balance and he fell, struck his head on the rock and for a moment blacked out. As he turned he saw the coyote on his right come at him, its mouth open and snapping. The animal tore the wool cap from his head and in biting wildly caught him in the head, the teeth sinking into his scalp as it tried getting at his face. He brought up his left arm to protect himself. The coyote seized the wrist in its jaws and tore at it, shattering the glass on his watch and with it the small bones of his wrist. The animal held him fast in its mouth, biting repeatedly and sending a searing pain into his arm. The pain traveled into his awareness so that he screamed more loudly in anger. He was rolling with the animal gnawing at his wrist. When they were near the fire he stabbed repeatedly at his attacker, plunging the eight-inch blade over and over again into the writhing fur until the animal released his wrist and lay gasping in a bloody mess. He turned and saw the last of the coyotes coming at the calf. When it reached the calf, the coyote bit its ear, held it fast and began pulling at the terrified animal, now mute, the fear causing her to freeze. He screamed and cursed loudly, rushed at the coyote and kicked violently at it until the coyote let go and he kicked it again as it tried to attack him. He felt a sharp pain in his right leg and with the last of his strength he stomped on the animal's rib cage, crushing the upper thorax and sending the animal whimpering away.

He looked at the calf. It was quivering and very likely in shock. The small animal stared pleadingly up at him. He put his knife back into its sheath and stroked the calf, covering it with her mother's hide. When he had done this and his breathing had become more normal he felt the pain and looked at his left wrist. The sleeve of the mackinaw jacket was torn to reveal the carnage above his hand. He was bleeding profusely and the skin was torn away, some of the bones visible. With difficulty, he removed the useless watch. The watch had stopped at ten minutes to five. The leather of the watch-band was chewed up badly. Later, the doctor said that had he not been wearing the thick leather band the coyote would have bitten through the wrist and very likely the hand would have had to be amputated. He reached with his right hand, twisting his arm behind him and pulled his large handkerchief from his back left-hand jeans pocket. He often wore the kerchief as a bandanna to hold his long hair in place. Although his left hand was intact, he couldn't move the fingers. He tried but he had no control of them. He raised the wounded wrist and wrapped the kerchief around it. Placing one corner in his mouth, he slit the loose end with his knife and was able to tie the makeshift bandage and halt the bleeding, fearing that he would lose consciousness from loss of blood or perhaps bleed to death. He touched his face and felt a gash near his cheek. His lip on that side was swollen. He touched his head and felt the wounds where the coyote's teeth had punctured the scalp.

He couldn't wait any longer. Let them come again if they wanted. Let the fucking bears come and get him if they also wanted to. He'd fight them as well but they weren't going to get his calf. He tried lifting the calf but his left arm was too weak. The calf would have been easy to carry were it not for the dead feeling in his hand. He'd hoist her up on his shoulders and carry it by holding its legs on either side of him. Or he could hold it in his arms.

*K*enny wasn't anywhere nearby and she became desperate and kept calling his name and yelling stupidly, *I love you, Kenny. Kenny, answer me. Kenny, Kenny, Kenny. I know you're there, Kenny. I love you. Answer me, Kenny.* She wanted to go into the woods but Gabriel said they should wait until they had more help. She didn't want to wait. She wanted him with her right now. No more waiting. *Kenny,* she screamed as Gabriel took her arm. *Let's go back,* he said. There should be more people at the house now and we'll go into the woods and look for him. They began to go down the hill with the sun coming up now and the farm gauzy in the early morning fog forming near the stream.

Going down the hill she felt as if she were abandoning him. What was she going to do if he was dead? She shouldn't think about such things. But what would she do? She'd end up like her mother. By herself with a baby to raise. Because there was no doubt now. She had missed her period twice now. She had a period the week after the end of June and then they started doing it and no menstruation in July and now nothing in August. She was going to tell him and now this was happening and it was like a punishment. She knew he wouldn't get angry and would tell her she'd be okay but she should've been more careful. His mother would hate her and wouldn't want to be her friend when she found out. She was sure of it. She would be alone if something terrible had happened to him. She couldn't figure out which prospect was worse. Being alone with a child to raise or the two of them together with a baby. Two more stupid teenage kids.

She began crying and couldn't stop. He was such a good person. So honest. He just came out and said things without worrying that she would be critical because he knew she wouldn't be. He didn't know what he would do in college. Maybe he'd want to graduate and become a teacher like his mother. Maybe he could play professional hockey. And he'd shake his head and tell her that he wasn't good enough. She said that maybe he'd get better in college. *Maybe,* he'd said, *but I don't know what I'll study in college.* She asked him what he liked best and he said he loved biology and the way there were so many animals and how some of them resembled each other and how they inherited the same characteristics from their parents. *Genetics,* she'd said. *That's right,* he'd said. *Something like that. Or maybe I'll become a farmer like Gabriel. I like being in the country. And you wouldn't miss the city?* she asked. *Sure, but we could go in once in a while.*

She knew he was talking about the future and about them staying together, living together, getting married and having a house and waking up next to each other every morning and the children would be there at Christmas. They would come into their bedroom and wake them up to tell them what Santa had brought them. That's how it had been the Christmas she'd spent at her father's when she was twelve and her mother had gone into the hospital. The kids had pulled her out of bed. *Come on, Claudia. Let's go see what Santa brought us.* And they'd gone under the Christmas tree and opened presents and howled at how exciting everything was and then they'd gone into their parents' bedroom and his new wife was there with her big boobs under her nightgown and they'd jumped up on the bed and told her what they'd gotten as presents. She stood by the door watching the three kids and their parents. She couldn't put the scene together with anything that had to do with her and she felt stupid and went back to her room to cry.

But it wouldn't be like that with their family, she thought. Gabriel was calling her and then she heard the voice, Kenny's voice, faint at first and then louder and she called out to him *Kenny, Kenny* and was running back up the meadow toward the woods.

*K*enny looked at the backpack, took out the bottle of water, drank from it and washed some of the blood away from his face. He gave some water to the calf, holding its mouth open and pouring some of it in, knowing it would become dehydrated if he didn't quench its thirst. When there was a little bit left in the bottle he brought it once again to his lips, drained it and threw the plastic bottle into the fire, where it melted and produced an acrid smell. He then took out the knife and over the next ten minutes he was able to fashion a sling from the backpack. He slung the straps around his right shoulder and knelt in front of the calf. Bending low so that he was almost lying down, he began to slide the calf into the sling. With great difficulty he maneuvered the calf so that its hindquarters were behind at his left hip and the front ones were at his belt buckle. With the knife in his right hand he held the calf's head in the crook of his left arm and stood up. The pain in his wrist was numbing and he tried blocking it out. He looked around for his compass and panicked when he couldn't find it. He felt in his mackinaw but he had placed it in his left-hand pocket, now pinned by the calf's hindquarters. He reached in front of him and methodically pulled at the mackinaw until he was able to bring the jacket around and remove the compass from the pocket of the jacket. Kneeling by the fire, he took a reading and recalled that the farm was down the mountain to the northeast.

He wanted to douse the fire but didn't, hoping that the light could help him find his way out of the deep woods. In the light of the dying fire he took one last reading of the compass, placed it in his pocket and once more unsheathed his knife and held it at the ready. He moved beyond the clearing and through the woods, stepping gingerly, avoiding a sudden drop, feeling for rocks with his boots and with his right shoulder for large trees. It was pitch black in front of him now but he continued, trusting his instincts. He tried to pray but the prayers made him angry and instead he cursed. He made certain not to curse God, but said son of a bitch, fucker, bastard and cocksucker liberally. He felt the ground descending and he slowed his pace. He once again exchanged knife for match and compass and took another reading. He adjusted his direction so that he was once again heading north-northeast and continued descending. He repeated the process three more times and continued, the ground becoming less steep.

He was functioning like a robot now, he thought, his mind torn by disconnected thoughts, some giddy, others filled with horror that the coyotes were trailing them and would attack again. Instead he heard a songbird and then another. He looked up and saw light through the dense woods. The sun was coming out and he hurried, stumbling once and nearly falling. And then he heard the voices calling his name, Gabriel and Carlos. He thought he heard Claudia but that couldn't be. He called out Gabriel's name and kept walking, the ground now more level. Two minutes later he had emerged from the woods. Down below he saw three figures and he walked toward them, crying again until he could no longer stay on his feet and he sank to his knees. He continued weeping, this time uncontrollably, and calling Jesus' name, crying for someone to help him.

She ran madly, holding the first aid kit against her chest. She lost a clog but she was able to reach him first and knelt in front of him with the calf between them. They cried together and she kissed his face. He winced and then she saw the swollen wounds and knew that he had been attacked by an animal. *Oh, my God,* she said and opened up the first aid kit. With a swab and peroxide she began cleaning the wound. First on his face and then his scalp, swollen and caked with blood.

Gabriel had rushed up now and then Carlos. Gabriel took off the sling and placed the calf on the dewy grass next to him. She made Kenny lie down and then she saw his bandaged wrist and removed the kerchief. What she saw horrified her and she couldn't speak. Gabriel spoke quickly to Carlos and told him to tell his father to call the doctor. *El doctor Anderson,* he said. *Tell him to hurry. Rápido. Corre.* Run, hurry. Carlos took off running down the hill, racing until he had descended into a dip in the meadow and emerged again near the first corral.

When Kenny was lying down Claudia worked carefully, cleaning the wounded wrist, pouring peroxide on it and then wiping it with a gauze pad. She then wrapped the wrist with gauze several times and taped it loosely. She was sure the wrist had been badly damaged. Gabriel asked what happened and Kenny said coyotes had attacked him. *How many?* Gabriel asked. Kenny said he didn't know. *Maybe eight or ten.* He wasn't sure. He asked Kenny if he thought he could walk back. Kenny nodded. *I broke the 30-30,* he said. *I'm sorry. I would have been okay if I'd had more ammunition, but I didn't want to wake you up looking for it,* he said. *I'm glad you're okay,* Gabriel said. *We have to get that wrist looked at. 571 is dead.* Gabriel said it was okay and he shouldn't talk.

Claudia closed the first aid kit, retrieved her clog, and helped Kenny stand up. With Gabriel carrying the calf and Claudia helping him walk down, they descended the meadow. He told her that the pain in his right leg was greater and he felt dizzy. He also said he was thirsty. She didn't know if this one symptom of rabies would appear so soon. She didn't say anything, wishing to have the doctor confirm her suspicions and not wanting to alarm Gabriel or Kenny.

Gabriel looked very worried. He was another mystery, Gabriel. He lived by himself and appeared to have little joy in his life. Between him and her mother they had probably accumulated more sadness than a hundred people. She often thought that maybe his mother and Gabriel ought to get together and put each other out of the misery of being alone. Even if they didn't like each other she wanted to lock them up in a room and bring them food until they at least talked to one another. What the heck was the matter with him? He wasn't an unattractive man, was bright, educated and evidently a good businessman, since he was making a go of the farm. Angie said he had been in the Peace Corps in South America. That was pretty cool. One of the first people to go into the Peace Corps from the area. Angie's mother, who went to high school with Gabriel, said he was a good student, ran track, went off to college to study and then got a master's in farm management or something like that. And then he went to work for the state, managing farm subsidies. Angie had asked if Gabriel had dated anyone. Her mother said he'd gone out with a girl named Lisa Diller for a while and then she stopped going out with him and after high school she married Steve Barnes who owned the gas station. After that he went to college and hardly ever came to town. Whenever he came home he went straight to the farm and stayed with the family that owned the place. The Vanderveers, Angie's mother said. And then he was gone and Angie's mother said he had joined the Peace Corps and went to South America.

And then she realized that Mr. Brunet had called Carlos his grandson. Either he had slipped up, considered the boy the grandson he never had, or it meant that Gabriel was Carlos's father. At least she wasn't the only one with a secret. Nobody knew what had happened to his mother. Some people said that Mr. Brunet had adopted him. Other people said that Gabriel's father and Mrs. Vanderveer had been lovers and Gabriel was really her son.

She continued leading Kenny toward the farmhouse, but he was fading now, the ordeal of the previous night beginning to take its toll on him. When they reached the barn he finally collapsed and she went down with him. She called out and three men came and helped to carry him inside. He was conscious but appeared dazed. When they had carried him inside he smiled weakly at her and told her he would be all right. They brought him to his room and helped him to remove his bloody clothes. When he was down to his underwear Gabriel had them bring him into the bathroom, where there was already a bathtub filled with warm water. She went to Gabriel and asked him if she could help him. Gabriel nodded and she removed his T-shirt and underpants and helped him into the tub, not permitting herself to admire his body as she did whenever they were nude, but instead thinking of him as her patient. He lay in the warm water and closed his eyes as she went over him with a washcloth and soap. When she was done the water was brown from the blood and then she saw the bite on his leg. She had to be sure to tell Gabriel and the doctor. She let the water out of the tub, refilled it and rinsed him until he was scrubbed clean. She asked him how he was feeling and he said he was happy to see her but felt very sleepy. She asked if it had been bad. *Pretty bad,* he said. *I hurt all over, baby,* he said. *I thought I was going to die.* She shook her head and said he was fine now and shouldn't worry. She wanted to tell him about the baby but didn't. She also wanted to tell him that she thought Carlos was Gabriel's son. He didn't have to know about the other thing. That didn't matter, or it shouldn't matter because maybe he would never want to see her again. There would be enough time later to tell him about the baby and about Carlos. She let the water out again, dried him while he sat and helped him to get out of the tub. Gabriel had placed clean underwear and a bathrobe on the toilet seat. She helped him dress and put on the bathrobe and then she heard a commotion outside and Angie screaming and people running through the house, their voices filled with concern.

reconciliation

*Kenny had asked about Gabriel's mother
but obtained little information from
either Gabriel or his father. He was
told she had died shortly after Gabriel
was born.*

C LAUDIA BROUGHT Kenny pea soup and a grilled cheese sandwich and he'd eaten sitting up on the bed with Claudia near him. She smiled and he felt better but he had such a bad headache. Angie came into the room and they sat with him and after he finished eating they held his hand and told him everything was going to be okay and they would go to the movies soon. Earlier that morning the doctor came and examined him. He took his pulse, checked his temperature, listened to his heart and lungs with his stethoscope and asked him a few questions. The doctor went into his bag, filled a syringe and took his arm. When he had done so he gave him a shot. He said it was an antirabies shot and he'd need five more in the next few weeks. He then took the bandages from his wrist and face. Claudia showed him the leg wound. The doctor told her she had done a good job. He asked for soap and water, and with gauze washed and rebandaged the wounds. The doctor gave him another shot, which numbed his whole arm down to his fingers. A few minutes later he stitched up his wrist where the coyote bit him. He said it wasn't as bad as it looked. *He may need some surgery to repair a tendon or two.* He sewed up the wrist but said it would have to be X-rayed, since there had been some bone damage. He should come to the office in the morning and then he'd determine whether he needed to go to Syracuse for the surgery. The doctor then made a few stitches near his lip and dressed everything, swabbed his scalp with disinfectant, gave him another shot and explained that it would calm him down and help him sleep. He fashioned a sling for his arm and told him he should limit movement in the wrist. *Not a problem,* he said. *I can't move it.* He slid down on the bed, looked at Claudia and smiled as she drew the bedclothes up to his chest and helped him rest the sling on his chest. *I'm sleepy,* he said. *I'll be right here,* she said. He began drifting away slowly.

One minute Claudia was holding his right hand and the next minute he was flying free of everything and traveling through a gauzy world in which huge butterflies of many colors filled the air, their wings transparent as they carried children here and there. Songbirds filled the air and there were no adults anywhere. The children were laughing and whenever one got hungry there was always something delicious to eat. The children were happy to see him and each one came up and touched him and said they were glad he had finally arrived. It was like a summer camp except that everyone was dressed in nice clothes as if they were going to Sunday Mass. And then he began to recognize all the children. Even Grandpa Martin was there as a little boy. They said hello and little boy Grandpa Martin asked him if he wanted to spin his top.

$g$abriel's mind was in a daze. The guilt over Kenny and what had happened would never be settled in his mind as it hadn't been settled all these years about the girl. In both instances, when he should have perceived the future he was too idealistic, too blind to reality, and he had overlooked the signs. It was like everything had suddenly come pouring in on him. Once again he had been given a responsibility and he had managed to screw things up. And now, in a blink, the old man was gone. He was grateful that Will Grisko had sent his two sons over to help, and that Albert Muller had shown up. They had milked the cows, set them out to graze and fed the rest of the stock. Maybe it had been too soon to bring Carlos into his life. At least he had met his grandfather and that was good. He hadn't believed the letter from Carlos's mother was genuine. It was another trick of fate to make him feel the horror of what had happened in the Andes. It didn't seem possible for her to have survived the mountains, but she had. And now she was there in Montreal, emigrated, teaching Spanish at a small college, still looking beautiful and once again drawing him into her world, still idealistic and now, not tired of her time in the mountains of her country, making contact with the Québécois separatists as she had made contact with the Shining Path guerrillas. Like a fool he had gone to her in Montreal and as if nothing had happened in their fifteen years apart they had taken up again. She insisted that she still loved him and he let himself be carried away as he had before. They had made love with difficulty but over the next few months he hired another worker, his father supervised the running of the farm and he made the trip, driving to Albany and then flying to Montreal.

It was months before she told him about Carlos. She showed him photographs and reassured him that Carlos was his son. Men never knew about their children's paternity but it didn't matter. It was a connection to her and that was important. *Where is he?* he'd said. She told him that Carlos was in Mexico, where they had gone after she left Sendero Luminoso. *How long ago? Ten years.* He asked her why she hadn't contacted him. She said she was married to a Mexican journalist who had helped her leave the mountains. It all sounded too strange and he felt as if he were back there again, naive, representing the United States, able to speak Spanish, knowledgeable about agriculture, learning Quechua and coming to Cuzco, one-time capital of the Inca empire, every month to get away from the poverty of the mountains, but drawn always to the majesty of the Andes.

One day, as he was in a bookstore, holding a volume of Borges's *Ficciones,* a young woman asked him what he thought of the book. He answered her in what he thought was perfect Spanish, but she immediately said he was American and laughed, not quite derisively but with enough irony to make him feel uncomfortable. She asked him if he had come to save the Indians from colonialism and if he was he ought to look at how the United States had held Puerto Rico in colonial bondage since 1898. She was a *mestiza,* with strong Inca features. Her name was Carmen Zamorra. They went to a restaurant and had dinner and talked literature and he told her he was learning Quechua and she recited verses in the native tongue and told him she'd studied indigenous languages at the university in Lima. She added that her mother was Inca and had spoken the language to her as a child until her father forbade it in the house. She then translated the poem into Spanish. She said it was a lamentation. He only remembered *auqa sonqo runakunataq llaqtanchiqta ñak'arichinku. But now, cruel men make our people suffer.* He knew she was directing the words at him as an American even though the verses referred to the Spaniards who had subjugated the Inca Empire. He wanted to protest and say he was only there to help. Instead, he asked why she was in Cuzco. She said it was her home and then added that her father was very wealthy and she had returned at his request to find a husband. He asked her if she had been successful. She nodded and held up a finger with a diamond solitaire. *I'm engaged. He's wealthy as well,* she said. *But he's in Colombia working in his father's business. I'm bored. You seem interesting,* she said. *What kind of business?* he asked. *Cocaine,* she said, and laughed. *Drugs?* he'd asked in apparent shock at her ease in discussing the issue. She chided him for being an innocent. *You Americans are so shallow in your idealism.* The words had hurt him but he said nothing. She suggested that they fly to Lima for the weekend and see the city. He pointed to himself and then to her. *¿Juntos? Together?* he asked. *Yes, together,* she replied. *Isn't it obvious to you that we need to? Yes,* he admitted and they went the following week. She bought cheap wedding rings and they wore them as if they were married. At the hotel they registered as husband and wife. They walked the city and went to the museum and bought books and had long conversations about the downtrodden. They discussed Franz Fanon and Karl Marx. They eventually made love and she bled and told him she loved him and hated her father and her future husband and said she wished she could join the guerrillas in the mountains and fight against the ruling class. She didn't call them the Shining Path because they were not yet called by that name but that's who they would become.

He told no one in the field office about his encounter with Carmen, fearful that what she'd said about the guerrillas would complicate matters for her. He did ask Baltazar from the mountain village about Carmen and mentioned her last name. Perhaps he shouldn't have but he trusted Baltazar. He was old and had introduced him to the villagers. He had been able to convince them about care of their crops and they were doing better. About a week later men in hoods came, blindfolded him and took him away, higher into the mountains. They traveled a long time. When he got out of the car they questioned him about Carmen. They said that he should continue to see her. She would be curious to see how he worked. He was to say nothing to her, otherwise they would both be killed. He was to create a pretext and bring her to the mountains. If she alerted the police and brought them they would all die.

He returned to Cuzco and while they walked he told Carmen what had happened with the hooded men. *They want me to invite you up to the mountains,* he said. *I think you should get away from here as quickly as you can. Go someplace else.* She smiled and nodded and it was almost like he had done her bidding. *I want to go up there where you work,* she said. There was no fear on her part. He did as he was asked and brought her with him. Again the men came in their hoods and took them away. They questioned her extensively. In the end, speaking fluently in Quechua, she convinced them that she was genuinely for their cause. She later told him that people thought her captors were Marxist guerrillas like Che. *But they're not. They just hate the government and the ruling class and want to wreck it and start an Indian government. They're noble,* she said. She convinced them that there was no value in killing her. What they ought to do was demand a ransom for her. Her father would pay it. They did so, and her father paid the ransom, an exorbitant amount. When it was time to return to Cuzco, she said she wanted to stay in the mountains. Shortly afterward they released him and she remained behind. A month passed and one day Baltazar said Gabriel had to leave the village, that his life was in danger. He went to the field office and spoke with Morgan and he was assigned elsewhere. Before he left he asked Baltazar about Carmen. He said she was safe, but nothing more. He never saw her again until he received the letter from her at the beginning of the year to tell him that she was in Montreal and wanted to see him.

Shortly after he came back from the Peace Corps, he was searching for direction. Being torn suddenly away from Carmen, certain that she had been murdered after the ransom was paid, he'd been walking around in Utica and someone stopped him and gave him a card. It said *Nam Myoho Renge Kyo.* The young man was very earnest and smiled and nodded at almost everything he said. He explained the philosophy of cause and effect to him. *We are the sum total of all the causes and all the effects we've made lifetime after lifetime. If you want know the kinds of causes you made in the past, look at the effects you're getting now. If you want to know the effects you'll have in the future look at the causes you're making now.* He went to a meeting and chanted and became a Nichiren Shoshu Buddhist, went down to New York City and received a Gohonzon, which was a scroll. His new friend came and helped him make an altar in his room at the farm and he studied and chanted and eventually stopped his practice, dismantling the altar, rolling up the scroll and placing it in a trunk. The only thing he came away with was that human beings had karma and that karma was the totality of one's causes and one's effects, lifetime after lifetime.

Was karma immutable? he'd asked once at a meeting. The Japanese man leading the discussion said that the only way one could change his destiny was chanting *Nam Myoho Renge Kyo.* Otherwise, the person was destined to repeat the same mistakes, over and over again. *No matter how many wives, always marry same person,* the man had said in his way of speaking English. *Does everyone have different karma?* The man smiled at the incisiveness of the question and explained that individuals had their own karma, but that families shared karma, as did towns and even countries. And then he explained that their Buddhism was the Buddhism of the Sun. Japan had turned away from True Buddhism, had slandered the Law of Cause and Effect. Hundreds of years later in the energy of the sun, harnessed in the atomic bomb, Japan received the effects of its slander in rejecting the Law.

He was stunned by the finality of karma. He continued studying and then began drifting away, examining other philosophies. Now that Carmen had come back into his life, he again wondered how much truth there could be to the theory of karma. And then he had begged his father to tell him about his mother. It was as if his father sensed that his life would soon be over. He'd told his father about Carmen and Carlos. His father, having held the truth for too long, wished to free himself from the deception he had lived and had forced his son to live. He had not mentioned the woman's name, but Jerry Boyle told him that Mary Boyle had to be his mother and he went to his father and Henri Brunet told him everything, unburdening himself of fifty years of his memories. Perhaps the stress had brought on his father's heart attack.

*H*e woke up and she was there in the room, her long frame curled up and covered in a quilt, sitting in an easy chair that they had moved into the room. The sun was streaming in through the curtains and he could hear birds in the trees and the turkeys gobbling out in the yard. One of the roosters was crowing and beyond that he heard the lowing of the cows. As if she sensed his waking she opened her eyes and stretched. She came to the bed, kissed him and asked him how he felt. He said he was okay but still had a headache. *It's still morning,* he said. She told him he'd slept around the clock and asked if he was hungry. *Starving,* he said, and she told him she'd go and make him breakfast. He tried to get up but felt dizzy and decided he was weak from not eating. He tried to recall the night in the woods but when he began to go over the events, the pain in his head increased and he pushed the battle with the coyotes away. He wanted to know about the calf. When Claudia returned with his breakfast he asked her about the newborn animal. She said the calf was fine. She'd fed it a bottle and Carlos was taking care of it. *He gave her a sponge bath,* she said. *She's standing and walking around. A little confused, but healthy and getting used to being alive. She asked about your name. She probably thinks you're her mother.* He laughed for the first time in a while but his lip hurt.

She brought him an omelet with potatoes and bacon. There was also toast with butter and marmalade, which she knew he liked. He drank a glass of milk and swallowed a couple of pills that Claudia gave him. *Doctor's instructions,* she said. She then brought him a cup of coffee and he sipped from it. When he asked about Gabriel she said that Gabriel blamed himself for what happened, but that he was glad he'd saved the calf. That it was a very brave thing to do. Kenny said it was his own fault. He shouldn't have gone into the woods. *I'd probably do it again but it was stupid,* he said. *I made too many mistakes.* And then she said she missed him and had lots of things to tell him.

At that point Gabriel came into the room and asked him how he was doing. He nodded and said that Claudia was taking good care of him. She lifted the tray from the bed and Gabriel asked him if he was strong enough to stand up. He gave the so-so sign. With Claudia on one side and Gabriel on the other they took him to the window and parted the curtains. Down below, Carlos held a rope that he'd placed around the calf's neck. He waved and pointed up at him in the window. *It's so small*, Kenny said in wonder. *It's no bigger than a goat*. And then he felt weak and said he was dizzy. They returned him to the bed and he closed his eyes. Through the haze of oncoming sleep he heard Gabriel ask Claudia if she had told him about his father. He wondered if something had happened to Mr. Brunet. He began to rise but Claudia pushed down gently on his chest and stroked his face and he was in a fluffy world, drifting and drifting like a feather in a blue breeze. The last thing he heard was Gabriel asking Claudia if she had slept all right and saying that her mother had called to see if she was okay. *We have to take him to Dr. Anderson's office when he wakes up,* he said.

*K*enny woke up a few hours later. He asked his uncle Jerry if his mom and dad knew what had happened. Jerry said they would be coming up to see him. Patrick said he should get up and stop being a lazy bum. Claudia helped Kenny to get dressed and they drove to Dr. Anderson's office. Kenny once again dozed off as he sat in the seat between them in the pickup truck. Jerry Boyle and his son followed behind in their car. On the way there she asked him about the funeral and Gabriel held a finger to his lips. Kenny woke up when they reached the doctor's office. He was X-rayed, examined again and his dressings changed. Dr. Anderson said the wounds were healing well. The nurse brought Dr. Anderson the X-rays, and he displayed them and nodded a few times. He said that Kenny should be admitted to the hospital in Syracuse to have an orthopedic surgeon look at the wrist. He was certain they'd have to operate in order to repair the damage. Claudia said resolutely that she'd like to go with him and keep Kenny company. The doctor thought it was an excellent idea and the following day, in Gabriel's car, they drove to Syracuse. Dr. Anderson traveled with Gabriel in front, insisting that his presence would ensure that Kenny received the best care. Kenny and Claudia sat in the back. Jerry Boyle said he and his son were flying back to New York and would return with Kenny's parents. Could Gabriel please call him and tell him whether Kenny had remained in Syracuse or had returned to the farm. Also, how soon would Kenny be ready to return to New York.

When they'd met, Gabriel had nodded and shaken Jerry's extended hand and then Patrick's. He was sure the Shining Path guerrillas had the same grave expression behind their hoods as Jerry Boyle. They were all warriors. Gabriel was moved by Claudia's devotion. She had the same idealism that he had seen in Carmen except hers was not a political zeal, but a personal one driven only by instinct. She was a fine young person and he was glad she was there to boost Kenny's spirits. Driving up to Syracuse, Dr. Anderson said that he had been on duty when Claudia was born at the hospital in Utica. Kenny asked if she was a pretty baby. Dr. Anderson said she was like most babies, wrinkled, but that after a while she had grown into a very pretty girl. He added that there had been problems with her mother, who was very private and refused to let the nurses change her. *Change Claudia?* Gabriel had asked. *No, change the mother,* Dr. Anderson had replied. *She wanted to do everything herself.*

Claudia was immediately talking a mile a minute, telling about her experiences as a volunteer and how much she enjoyed helping people and asked Dr. Anderson which college was the best for her to study nursing. Dr. Anderson, not aware of Claudia's need to change the subject, discussed several options but it was obvious to Gabriel that Claudia had wanted to steer away from her mother. The subject of her parents obviously pained her. He remembered Karl Bachlichtner as an oaf, a big hulking red-faced man who showed up in town one day and began working as a car mechanic in Steve Barnes's garage. A few months later he had taken up with Eva Green, a pretty girl who was very shy and had come to work for the Cortland family, who owned several factories and lived in one of the most beautiful houses in the area. Eva had come up from New York to work as an au pair for the Cortland children.

Gabriel recalled the time because a Negro woman came to work as a cook for the Cortlands around the same time. She had a son who was an excellent athlete. He had taught Larry Creighton, her son, how to use a short lacrosse stick. Larry became the star athlete on the high school team. He was good at everything. Kenny reminded him of his friend Larry. He graduated from college, was in ROTC and eventually joined the army, became a helicopter pilot and was shot down in Vietnam. He was still listed as MIA. His mother continued working for the Cortlands until two years ago, when she died in her sleep.

But Eva began going to night school and when she graduated, decided to strike out on her own and got a job as a bookkeeper in Utica. She was living in a rooming house for a year when Carl Bachlichtner came to live there. Within six months they were married and rented a house on the edge of town. The following year, Claudia was born and four or five years later he was gone. Gabriel didn't know why. Some people said he'd met another woman in Buffalo. He could understand perfectly, but at least Claudia had known her father and visited him from time to time. He wished things had remained as they were and his father had not invited Kenny to the farm. He had the greatest affection for Kenny but he wished he'd known about the connection between Kenny's grandmother and his father. He did not like Jerry Boyle even though it was now obvious that Jerry was his half-brother.

*d*r. Flanders, the orthopedic surgeon, looked at the X-rays, consulted with Dr. Anderson and wanted to know how soon they'd have the results from the rabies tests on the coyotes. Dr. Anderson said it usually took ten days to two weeks to get the results. There had been eight coyotes. *The boy killed them,* Dr. Anderson said. The surgeon asked where the heads had been sent. When Dr. Anderson let him know, the surgeon made a few phone calls and said that they should expedite the results. He examined Kenny's wrist and determined that the sooner they operated the better. He was admitted to the hospital immediately. He added that Kenny might need several operations over time but with physical therapy he should regain not perfect but at least functional use of his hand. He asked the surgeon what he meant. Dr. Flanders said that in time the boy would be able to grasp tools, utensils, button his shirts and coats, and with practice use a typewriter. *Sports?* he asked. *Perhaps over time. I have a colleague who does sports medicine. Maybe we can consult with him after a while.* The doctor made some more phone calls and an hour later Kenny was assigned a bed in a ward. Claudia stayed with him throughout, telling the nurses that she was a volunteer in Utica. When he was in his hospital gown and in bed she was allowed to stay with him after visiting hours were over. The nurses liked her immediately and gave her small tasks to perform to ease Kenny's stay.

Gabriel said he would take Dr. Anderson back home and return in the evening to get her. He asked if she had enough money for snacks and supper. Claudia nodded and the nurses said since they were so cute together she could have pretty boy's dinner because he had to have surgery. The remarks made Kenny blush and Claudia rolled her eyes and laughed. *Like he doesn't know it and needs more women paying attention to him,* she said, and the nurses laughed and accused her kiddingly of being jealous.

He closed his eyes and wondered why he still had such a headache. He told the nurses and they brought him pills and said he'd be fine and that it was normal after what he had endured. They looked at his scalp and said he was healing quite well. *Dog?* she asked. *Coyote,* he said and she joked that she hoped he wouldn't start howling. He tried laughing with them but his head hurt too much.

In the evening they came to get him, helped him onto a gurney and took him away. The operating room was cool and it made him shiver. They covered him with a sheet and placed his arm on a stainless steel table. They now placed a mask over his nose and mouth and asked him to count. By the time he got to fifteen he was traveling across an arctic landscape, everything blindingly white and barren. He was gone a long time and then the next day he woke up in the hospital room and his mother and father were there with his uncle Jerry. He wondered why Claudia wasn't there. His mother said that she'd gone to call her mother and tell her she was still in Syracuse. He asked about the kids and his mother said Grandma Rosa had come over to stay with them. His wrist was bandaged, had been placed in a cast with a splint and a sling. He said he felt fine and his headache was gone. Dr. Flanders said the headache might have been caused by a damaged nerve in the wrist.

*h*e didn't know why, but he thought again that Jerry Boyle reminded him of the hooded men up in the mountains of Peru. There was an arrogance to Jerry that intimidated him and made him feel as helpless as he'd felt then. It was as if they were a special kind of men for whom compromise was not part of dealing with life. Like the men in the mountains there was to Jerry's eyes a danger that went beyond the fear of punishment or even death. His eyes had a sort of damnation to them, much as if he were judge and jury, and beyond that, God Himself. Their first meeting had been truly uncomfortable. He'd come, ostensibly, to visit Kenny in the middle of the summer, driving up in a big car with another man whom he introduced as Teddy Grady who was as dangerous looking. Kenny came out of the barn where he'd been repairing a saddle with the elder Brunet. Jerry had sent Carlos to get him. *Tu padre,* Jerry'd said, referring to him in the rudimentary Spanish he was learning from his girlfriend. He had no idea how Jerry knew that Carlos was his son. They sat down to lunch and Jerry talked about Kenny and what a wonderful athlete he was. Jerry asked him about the Peace Corps and where he'd been. He told him that he'd been in Peru and he nodded and said there was a lot of drug traffic down there. *The Indians chew coca leaves,* Jerry said. He added that the drug trade was lucrative but dangerous. Jerry asked him what'd he done in the Peace Corps. He told him that he'd helped farmers improve their crops and set up a cooperative so they could sell the things that they manufactured. Jerry said the Peace Corps was Special Forces for liberals and that Kennedy had understood this, realizing most Americans wanted freedom but were unwilling to fight for it. *The Pink Berets,* Jerry said, mirthfully looking at Teddy Grady. *No offense,* he added looking back at him, light sarcasm in his disclaimer.

Kenny had seen how disrespectful his uncle was being and said that when he graduated from college he might join the Peace Corps. He asked him where he wanted to go.

Kenny said that he'd like to go to Africa and Jerry said that he should be careful and not end up getting involved with some safari honey like his son Patrick. The only person who laughed was Teddy Grady. His father got up from the table and asked if anyone wanted coffee. Jerry said he did and then told Kenny to show his cousin Teddy Grady around the farm while he spoke to Gabriel. He and Jerry got mugs of coffee and went and sat on the porch of the house. When they had been sitting a while Jerry commented that it was a nice farm and asked him if he'd lived there all his life. Gabriel nodded. He wanted to be away from this situation. It was like he was being menaced with a branding iron, the red hot tool coming closer and closer to him. He didn't want to talk and recalled that he had gone out west to Wyoming with Trip Fuller to see if he liked ranching life. He and Trip had been in Peru together and became friends. During his stay he had worn western boots and chaps and had learned to herd, rope and brand cattle. He was there nearly two months but hadn't liked the life, too austere, the land foreign to him, the people's attitudes so independent that he wondered if he lived in the same country as they did. Trip's sister Martha had liked him. She was pretty and shapely and they had wonderful conversations about world politics and even made love one time when they rode way out on the range and went into a hunting cabin. This happened the second month of his stay at the Fuller ranch. Martha was passionate and he thought that under different circumstances things could have worked out between them, but he couldn't stop thinking about Carmen. When Martha realized that things wouldn't work out between them she withdrew and one evening at dinner she announced she was going on a spiritual retreat to Nepal. They said good-bye stiffly. Out of politeness she said they should stay in touch, both knowing that they could not. She was gone

EDGARDO VEGA YUNQUÉ

the next week. Three weeks later he thanked Trip's parents and embraced Trip and he returned to New York.

You don't like me very much, Jerry had finally said. He'd shrugged his shoulders and said he hadn't given it much thought. Jerry laughed and said that it was all he'd thought about since he'd driven up. He didn't answer him and instead asked him why he'd come up. *Are you afraid that we're going to convert your nephew to some sort of strange cow cult?* he asked. This amused Jerry and he laughed uproariously and asked if he knew that he'd been a detective for a time with the New York Police Department. *Damn good one,* he said. He replied coldly that Kenny had told him that both his uncle and his father had been policemen, but said he didn't know why they were no longer working for the city. Jerry laughed and said they'd had a parting of the ways and added that Kenny's father had been a damn good detective as well. Gabriel said that this was obviously leading somewhere but he didn't know quite where. He found himself becoming angered by Jerry's arrogance.

Jerry Boyle said that he'd found out certain things and wanted to verify them with him. *When were you born?* he asked suddenly, not abruptly but with kindness. Gabriel looked at him and told him that it was 1935. *Impossible,* Jerry said. *I was born that year. And why not?* he asked. *Millions of people were born that year. What's this about?* Jerry said that he might as well come out with it and remove the mystery from the conversation. He said his mother had been a novice at the Convent of St. Ann's nearby. *It's no longer there,* Gabriel said. *Burned down quite a while ago. I know,* Jerry said. *They moved closer to New York City. My mother was up here at the convent from April 1931 to roughly December 1933. A total of thirty-two months. What month is your birthday? December,* he said. *So you were probably born in December of 1933. Okay,* he said, *now that you've made me older*

*what do you base this on? Good question. My mother married my fa-
ther in May 1934. I figure she got pregnant in October of that year
and I was born in July of 1935, so you couldn't have been born that
year unless we were twins and the births were seven months apart.*
Gabriel nodded, still attempting to seem puzzled. *Okay,* he
said. *And?*

Jerry laughed again. *Well, Gabriel, as much as it might pain
you, it's likely that we're brothers.* Gabriel asked him to explain
and Jerry went into his jacket pocket and took out an old
notebook and told him to open it to the page where he'd
placed the bookmark. He did as he was asked and read the
words. They stood out as if they were written in red ink.

> *I have prayed and I have decided that I have to
> leave this life. I don't know if I love H.B. but I
> am determined to have this child. I'm not sure
> that I will be able to keep the baby after I have it.
> Perhaps a good family will raise it but I don't
> know how to find such a family. I certainly can-
> not return to my mother's house. H.B. has said
> he will take care of the baby and that he will al-
> ways love me. He has not offered to marry me,
> nor do I believe I would accept, but he's said
> that I can remain at the Vanderveer farm where
> he works. I should have remained chaste and
> have no one to blame but myself. It has become
> too difficult to live a life of deceit. My habit
> keeps me from being detected but soon someone
> will learn of my condition. Sister Antonia has
> noted that I've gained weight. I've explained
> that working in the kitchen has led to certain
> temptations. She laughed but I'm certain she's
> not being taken in by my mendacity. H.B. has
> said that he will wait by the well each night as
> before and help me any way that he can. Al-
> though he has not mentioned marriage, he is
> certain that he can make me happy. I don't*

*know that I can ever be truly happy. It is not in
my disposition to be happy even though I love
laughter and joy. I often wish I were a man and
could simply come and go without the con-
straints placed on women.*

Gabriel turned the pages but the rest of the entries were
uninteresting notes on life in the convent. He asked Jerry if
there were any other entries like this. Jerry nodded and he
said there were a great many other entries that pointed in
his father's direction. *They're not totally clear but give a pretty
good indication.* He wanted to say that H.B. could have been
anyone but knew that it had to be his father, Henri Brunet.
Before he could ask another question Jerry said that he didn't
want to alarm him any further but that he looked very much
like his own grandfather Jerome Grady. *My mother's father. I'm
named after him but don't call me Jerome or I'll knock you on your
ass. Same jaw and nose. You wanna see?* He shrugged his shoulders and handed Jerry the diary. Jerry took it, and, from another pocket, produced an envelope with photographs.

There you go, he said. *From my mother's album.* He took the
envelope, opened it and extracted several photos. In one of
them there was a big man and with him an equally large
woman. The man certainly looked like him. He held it up and
asked if this was the picture. Jerry nodded and said there was
a close-up that was even more telling. He pulled out one of a
man in a winged collar, tie, his hair parted in the middle and
his eyes opened as if expecting the flash from the camera to
blind him. He nodded as he saw the line of the jaw and the
nose exactly as Jerry had said. *I always wanted a little brother,*
he said. Jerry was convulsed with laughter. *That's more like it,*
Jerry said. *What?* he'd asked. *A little Irish wit. Dry, caustic, to the
point. It lessens the pain about these things.* He asked if Gabriel

thought they should bring this up with their mother. He honestly didn't know and instead asked if he had a photo of his mother.

Jerry went into yet another pocket and brought out a postcard-size portrait of his mother at the age of eighteen. She wore a dress with a high collar and a bow at the neck. Her hair was cut in a bob with bangs. If not pretty, Mary Grady was certainly sensuous. She had a full figure, her lips were thin but pouting, and her eyes wore a wicked *step-into-my-boudoir* kind of look. She was like the girls in Rudolph Valentino films. *Can I keep this for a little while?* he asked. *I'm sure someone else in this household would enjoy looking at it. Sure,* Jerry said. *Maybe you can make a copy of it. You got Kodak up here, don't you? Rochester,* he said. *So who else is there besides you and Kenny's mother. Oh, hundreds, but siblings besides me you have Maureen and Michael,* and then the baby, Frankie. *Frankie?* he said. *Yeah, Kenny's mother. Frances. I call her Frankie. Why?* he said. Jerry had replied quickly: *I guess I wanted her to be a little tomboy, but she was this delicate little girl, very much female. But anyway, you're our big brother.* Gabriel laughed and stuck out his hand. Jerry shook it and Gabriel was amazed by the size and strength of the hand. His own father had small, almost delicate hands. *Your father must have big hands,* he said. *Huge,* Jerry said. *Kenny does as well.* They both nodded and he returned the envelope to Jerry. He looked once more at his mother's photo and placed it in his shirt pocket, folding the flap of his shirt over it. Karma, he thought. Family karma.

*h*aving his mother and father near him made Kenny feel happy. His mother couldn't stop touching him and kissing him and asking how he was feeling. His father nodded and looked more worried than he'd ever seen him. The doctor came in and the nurses chased everyone out because visiting hours were over. He was again alone. He turned on the television and began watching a Yankee baseball game. In the middle of watching the game, he fell asleep and was again traveling far away, his body light as a feather. This time he was among penguins and he was dressed just like them. They were waddling around but they were obviously part of a dance group and kept nodding their heads and slapping their feet like they were tap-dancing but instead of tapping it was slapping as if they were tap-dancing on water. The whole spectacle made him laugh and then he saw Claudia and she was also a penguin. She came over and they danced together. She was the tallest penguin he had ever seen. He was dancing with her and then they were lying down inside an igloo and they were making love. He thought that this was totally wrong because igloos are Eskimo houses in the North Pole and he didn't think there were penguins on the North Pole. The music was beautiful and after they made love they were once again dancing with the penguins. This time all the penguins were as tall as they were. Some of the penguins were New York Knicks and they were shooting baskets. Willis Reed, Bill Bradley, Walt Frazier, Dave Debuschere, Earl Monroe and the rest shooting baskets but they were penguins. He kept looking for Claudia but she was gone. He tried calling her but his voice became weaker and weaker and the singing of the penguins was louder and louder as they sang, "We all live in a yellow submarine."

*A*s they were heading for the elevators Tommy Romero said Kenny might have to stay in the hospital. He told him that the doctor said that they were still waiting on the results of the rabies tests and it could be another week. Frances was disappointed. Claudia reassured her that she'd drive up and see Kenny every other day and call New

York to tell her how he was doing. Fran nodded and hugged Claudia. Downstairs he said good-bye. Claudia stayed with Tommy and Fran. When Gabriel returned to the hospital the next day, they were there huddled in a hall outside Kenny's room. Claudia was holding Fran and Jerry and Tommy were standing next to each other looking pretty grim. He approached Jerry and asked what was wrong. Jerry said that the doctors told them that Kenny had sunk into a coma. *How do they know?* he asked. *He's not responding,* Tommy said. *They think that maybe he was affected by the bites. His brain. They're not sure. The doctor explained that if it was rabies maybe Kenny's body had induced the coma to protect the brain from the virus. He thinks the coma could've also been caused by an injury to the head while he was fighting the coyotes.* Tommy said that he and Fran were going to stay. Fran nodded but looked at Tommy and said she needed to get back to the children. Tommy said that the kids understood and were in good hands with her mother. Fran shook her head and said she'd also made a doctor's appointment and had to keep it. Tommy said that she could reschedule the appointment and felt that it was important for them to stay. He looked at Jerry but Jerry threw up his hands and said that it was up them and that the airplane was at their disposal, whenever they wanted to go back.

It seemed to him at that point that Jerry, ever the detective and alert to the unusual, noticed that his sister was acting in an uncharacteristic manner. Tommy took her aside but she simply continued to shake her head and they were now arguing in whispers. Claudia had walked away and was standing by a window in the visitors' lounge. He asked Jerry what was going on. Jerry shrugged his shoulders and said that Tommy thought Fran was pregnant again but she had denied it. He asked Jerry if Fran knew that he was their mother's son as well. Jerry said he hadn't yet discussed the issue with her. He said he hadn't even discussed it with his mother. He asked if he was going to ever do so and Jerry looked at him and smiled. *I don't know,* Jerry said. *I see,* he said. He had the urge to run from the situation. He was better off alone rather than being involved in the emotions of a large family and the complications they created.

He had grown up with the Vanderveers and although they were simple people who lived by a strict code that they followed without the slightest deviation, family intrigue, sibling rivalry, disappointments, broken promises and alienation were common. They worked and studied and attended church and did not speak ill of anyone in the hopes that upon death they would be rewarded with the Kingdom of Heaven, but their silences and quiet hatreds were evident. He was grateful to them but had not truly felt a connection to life with the Vanderveers. It had been he and his father, especially after the Vanderveers left. In the past two months he had barely gotten used to being a father and having Carmen back in his life. Now he had inherited more relatives than he needed.

Suddenly, he was tired and his forty-five years, or forty-six if Jerry was right, weighed upon him and he felt as if he had ended his middle age. If he was born in 1933 instead of 1935 then he was forty-six in December. Now that his father was dead and he had inherited the farm, he had also inherited his father's old age. He had seen too much, had read and studied too much and his life, without wishing for it, had become complicated. He excused himself from Jerry and said he had to go to the bathroom. He went down the hall, found the men's room, urinated and returned. Only Claudia, Tommy and Jerry were there. He inquired about Fran and they said she had gone downstairs to the hospital chapel to pray. He told Claudia that one of the Grisko brothers, working at the farm permanently during the emergency, said that her mother called again and asked how she was doing and that she should come home because it was time for her to start getting ready for school. Claudia said she'd go home that night after she checked on Kenny's condition and was he driving back. He said he was.

Jerry said it was late and they should all get some rest. Everyone agreed and they took the elevator downstairs. Tommy said he was going to get Fran and that they'd be right out. He went off and they walked out into the late August night, the air still warm but a wind from the north issuing a warning that the weather would soon change. A few minutes later Tommy came out with his arm around Fran's waist. She smiled weakly and said she felt better. They drove to the Holiday Inn and ate supper and everyone said good night. Tommy and Fran went to their room, Claudia to hers and he and Jerry to theirs. It was odd sharing a room with this man who was both a stranger and his brother, both of them approaching fifty and not knowing how much time they had left to their lives. Jerry threw himself on the bed and immediately turned on the television set.

He sat on the other bed, his head in his hands, seething and not knowing what to say. Why hadn't he told the others about his father and their mother, especially his mother? Why was he dragging this out? He suddenly stood up, childishly placed himself in front of the television set and said they needed to talk. Jerry was understanding and turned off the television. He stood up and asked him if he felt like having a drink. He nodded and they went back out of the room and downstairs to the bar. The place was empty. They found a booth toward the back that looked out on the highway. When the waitress brought them their whiskey, he scotch with soda and Jerry's on the rocks, he asked him why he hadn't told the rest of the family about him. Jerry said it wasn't the right time. He took a long sip from the scotch, draining half of the glass, the cold hurting his throat, and said that he realized that this thing with Kenny was tearing everyone apart and that he should have been more insistent with their nephew, but he hadn't and now all he had were regrets and guilt. He had dared to call Kenny his nephew, trying out the shared owner-ship of the family. Jerry was oblivious to his passion and said that he had lived a fairly guilt-free life and that he realized that perhaps he was in many ways a psychopath, but that no one was totally one thing or another. Jerry said guilt was for people with too much time on their hands and no real inter-est in life. Some people need to feel guilty to affirm their ex-istence. He said he felt no guilt because he always considered the necessity of his actions and that he hadn't told his mother and Fran, the ones he was most concerned with, because it wasn't the time.

He protested and said he'd had a month. Jerry was very quiet, smiling at him as if he were being tolerant. He mo-tioned to the waitress and when she came over he ordered an-other round. When the waitress returned with the new drinks and he'd paid her and tipped her generously, Jerry said that he genuinely liked him, that he possessed the same qualities as his sister Frances, using her name and not the nickname Frankie. *She's a very strong woman but an idealist, which I admire in the same way that I admire you.* Jerry said he'd always fought for her and he'd fight for him in the same way because he was a naive son of a bitch. He said that there was a difference be-tween one and the other. His sister is pure about her beliefs and he was just posturing, not truly believing but acting as he was expected to by some code he didn't even understand. He shook his head and told Jerry *he* was wrong. Jerry sipped from his glass and said that their mother was due to have a double mastectomy later in September. *Did she tell you this?* he asked. Jerry shook his head and said Mary Boyle had not but that was the reason he had not informed her that the cat was out of the bag and her immaculate conception had a name and it wasn't Jesus.

And she didn't tell you about her operation? he asked. *Are you assuming this? I found out,* Jerry said. He asked how he'd found out. Jerry laughed and said that maybe he wasn't going to like what he was going to tell him. *Take your best shot,* he'd said, trying to act tough. Jerry said that the notion of service to the Catholic Church had escaped three generations of his family. No nuns and no priests, and that their mother was the closest they had come to complete Catholic devotion. *Until now,* he said. *Is one of the kids going to enter seminary?* he asked. *I'd kneecap them first. Maybe ankle-shoot them. It hurts more and it's all the rage for dealing with renegades these days.* He didn't understand the oblique reference but guessed it had to do with Jerry's obsession with Ireland. What a need for identity. But again maybe being Irish was an antidote to being swallowed up in the anonymity that being white brought with it. *Who, then?* he'd asked, the scotch making him bolder. Jerry pointed at him. *You're the priest we never had,* he said. *And because of that I am going to confess to you that among my many skills I am an accomplished burglar. I could tell my mother was not well and I asked her what was the matter. In her usual way, she manipulated and talked without stopping for nearly twenty minutes as if she had not only kissed the Blarney Stone, but had bitten into it and taken a large chunk out, chewed it and swallowed it, weaving a tale of deception so complex and the language so brilliant that you felt as if James Joyce had consulted with her before writing the end of* Ulysses *even though they were not contemporaries, but Jimmy Joyce had tapped into her future psyche as it flitted about in the ether of time with full knowledge of Mother Ireland and her stories embedded in our mother's devious*

*mind; and I know you're going to ask me, what does a dumb mick
like me know about Mr. Joyce, God bless him, and I hope he found a
good oculist in Heaven, and I will respond that I have numerous
friends, some of them terrible people and others of excellent character
and literary acumen, the latter, who, with great kindness and in
recognition of my barbarian nature, my truly Celtic insanity and Hibernian psyche, invite me, with great kindness and consideration for
my cultural lacks and in recognition of my uncouth temperament, ask
me to join them on Bloomsday, where, with great style thespians and
scriveners of places like Greenwich Village, SoHo, the East Village
and Tribeca declaim the words of this strange and honored Irishman
in saloons replete with out of control tattooed and pierced communist
East Village denizens in the borough of Manhattan, not too far from
the one time Five Points section down near City Hall that was once
an Irish enclave of poverty and depravity that spawned fine Irish men
and women on both sides of the law, and these people take me into
their confidence and enjoy my company and we go there on the morning of that June 16 literary date and have bangers and potatoes and
eggs in middle class abundance and chew thick, rough, cleanout-
yourbowels Irish bread and drink morning stout without guilt and listen to passages from* Finnegans Wake—*but our mother talking like
that and God help you if you ask her to explain anything because no
matter how innocent the question you're in for another extensive dis-
quisition.*

He couldn't stop laughing and said: *Well, it appears that you
have bitten into the rock yourself.* And Jerry said: *I sprang from her
loins babbling in this devious manner as if her blood were the one
speaking and I having no volition except to discourse with the same
verve.* He called the waitress over and ordered another round.
Are you telling me, he asked, *that you broke into a doctor's office and
read your mother's medical records? I did,* Jerry replied, and asked
him to imagine what that must be like to a woman who had
been enormously gifted by Providence with melons for

breasts to find herself suddenly flat as a wall. *And she's our mother, boyo. Yours and mine.* He sat a while absorbing the information and said that he had been watching him when Fran said she had to return to New York, which seemed uncharacteristic for her, and that he detected enough of a change to make him suspicious and that is why he was asking. Jerry laughed and said that he was indeed perceptive and that he was correct. *And?* he asked. *Bad news there as well.* He said that Fran was terminating a pregnancy. *Down's syndrome,* he said. *Jesus,* he said. *Did you break into her doctor's office as well? Same doctor,* he said. *They've been going to him for years. There they were, both of them under Boyle, Frances Ann and Mary Katherine. She's due to go in and have the thing done later this week. She obviously wants to get it over with. I don't blame her. Knowing what I know today I would have done the same thing.* And then Jerry went into his pocket, removed his wallet and showed him pictures of his children. One of the girls had Down's. *She's a sweetheart,* he said, softening for a moment. *I would probably have done the same had I known,* he repeated, a momentary sadness passing across his eyes. He said he didn't know whether his wife would have gone along with the abortion.

And you've chosen to tell me, he said. *I have, Father Gabriel,* Jerry said. *Have you told them that you know? No, I haven't and I won't.* He asked him if he had told Tommy. *No, and I won't. But you've told me,* he said. *Why? You're ethical and I'm going to ask you to keep silent about what you've heard. Nothing can be gained from revealing such things. For our mother it's the third most difficult thing she's done in her life. And for Fran? This is her second. I think the first one was marrying Tommy and taking on the life that she's had. Marrying a Puerto Rican?* he'd asked. Jerry nodded and said that no two people carried so much baggage. *Fran and Tommy?* he asked. *No, not them themselves,* he said. *They're the innocents. I mean the island colonies.* He understood and felt as if Jerry wanted to tell him more. He drained his glass and said he should sleep.

*h*e was underwater swimming with clown fish. There was a soundtrack as there was in films. The music was that of Bach, which Claudia loved, and she explained about fugues and he listened, loving the deep sounds and closing his eyes as they held each other and kissed in her room as her mother sat in hers down the hall, worrying. They never did anything in her house except kiss. The clown fish were beautiful. Some of them were as big as poodles and they kissed each other and swayed to Bach's music, the orange-and-white bodies undulating. He could hear his mother and father talking and worrying next to his bed and he wished he could tell them that he was resting and would soon be up, but he couldn't will his body to move or his eyes to open. The coyote tests had come back and the score was 8–0. A shutout. He had won again but the doctors said that they couldn't figure out why, if none of them had rabies, why he'd drifted into a coma or whatever state he was in. He wanted to tell them that maybe the one that had bitten his ankle and had gotten away was the culprit. He hit on the idea of writing them a note but he could neither open his eyes nor lift his hand to write. Maybe he should have played baseball. He loved the responsibility of playing shortstop. He liked gliding toward second base, taking the throw from the second baseman, barely brushing second base with his foot, avoiding the sliding runner, and throwing to first base to complete the double play. And he could go to his right, dive and rise up and, his throw like a clothesline, fire to first to get the runner. The clown fish shook their heads in synchronized disapproval. Hockey, hockey, hockey, they mouthed and danced some more to Bach's music, the fugues repeating the themes like they were singing *Row, row, row your boat gently down* *the stream* in three parts with his mother singing the first part, and then he in the middle and Peggy the end when they were little. *Merrily, merrily, merrily, life is but a dream.* He smiled and remembered that Bach meant stream in German and Claudia was Bachlichtner, which meant stream of light or perhaps shining stream if he was recollecting correctly. And she was a shining stream of life in him and he was a pilgrim, a Romero, but she said peregrine, which was a hawk, and he liked that. A peregrine searching for a stream of light to drink from and be whole.

$g$abriel had driven Claudia to her house and then he drove to the farm, checked to see how Carlos was doing and how things were going. He lay down on his bed, drained by everything that had happened. Later, much later when he got to know Tommy, his now brother-in-law told him about his last trip, truly convinced that he had contributed to what happened to Kenny by the pressure he'd put on him. Of all of them Tommy had been the most distant, perhaps because his only connection to them was through Frances and Kenny. But he was as much a part of his life as the others. Tommy told him that the entire trip through New Jersey, Pennsylvania, Ohio, Indiana and then Illinois had the sameness of America, the extent of its geography tiring, and he had wondered why this small, seemingly insignificant island of Puerto Rico, a speck in the ocean compared to the United States, should wish to free itself. One hundred miles long by thirty-five miles wide against over three thousand miles from sea to shining sea; from top to bottom over seventeen hundred miles from the Canadian border to the tip of Texas. The United States was 3,615,211 square miles against 3,421 square miles of Puerto Rico and the United States still had to use part of the land for military purposes. He wasn't that good at mathematics but he figured it was possible to fit Puerto Rico's landmass over a thousand times into the United States. Odd number that one.

Gabriel said he now understood the anger of the Puerto Rican people as he had understood that of Carmen and the Shining Path forerunners in Peru, and his father's rage as a Québécois, and Jerry's defense of the IRA, and now Tommy Romero, conflicted about his loyalties. His own father had left Quebec after he protested treatment by a pro-English judge when he defended his sister, Simone, against a policeman, injuring the policeman with a stick. He was seventeen years old and he ran and hid and eventually came across the border and made his way south to New York State. After he told Tommy about Carmen and being up in the mountains in Peru, Tommy opened up, and although he never mentioned what he and Jerry did, he said he was done with it now that Frances had gone back to teaching to ease their financial burden.

Tommy said they reached Chicago early in the afternoon of the next day and drove first to the Humboldt Park section, picked up another carload of men and drove in a convoy to a farm near Evanston. They drove the truck into a barn and the men unloaded the merchandise. When they were done, they ate lunch. He couldn't believe it. Here he was in the heartland of America hobnobbing with urban guerrillas who spoke Spanish and quixotically wished to liberate the land of their ancestors, some of them born there and others born here, but all of them united in a common purpose. He was served the most delicious rice and beans he'd ever eaten and a codfish salad with fresh avocado slices and onions, everything soaked in olive oil. There were *viandas* as well: potatoes, green bananas, and tanniers and *ñame* and *malanga,* which he didn't know what they were called in English but were huge tubers and tasted great with the codfish. Maybe certain things were untranslatable to English. Certainly, the love that his father and these people felt for Puerto Rico was untranslatable. Everyone was so kind to him and an older woman said she and his father had gone to junior high school in Cacimar. *Have you ever gone there?* she asked. *No, but I will soon,* he said, his heart breaking a little by the love in the old woman for a land she'd probably never see again.

Tommy said that toward the end of the day he told Sean Rivas that whenever they needed him he would be there. They had hugged and he slept in the farmhouse. In the morning he got into the truck and drove back through this huge country, which was the third largest in the world behind Russia and Canada. He hated bullies and now finally he understood his father's quiet dignity and insistence that no matter how long he lived in the United States, he felt that a great wrong had been committed against Puerto Rico. *They could've accomplished the same ends with Puerto Rico being independent,* he said. *We're a friendly people. There was no need to abuse us as they have.* He'd thought that perhaps Puerto Rico could become a state. Now he knew different and Puerto Rico could never truly be part of the United States. Sean had explained this clearly. If Puerto Rico became a state it would have a federal budget larger than twenty-two other states. It would have two senators, seven congressmen and a substantial lobby. Why would you permit a minority that kind of power? Any time Puerto Rico gained an advantage, the other minorities would demand the same. *The cheapest alternative was independence but it would come grudgingly,* Sean had told him. It's just like the Irish, who couldn't permit their country to be divided into North and South, one free and the other held in bondage by the English.

He drove back and stopped off when it got dark, found a

motel and called Fran. She told him that something had happened to Kenny and he should get back as soon as possible. He said he was too tired and shouldn't be driving but he'd get a few hours sleep and then get in the truck and would be home late the following night. Tommy told her he loved her and then he called the farm and he'd told Tommy what had happened and that Kenny was okay. He worried about the wrist but at least he was alive. Tommy slept and in the morning was on the road again and finally got home. They'd flown upstate with Jerry the following day.

*t*he rain fell in long lines through the smoke and they continued walking toward him as he sat on the glass chair inside the glass globe, sitting calmly and everyone calling him to come out. The voices sounded closer and closer and he continued sitting in the glass chair trying to figure out how he could come out when there was no door. They kept saying: *there, there. Come out, come out.* They were talking and the voices were clear, so that he could tell that it was his father and mother and his uncle and Gabriel and the doctors, but Claudia wasn't there because she had left for New York but didn't want anyone to know. She had told him, bending close to him and whispering in his ear. It was their secret. She had come and told him that if they were going to move him to New York, then she would come and take care of him there. He wanted to tell her not to worry. She kissed his lips and he wanted to open his mouth and touch her tongue with his but he couldn't make his mouth open. He could smell her and remembered how her body felt but nothing happened except that he knew he loved her. She left and then the doctors came with the nurses and they had bathed him and got him ready and then he was on a gurney rolling down the hall and then in the elevator, and then downstairs and into an ambulance and eventually into an airplane and then he fell asleep and they said they were in New York City and he was in another ambulance, and another gurney rolling into another hospital and into another elevator and onto another bed with other nurses and doctors but his mother and father and his uncle were the same. Gabriel had remained at home but said he would come and see him soon. Later, after he had slept a long time and became music, his grandmother came to see him with his mother and Peggy and Rose and Rose wanted to know how he ate and then he heard Claudia's voice and she said they fed him intravenously. He wanted to eat bananas and have a sandwich or a hamburger and drink a cold glass of milk or lemonade but they wouldn't give him any but he wasn't hungry. He wanted to sit up and tell them he was all right. His grandmother said he looked like an angel and he wondered if he had died.

*h*is father had told him his version about a month before he died. He fell in love with Mary Grady when he was delivering milk in his wagon. She had come to him in the moonlight of that spring when the air was warm and fragrant and he fell in love with even more passion. *You can't help it when love happens,* he said. They walked together not yet touching and he'd spoken to her about his love and said that love was not a sin and she listened, her body aching to be touched and then they were on the side of a hill with a million stars above, the moon hanging low and yellow. They remained there for a while and then he took her hand and he led her away over the hill toward a stone hut where he often slept. There was a wooden bed and a mattress made of canvas. It was filled with straw and covered with a quilt that old Mrs. Ilse Vanderveer had given him. This was the mother of Hans

Vanderveer, who had married Marike Bueken two years earlier and run the farm and eventually owned it after his mother's death, subsequently selling it to him and Gabriel. When Marike was nursing their son, Peter, she had nursed him, Gabriel, alongside her own son and was the same Mrs. Vanderveer who helped raise him.

His father couldn't help himself and had walked six miles each night to the convent and stood waiting for her by the well and when she didn't come he would go to the stone hut and sleep fitfully, dreaming of her body until just before dawn when he returned to the farm. He went each night for a month and then she finally appeared, only her white face shining in the moonlight, her habit like the night.

He said she finally came to him one moonlit spring night and they went to the stone hut and made love. He was not a virgin, since he had been with girls before coming from Quebec and there had been a farm girl in the area, but Mary Grady was a virgin and the stains of her blood remained on the mattress like dead roses. She had come to him many times during the spring and summer, never saying anything but wanting him with a hunger that he had never experienced in a woman before or after, because there were others, including Mrs. Vanderveer, Marike, who came to his bed when her husband went away twice a month to help his brother with his farm in New Hampshire, and he hoped he didn't think badly of him for telling him, since marriage was a sacred thing even for him, who scoffed at the idea of God and saints, or angels and devils. One day in the fall of 1933, he went to deliver the milk with the horse and wagon and she told him that she was going to have his baby and she couldn't keep it and he had to take it and give it to an orphanage and could he help her when the time came. He said he would and brought blankets and took some baby clothes from the Vanderveers and brought them to the hut. He stored water and wood for the fireplace.

He went to the well and waited for two weeks and then on the fourteen day of December she came shortly after sundown. In terrible agony, nearly eight hours later, she had a son who was he, Gabriel, whom she named and together they were able to deliver him. *She named me?* he asked. His father nodded and sighed as if the effort of talking had become too much of an ordeal.

The baby whimpered and he knew to cut the umbilical cord and tie it as the midwife had done after Peter was born, the younger Mrs. Vanderveer's first son, whom she had nursed alongside himself. He did so with a pocketknife and some string. He then wrapped the baby up and held it. *She looked at the baby and said she had to go back,* his father said. She left and a few minutes later she returned and took the baby from him and cradled it. After a few moments she asked him to help her unbutton her habit and she nursed the baby and held it and cried and his father said that she was like *la vierge,* the Blessed Virgin, even though all of that religion stuff was nonsense and he had never seen such magnificent breasts in his life. He said he was sorry he was not able to convince her to marry him. She left the order the following week and lived in the stone hut, where he brought her food each day. One day he came to the hut and she was gone and the baby was lying under the quilt among the roses of her blood.

Ten years later, during the war, Mary Boyle had contacted him through a priest in the area. He had gone to see her in Utica, where she came on a bus and for a few days stayed in a rooming house. *She asked if I could bring you so she could at least see you,* Henri Brunet said. He asked her if she didn't want to meet him and she said: *no, because he would have to tell him she was his mother and that wouldn't be right.* His father brought him to Utica a few times and they ate ice cream and she sat there watching them. He told his father he had no recollection of those events. His father asked him to bring him a small wooden jewelry box in the bottom drawer of his dresser. When he'd brought him the box he searched through it and extracted a silver ring with an Irish knot on it, the silver intertwined in loops so if you wore it you could see the skin of your finger under the loops. His father said that Mary Boyle had given it to him after he was born. She said her grandmother had given it to her. For a time he had thought that perhaps his father had gotten Mrs. Vanderveer pregnant and he was really her son. That would have been fine, but after his father gave him the Irish ring he knew that this was enough provenance and Mary Boyle had to be his mother. His father said his birth wasn't registered for more than a year and that is why the certificate said 1935, but he was born on December 15, 1933. *No Marguerite Bouillet? No, no there was no such person,* his father said.

A month after Kenny was transferred from the hospital in Syracuse to New York City, he drove down to see him and agreed to meet Jerry. Kenny was still in a coma. Jerry said that their mother, a term he enjoyed using, had her surgery a few days after Kenny was transferred to New York. She had been home two weeks and was feeling better. Was he interested in visiting her? *She's pretty much a hundred percent,* he said. *She's going in to get fitted for a falsies bra.* He nodded and when they finished looking in on Kenny at New York University Hospital they got into Jerry's car and drove up to the Bronx. On the way up Jerry said that he had finally talked with his mother the previous week. He told her he knew about her time at the convent. She'd looked at him and after a while she said he was a darn good detective but a very nosy son. He told her that he knew about Henri Brunet and his son. She said that she could explain and told him a bizarre story about Henri Brunet forcing himself on her and that is how she had become pregnant. *Rape, Mom?* he'd asked. She had shaken her head violently, said that rape was a very ugly word, and that nothing at all like that had taken place. *But he forced himself on you, Mom?* Jerry said. His mother went into one of her dissertations and ended up asking him if in the course of his relationship to his wife, Sheila, he had never imposed himself on her and would he consider that rape. *Are you saying there was consent on your part?* he asked. *I didn't say that,* she had insisted. *If it was anyone other than my sainted mother I'd have called her a devious bitch,* Jerry said.

When they reached the apartment Claudia was there helping Mary Boyle. When his mother saw him together with Jerry she smiled and asked them if they wanted tea. They said they did and she made tea and served it with store-bought cookies. They made small talk about Kenny and about Fran going back to teaching and then Jerry said that Claudia ought to come with him to see if they could buy some bedroom slippers for Kenny because he was sure any day now he'd wake up and want to take a walk around the hospital. Claudia got very excited hearing such a positive prospect. He was left there with Mary Boyle, who was his mother but not his mother.

He asked her what had happened. She wanted to know how much he knew. He said that he knew that she was his mother and that it was very likely that Henri Brunet was his father. She then told a different story. She said that she should have been stronger but that Henri was relentless in his pursuit of her. That she finally gave in and went to him and they went to a stone hut where he often stayed but that they had been intimate only once. *What made you give in?* he asked. *Did you love him?* She was silent for more than a minute and then said that it had been a strange passion, part love and part rebellion against the Church. They both regretted what happened the first time and although they met twice more there was no subsequent physical contact between them. She regretted greatly what took place and returned to her life and although he came to see her each day she would not speak to him. She had bled and then stopped bleeding regularly during the month and knew she had sinned. She couldn't go to confession and began feeling sick and eventually she had to admit that she was pregnant. She continued to function in the convent and one day when he came to deliver milk she told him about her condition and he said they should run away and get married. She couldn't and kept her secret at the convent and eventually she gave birth to him, Gabriel. She said it was her misfortune, or fortune, she added quickly, to become pregnant and she hoped he forgave her.

She said she hid her secret from the other novices and nuns, keeping busy and becoming invisible in her silence. With scissors, needle and thread she let out her habit to conceal the pregnancy. She said that her breasts, now plucked from her so she could go on living, were prominent enough that they kept her habit sufficiently protective of her pregnancy. Summer ended and fall came and she told Henri Brunet that she was going to have the baby and that he should give it a name and care for it because she couldn't keep it. He said angrily that he would do so and she should come to the stone hut where they had met that one night and he would help her. She said she was glad that his father had named him Gabriel. *Like the guardian angel,* she said. He wondered who was telling the truth about giving him the name Gabriel.

She said that when the baby was born, Henri was angry at her for not marrying him and literally snatched it from her.

She wanted to take care of him but Henri took the crying baby to the farm. She went back to the convent with the guilt of what she had done eating at her so she couldn't concentrate and finally went to confession and after praying and not being able to reconcile her sin, she left the convent and returned to New York. *Because it's one thing to be forgiven by a priest and quite another to forgive yourself,* she said. *And did you?* he asked. *Eventually, after seeing you, I did,* she said. *Did you love me?* he asked. *Very much so,* she said, but he couldn't be sure that there was any truth to her words, nor could he detect falseness in them. Instead there was a foglike haze that extended from his birth to that moment and made him think of the metallic cold and imposing mystery of the Andes. He went into the pocket of his jacket, took out the knotted ring and extended it to his mother. She recognized it immediately. She took it and slipped it onto her left ring finger as if she were accepting a wedding band. *Thank you,* she said. *I think my great-grandma would want you to have it back,* he said, and noticed that Mary Boyle's eyes were filled with tears but as always she remained stoic in appearance.

*t*he bird had bright blue feathers. It looked like a large pelican with a big beak that was an even brighter blue with golden specks. He would soon board the bird and fly home. But first he had to say good-bye to his family. They were all there. Little boys and girls and they were all dressed in pretty clothing. The boys had short pants and stockings with beautiful coats and ties. The girls wore pretty dresses in many colors and had matching ribbons in their hair. Tommy, Franny, Peggy, Rose, Katherine, Diana, Tommy, Jr. and Claudia. Grandpa Martin and Grandma Mary, and Grandpa Tomás and Grandma Rosa and all his aunts and uncles and cousins were there, the Puerto Ricans and the Irish, dressed so prettily and they all had flowers and there were beautiful wreaths and the breezes were dancing in the trees, but the baby was gone. He asked Franny about the baby but she shrugged her shoulders and pointed at him. *Me?* he'd asked and Tommy had nodded. *I'm not the baby,* he'd said but they all clapped and cheered and the bird sang: *It's time to go, no more tarrying, little boy, it's time to go back home.* It's not possible, he'd thought, but the large bird called again and he went to each of the boys and girls and kissed them and they all said *I love you* and he said *I love you.* He went to the bird, lifted himself up, and slowly he sank into the blue feathers until only his head showed. He waved at the boys and girls and then the bird stood up, opened its wings, and it was soon rising above the ground into the brilliant sky. Higher and higher it went until the boys and girls were very small and then he couldn't see them anymore and he felt sad. And then they were beyond the clouds and he fell asleep and knew that when he woke up again he would be home.

$g$abriel couldn't believe Claudia's voice on the telephone. He and Carmen and Carlos had just sat down to dinner when the phone rang. Carlos answered it and said it was for him. Claudia couldn't stop crying and after a while she said that Kenny was awake. He asked what the doctors had said. Claudia said they were amazed that he had recovered, that they had to run more tests on him and that he sounded hoarse from not having talked all this time. She said that he wanted to know why it was snowing. She told him it was November and he couldn't believe it. He asked if everyone knew that he had come home. *Everyone knows,* she said. *They're on the way over. And you?* Kenny asked. *I'm fine,* Claudia said. *Has he noticed, Claudia?* he asked. *No, not yet,* she replied. *I'm not showing that much. I'll tell him later. Do you think he'll be angry?* she asked. He said that he didn't think Kenny would be angry.

When he was finished talking with Claudia they wanted to know about the phone call. He explained and shook his head as if it was impossible that Kenny could have recovered. Kenny had been in a coma since the end of August until the middle of November. *Nearly three months,* he'd said. *A medical improbability given the situation,* he'd said. Carlos said that perhaps he had developed an immunity. Carmen was pleased and talked about hybrid vigor, and he understood she was talking about them and how bright their son was.

They had traveled down to New York to see him. He was weak but in good spirits although a little strange, much as if he had gone on a long trip and was not yet accustomed to his surroundings. He kept staring out the window at the falling snow. He would be going home the next day. He kept flexing his left hand, which looked not quite right but was functioning; some of the fingers lacked articulation but were otherwise okay. Seven operations, until they reconnected the ligaments and tendons. It was unlikely that he would be very good at athletics but he was alive and alert again. His mother couldn't stop touching him and his father stood by, stoic as ever.

*g*abriel stood with Mary Boyle wondering if she had the same toughness as Kenny and whether it had helped her to withstand the cancer that doctors said was in remission but which they also said could return. She was in good spirits and overjoyed that Kenny had recovered. They agreed that perhaps they could drive up and have Thanksgiving at the farm. And that's how it went that year. They cooked two of the turkeys and there were two long tables end to end. Three Brunets, eight Romeros, one Boyle, and two Bachlichtners, Claudia having dragged her mother out of her house. Kenny's calf had grown in the past three months and he petted and fed it. He helped with some of the chores around the farm but he seemed abstracted from the tasks he once enjoyed. Gabriel drove Mary Boyle, Kenny and Claudia, Carmen and Carlos to the cemetery and they placed flowers on Henri Brunet's grave. She noted the year of his birth and with her usual dry humor said that he was a year younger than she was. She said that among her many faults she had also been a cradle robber. They laughed and Claudia hugged her but neither Carlos nor Kenny knew then their relationship to each other, nor was Claudia aware of the complications until years later.

Kenny returned to school, apologized to his coaches and picked up on his studies, hoping to graduate with his class. He began running and lifting weights and skating with the team at practice. Although his wrist hurt him he was able to hold a hockey stick, stickhandle, pass and shoot. In spite of his efforts he was nothing like before. He was disappointed but thought that perhaps with more physical therapy he could play when he went to college at a Division II or Division III school. The chances of playing at Division I level were gone and the letters stopped coming. Everyone returned to the city Sunday night and he drove with Carmen and Carlos to Montreal. They married in a civil ceremony. He had wanted her to come and live with him at the farm, but she said she couldn't, that she had responsibilities to her college. Carlos was enrolled in a private French-English school and twice a month Gabriel traveled to Montreal and stayed with Carmen. During the holidays she and Carlos returned to the farm. He thought of selling the farm, not wishing to go through the loneliness he had endured.

In spite of Claudia's condition she and Kenny agreed that

they didn't want to be married yet. As for his parents, he was no longer obliged to follow their wishes. Things had changed. His ordeal had elevated him to a more respected position in the family and his wishes were hardly ever questioned, his demeanor and seriousness of such intensity and his grace so abundant that they knew he would not bend to anyone's will but his own and should they try to convince him otherwise they would be met with tolerance but he would remain inviolate in his stance. He knew now that it was this type of dignity and respect that all people of the earth wanted. It was a simple wish and yet so difficult to allow, each person wishing to control the other to ease the burden of responsibility to themselves.

memoir

BEGIN this remembrance not quite knowing where I should start. I feel humbled by my good fortune. There is no earthly explanation why I should be alive. I do not believe, however, that there is a divine reason for my existence. My uncle Gabriel says it was my karma. He's a Buddhist. I am not a religious person and have drifted further and further away from all beliefs except the ones that support absolute kindness toward other human beings. I realize that I am not a remarkable person but one who was fortunate enough to be born to good parents, flawed to be sure, but with a core of goodness that permitted them to protect their children and help them to grow. Love is a powerful weapon against evil, this much I know.

President Clinton was inaugurated earlier in the year after defeating George Bush. Politics don't interest me very much. The Florida Marlins are about to face the Cleveland Indians in the World Series. I still love baseball and will watch the games and again wonder how far I could have gone in the sport.

After I came out of the hospital the world seemed quite different. I recalled experiences while I was in that dream state that the doctors identified as a coma. To me it seemed as if I needed to sleep and dream and understand things at a deeper level so that I could be more awake in my life. I don't know where I went during that time, but when I returned I knew that I had changed. The difference between good and evil became clear except that I could see that sometimes people do evil things for a good purpose, and people sometimes do seemingly good things for evil purposes. I also know that people have deep secrets that they cannot reveal. Before he died, my father told me things that I wish he hadn't told me. They came as a shock to me until he explained that he had done everything for his family and for my uncle's family. I don't know that I could have done what he did but I've never been in his situation, so I cannot judge him.

I did not tell my mother, nor did I tell Claudia what my father said to me. I hope I never have to be in his shoes. No one needs to know those things. I will keep his secret and mourn his passing each day. Did I learn anything from my battle to save the calf? I learned that human beings are capable of anything, that they are a combination of good and evil, of love and hate, of kindness and rage. I learned that human beings should not deny who they are but should make good use of whatever passion rules their life. I know that sounds strange but it is what I believe.

Since then I have never been as angry as I was when I was fighting to keep the calf and myself alive. I can understand people being angry and don't believe like others today that anger is a bad thing. I believe that the more you tell people that their anger is wrong, the more they suppress it and then it explodes in our schools and in neighborhoods and children shoot each other. I have often wondered if I have the capacity to kill another human being. I have no doubt that I could if the situation was one in which I had to defend the people I love against a real threat. Knowing that I am capable of killing, I do my best to guard against creating situations in which I would have to. I do not advocate anger and violence, but understand people who feel they have been wronged and direct their anger and violence at injustice, particularly in defense of ideals. Ultimately, the decisions we make are personal ones and only our hearts determine the right and wrong of an issue.

Two years ago, my mother told me what she had told no other person except a priest. I was not shocked and told her she had done the right thing in terminating a pregnancy that would have caused the family, already beset by financial difficulties, greater hardship. She cried and thanked me for being understanding. She's retiring this year as a school principal. My father's death has affected her greatly and she's come to live with Claudia and me and our family. Both of my parents revealed secrets to me they had not revealed to each other. Eventually, I learned everything there was to know about my family, including my uncle Gabriel, whom we still visit in Montreal. Claudia's mother has moved to Albany and lives a quiet life, in a more supportive atmosphere with people who understand her suffering. She is no longer a Lutheran.

My brother and sisters are doing well. Peggy studied literature and has had two small but respected volumes of poetry published. She married an Irish scholar and lives in a cottage on the western coast of Ireland. Claudia and I have visited them. They have two daughters and seem happy. They look like little Irish girls and speak English beautifully in the way that Irish people speak. Peggy has learned to speak Irish and at times all four speak the language among themselves. Both Peggy and her husband, James, teach school. Rose tried being a lesbian. She didn't like it and became a personal trainer. She never married and has a boyfriend who is a jazz musician. He is Japanese. They live in San Francisco. Katherine is an actress and you can see her in soaps on TV. She plays a villainess, conniving and without pity for her victims. Diana received her Ph.D. in Romance languages, teaches at an Ivy League college and is presently on sabbatical, writing a book on the Celt-Iberians. Tommy Jr. went to St. John's University. In his sophomore year, after pitching a no-hitter, he was signed by the Boston Red Sox. He's six foot three and his fastball has been clocked at ninety-eight mph. Our father saw him pitch one minor league game before he died. He was happy. After my brother got a single and was putting on his jacket at first base, my father looked at me and shook his head and smiled. The look wasn't one of pity for me but a sadness about his own life. He was probably right and I should've played baseball. But then I would not have been on the farm and made the choices I made. I also would not have met Claudia, and that to me is of the greatest importance.

Paulie, our son, arrived prematurely in late January of 1980. He weighed a little more than three pounds and was in an incubator for nearly a month. Claudia and I had two more children, a girl and then another boy. Eva Frances, after our mothers, and Thomas for my father. For the sake of our children Claudia and I were eventually married in a civil ceremony. Our children are all thoughtful people and excellent students. Eva is the athlete and she is good at everything. At six feet tall she has the same kind of looks as her mother, exotic and haughty. She pitches windmill softball, and is on the basketball and volleyball teams in school. Even though she is only fourteen she has been invited by the Junior Olympic Softball team to their summer camp. We are already receiving letters from colleges. Eva is also a gifted pianist.

In the winter of the year that our son was born and I turned eighteen years old, Claudia and I, together with our baby, traveled to Long Island to stay at my uncle's beach house. We were living at my grandmother Mary's while Claudia finished high school. After Thanksgiving we needed to get away for a while. In early December we took a week off from school. The weather was becoming colder and we packed up clothes, put the baby in a small cradle in the backseat, and in Claudia's Volkswagen we drove out to the beach house. Claudia had never spent much time near the sea and she was excited. She was seventeen years old and a mother, but she was like a little girl about the sea and I loved her more for it. She has never lost her enthusiasm for life. She's very much like my mother but fierce in her defense of people.

In time Claudia decided that she didn't want to become a nurse after spending so much time in hospitals because of Grandma Mary Boyle and then me. She attended Hunter College at night. It took her five years to get her degree but I've never been prouder. I was at the graduation with Paulie sitting next to me and Eva on my chest strapped into a carrier. Eva slept during the ceremony. Claudia went on to law school and even though it took her another four years she became a lawyer. Six years ago she met another woman lawyer and they've established a practice out here where we live.

I have so many memories but none stands out more than the one after waking up and seeing Claudia sitting on my bed at the hospital. It was as if I was at the farm and she had given me sleeping pills and I had woken up a few hours later except that it had been three months. During those months when I was sleeping I had been in a hospital in Syracuse, had several operations on my wrist and was transferred to a hospital in New York. Eventually, I learned that my uncle Jerry paid for the hospital bills. We have never been close but I owe him a debt of gratitude. He too is capable of great good, although I suspect he's had difficult choices to make. The wear and tear of living shows in the pained expressions of his face. With physical therapy the movement in my left hand improved but it was never the same. But that afternoon in November I opened my eyes, moved my head and touched Claudia's arm as she sat reading. Claudia turned, called my name and began crying. She then threw her arms around me and kissed me and told me not to fall asleep again. She rushed to call a nurse and pretty soon the doctors came to examine me. They poked my body, looked into my eyes and asked me questions. My body felt uncomfortable and out of synch with my brain. Nothing seemed right and I hurt all over. Even my voice was hoarse and sounded strange to me.

Claudia went and began calling people to tell them I had woken up. I kept thinking that she looked different but I couldn't figure out why. Her hair was shorter but something else had changed. When the doctors went off to consult with each other, she came over and sat on the bed. It was then that I saw that her stomach was not as flat as I remembered it. I touched her, not quite knowing what it meant. She said she had been planning to tell me back on the farm, but I had never woken up. She held up her left hand and with her right index finger she counted each of her outstretched fingers to tell me that she was five months pregnant. She said she'd wanted to discuss with me whether she should get an abortion but kept thinking that my mother and my grandmothers would be disappointed. After she told them she was pregnant they all said that they were sure I'd want the baby. I shook my head violently at the thought of Claudia having an abortion of our baby. She cried and said that she was glad because she wanted to have the baby. *But what are we going to do with a baby and no jobs?* I said, *What's going to happen to us?* She shook her head and said she didn't know but the important thing was for me to finish school and go to college. I never went to college but have continued reading and learning and being amazed by people's capacity for creativity in all sorts of fields.

I finished high school and asked my father if I could work with him. He said he didn't have enough work to take on another person. Given what he eventually told me, it was obvious that he didn't want me involved in his dealings with my uncle, although I later learned from my mother that his trip to Chicago had been his last one of that type. He said maybe I could work with my grandfather. We went to see him and my grandfather was happy to have me as a helper. He paid me well and I suspect that he often gave me the entire amount that he earned from his jobs. He was still installing cabinets and floors, building extensions to houses and repairing stairs. I learned everything about carpentry from him and then he told me about working on boats during the war and I asked him if it was difficult to build boats. He said it was a special kind of carpentry. He said he had friends that could teach me if I was interested. I said I was. I worked with my grandfather for four years and when I had learned enough about wood and tools, we drove out to Long Island. He introduced me to his friends and I began learning to build boats. I now own a modest business with two partners. We make sailboats and have commissions to build several large yachts.

Grandpa and Grandma Romero moved back to Cacimar, their hometown in Puerto Rico. We have visited them. Our children are fascinated by Grandma Rosa's cigar smoking. Claudia and I do not smoke anything. Grandma Mary is a mystery. She was born in 1912 and is now eighty-five, appears healthy and as if she'll live forever. She still tells long stories and you can never tell what is true and what isn't.

I jog and play softball and stay in shape. Claudia and I

travel when we can. Besides going up to Montreal to see my uncle Gabriel and his wife, Carmen, we visit relatives in Puerto Rico and in Ireland, and we've been to other countries in Europe, Latin America, Africa and the Orient. We have plans to see the Great Wall of China and we are scheduled to take a cruise to Alaska. Oh, my cousin Carlos went to McGill University and then to their medical school. He has a practice in rural Quebec and has married a French-speaking young woman. They're expecting their first child.

My cousin Patrick made a ton of money on Wall Street. He owns Boyle's, an upscale Irish saloon in the area, and is still involved in the cause to unify Ireland. He married an Irish Catholic girl. They have five children. His father and mother are still together. My other cousins on both sides of the family are doing well. No scandals and nothing spectacular except for my aunt Evelyn's youngest, Mark, who is a pianist and plays in a salsa orchestra. I still play the harmonica but the children walk out of the room when I do. Claudia remains and encourages me. I realize I'm not a very good musician.

In the summer our family sails out on the Sound. The children have become excellent sailors. We swim and have thought of sailing up the coast to Canada. The ocean delights Claudia. We have snorkeled in the Mediterranean and the Caribbean. She is like a siren in the water, slender and alluring, and I am consistently awed by my feelings for her.

But I'm digressing. Discipline. I'm taking a course on writing at the community college and I have books on the subject. They all say that discipline is of the greatest importance. I write a little every day.

Claudia, the baby and I drove to the beach house. We stopped off and bought groceries, baby food and disposable diapers. When we got to the house we fired up the woodstove. I repaired the plastic seals on the windows and made sure the

waterpipes and faucets were in working order. We went outside and with the baby we walked near the water. Claudia
loved being there and asked me if sometime, when we had
money, we could live by the sea. I said that we could. I think
wanting to please her is what led me to want to build boats.
We own a large house no more than a block from the ocean.
I know that I will have to delete this but it's impossible to
build boats and not be near water. Saying so creates a redun-
dancy. Then again, perhaps there are such things as necessary
redundancies. I like the sound of the phrase. I think maybe
life is a series of necessary redundancies. I recalled being in a
coma and thinking of listening to Bach fugues and wondering if perhaps life is about the repetition of stories and our
connections to each other.

We sat on the beach and watched the sunset. After a while
a wintry wind came up and the baby began crying. When we
got back the house was warm. In spite of that I knew it would
get colder and while Claudia was cooking supper and feeding
the baby I made a fire in the fireplace. When we finished eating supper we changed the baby and watched him fall asleep
in his cradle. We sat in front of the fire and held each other
and talked about the upcoming Christmas, our first as a family. I remembered that before I went away into my dream-
world Claudia said she had many things to tell me.

She tried to remember but couldn't and I kept helping to
jog her memory. I said that Angie, her girlfriend, had been
there, and she, not Angie, but Claudia, had given me a bath
and the doctor had come and sewn up my face, my wrist, and
my leg. She remembered and said that she was going to tell
me about being pregnant and that Mr. Brunet had died but I
wasn't in any shape to hear those things. And then she was
still for a few moments and quite suddenly she began crying,
sobbing like a baby and saying she was sorry. Her sobbing be-

came so loud that Paulie woke up and I had to hold him until he calmed down and went back to sleep. Claudia got up, went into the bathroom and remained there for nearly ten minutes. When she came out she sat cross-legged in front of me. I placed another log in the fire, held her hand and asked her what was the matter.

She said that she hadn't wanted to tell me but she had to. It wouldn't be fair and if I didn't want to I didn't have to marry her. She said she would always love me and take care of the baby for me and would never marry anyone, no matter what, just like her mother. I told her I would never want to be with anyone except her.

Once I had reassured her of this she said that her mother always wore long-sleeved dresses and blouses and never went swimming because she had numbers on her arm. I didn't know anything about such things and she explained that Jews had been rounded up during World War II and had numbers tattooed on their forearms when they were sent to concentration camps. She said her mother's name was Greenberg. She was just a little girl when it happened. Maybe eight. She had hidden under the barracks where they were being held in the concentration camp. That night it rained. She found a ditch that ran under a fence and crawled out. Mother, father, brothers, sisters, uncles, aunts, grandparents on both sides died in Hitler's ovens, she said.

I had read about Hitler but had never met Jewish people who had experienced such horrors. If I had I didn't know about it. In Williamsburg, the neighborhood where my grandparents lived in Brooklyn, there were many Jewish people and some of my grandfather's friends called the area *Tierra Santa* or Holy Land because of the Jews. I had too many things on my mind and did not concern myself with anything but trying to finish school and make a little money after school to help my grandmother and feed Claudia and the baby. At that age I was totally ignorant about what happened with the Jews in Europe. That evening Claudia told me.

Claudia's mother had escaped and lived in the woods eating berries, hiding and being frightened and stealing food from houses while the people were out. Luckily this was in early summer toward the end of the war because she wouldn't have lasted the winter. It still made little sense to me. I felt bad for her mother and understood Claudia's distress but her mother had survived and that is what counted. And then Claudia let out a sob and said that her mother was Jewish.

The information didn't mean much to me and then, without turning around, she said that if her mother was Jewish, so was she and that she felt ashamed and should've told me and maybe I wouldn't have gotten so involved with her. She felt that she had been deceitful. I stood up and went to the window and stood looking out at the night. She called my name but I couldn't answer her. She came to me, as usual concerned with my well-being. She asked me why I had turned away from her. I told her that it was because I remembered crying when I was alone in the woods and fighting the coyotes and wondering if I'd ever see her again. I turned around and told her that I was angry that her mother had been left without a family and this caused Claudia so much pain.

She asked me if I was angry at her for not telling me. I shook my head and said it didn't matter. Everyone has secrets. When the secrets come out it makes more pain for everyone. Eventually, people go on living and if they want to concentrate on the secrets and torture themselves they really don't understand love. It doesn't matter if the secrets ever come out. When they come out you have a choice whether the secrets are going to ruin your life or make you stronger. It doesn't matter what you are or what I am, I said. We're blood and that is what counts. She was genuinely surprised. She let out a big sigh and then cried a little more and told me she loved me. She asked if I knew how she felt when people said terrible things about Jews. I said that I loved her and loved our son and we would be okay and that even though I looked as I did, yes, I had an idea because people often said things about Puerto Ricans or other people in front of me. Sometimes it hurts but after a while the pain is about the people who live with that kind of hatred and prejudice.

She asked me if we had to go to church and raise our family in a religion and that if I wanted she would be glad to. I said we did not. That we should make sure our children had music lessons and read good books and learned to respect others. We went to bed, made love and fell asleep in each other's arms. We must be the only people our age who've never had sex with anyone else other than each other. In the morning, while we were making breakfast we listened to the radio. We were singing to the baby and the baby was smiling and making little noises that sounded like he was trying to sing. Then the news came on. We listened intently, not speaking and not quite believing what we heard. The previous night, in Manhattan, John Lennon had been shot to death.

The news stunned us and that is how we began our life as adults.

AUTHOR'S NOTE

ON MAY 19, 2001, as I was correcting the first draft of this book, I learned of the death of Susannah McCorkle, a jazz singer of remarkable sensitivity, an artist with the soul of an angel and a voice that touched me and who, tired of this long trek that is life, ended hers as a tortured dove. I never met her nor do I know her motivation for ending her life, but I am devastated and grieving over her death. I am convinced more than ever that our society, with its concerns for goodness, has forgotten that we are still young as a species and rather than trying to sublimate violence ought to figure out ways to permit the violence to be expressed in the destruction of ideas and systems that harm humanity rather than have the violence turn inward to destroy those we love and ultimately ourselves. I wish I had met you, Susannah McCorkle, and explained to you what I know of despair and that many times I contemplated the same. I shall miss you, Susannah McCorkle. May you always know that I love you and would have fought to keep you alive. I am certain you would have enjoyed this novel because it is about our families.

ACKNOWLEDGMENTS

As ALWAYS my sincerest gratitude to my agent, Thomas Colchie, and his wife, Elaine Colchie. Their kindness, friendship, and respect for the novel as an instrument for humanist dialogue always inspire me to go beyond myself in this process. For his interest in this novel and its publication my thanks to René Alegría, head of Rayo at HarperCollins. His sensitivity, support, and understanding have eased the process. To Andrea Montejo and the rest of the Rayo staff, my heartfelt thanks as well. To my son, Matthew, to whom this novel is dedicated, my appreciation for having lived part of the main story and telling me about it. His courage, his grace under pressure, and his benevolence have always served as an inspiration for me.

bonusPAGES

Born in Puerto Rico in 1936, **EDGARDO VEGA YUNQUÉ** grew up in the mountainous town of Cidra. In 1949, he came to the United States when his father, a Baptist minister, was employed as the head of a Spanish-speaking congregation in the South Bronx. After high school, Edgardo joined the Air Force and was stationed overseas in the Azores and Greece. Upon his return from the Air Force, he attended Santa Monica College, where he played baseball and met his future wife. In 1962, he returned to New York to attend NYU. But he soon dropped out of school after the JFK assassination and went to work for the war on poverty as an organizer in East Harlem.

In 1977, at the age of 41, his first short story, "Wild Horses," a reference to Faulkner, was published by *Nuestro* magazine and, in 1985, his first novel, *The Comeback*, was published by Arte Público Press. Since then, he has published several works of fiction, including *No Matter How Much You Promise to Cook or Pay the Rent You Blew It Cauze Bill Bailey Ain't Never Coming Home Again*—a *New York Times* Notable Book, *Washington Post* Best Book of the Year, and Winner of the 2004 Latino Book Award.

Edgardo Vega Yunqué works on five or six novels at a time and states: "Since my work is about people and my affection for them, I don't lose track of who they are, just like I don't lose track of my children or other relatives and acquaintances. I have friends—and characters—whom I don't see for a long time, but as soon as we get together we pick up where we left off."

AN INTERVIEW WITH EDGARDO VEGA YUNQUÉ

How did the idea of fugues work their way into your novel?

The structure of the novel is such that it resembles this particular musical form. The book has seven major characters. Each of the seven inner parts, excluding the first (Prelude) and last (Memoir) is the inner dialogue of the characters of the tale. Each part has a theme, and each of the characters has his or her own concern played out against the struggle of the main character. With each repetition of the theme, new information is revealed about the other characters.

In the Author's Note, you express your grief over the death of jazz singer Susannah McCorkle and state, "I am convinced more than ever that our society, with its concerns for goodness, has forgotten that we are still young as a species and rather than trying to sublimate violence ought to figure out ways to permit the violence to be expressed rather than have it turn inward to destroy those we love and ultimately ourselves." Will Ms. McCorkle and/or this theme appear in any of your future novels?

In spite of all the goodness professed by the ethics of monotheistic religions, there is greater and greater violence today in the world. All of my work is concerned with this contradiction. I believe strongly that the Greek ideal of the *daemonic* composed of *eros* (love, but also creativity) and *thanatos* (death, but also destruction) is a much more sensible way of looking at the human condition. In other words, monotheism seeks to suppress the destructive elements and elevate those of creativity, that is, quiet the devil and give voice to the angel. It is significant, and an apt metaphor that the highest prize for creative accomplishment in most important fields of endeavor is named after the inventor of dynamite. In other words, each human being is capable of great creativity and great destruction. Suppressing destruction obviously does not work. Why not teach people how to use their natural tendency to destroy in productive ways? Aren't there institutions and ideas in the society that need destruction? Destruction of something does not necessarily mean that violence should be employed. As a matter of fact, what happens with artists when faced with this dilemma is that they turn the anger and violence inward and either hurt themselves or the ones they love most. What should happen, instead, is the artist, and indeed, everyone, must level their destruction at those things in society that impeded progress and the well-being of the majority of the people. As for Ms. McCorkle, I was simply paying homage to a fellow artist and mourning our loss.

New York is obviously an important place to you as it is the setting for much of your fiction. How has the city influenced you as a writer?

I have always been a writer mired in poverty. I have never had a driver's license and have never owned a car, let alone driven a car in the United States. The two factors have kept me in New York City. If I had a choice I'd live on southern coast of Spain in winter and on the western coast of Ireland in the summer. But although I do write about New York, I also write about other parts of the U.S. I believe *Bill Bailey* has many different locales, including several in southern states, places that I've visited. I have an unpublished novel that takes place pretty much in Puerto Rico, one in the Biloxi, Mississippi Bay Bay area, another which takes place on Martha's Vineyard, another in southern Spain, parts of Europe, the Levant and other areas of the Sephardic Diaspora. I write because I need to explore ideas, that I can use a locale to further the exploration of ideas is not as important to me as the ideas that I am exploring. New York City is an invigorating environment that keeps you on your toes. I have always looked at writing from four very distinct vantage points: a) as part of the humanist tradition of letters, that is the novel as a place for discussion; b) as a way of painting with words, c) as the composing of musical forms, because, if truth be told, I hear language rather than know it technically, and

d) as a way of emulating the motion picture arts. In other words, in the latter case I get to be the actors, director, producer, cinematographer, art designer, set designer, lighting designer, and every other person involved in this collaborative art form. As such I'm not only interested in telling a story but in creating a confluence of the arts that produce a mimesis or synthesis that goes beyond the written word.

Do you find that it is more difficult to write objectively about a culture of which you are a member, or one, like the Irish, in which you are only an observer?

To write about the Irish requires much more research if I'm going to talk about the culture at a mythical or linguistic level. However, the Irish and the Puerto Ricans are amazing storytellers. I have sat with both and listened to individuals young and old, male and female tell their stories and they have stayed with me. I have never felt at home anywhere in the world. It has always felt that I was an observer everywhere I've gone. Even growing up in the small mountain town in Puerto Rico I felt like a fish out of water, as if I didn't belong there. So coming in contact with the Irish when I first came to New York didn't seem all that strange. In fact it felt just like it did in Puerto Rico in that I felt like a stranger. But I believe that there are great similarities in the two cultures and that is why I've been writing about the Irish, both from personal knowledge, from having relatives by marriage and blood who have an Irish ancestry, and from study I feel that I can write about both groups with objectivity since ultimately the emotions of all human beings: their joys and sorrows are one in spite of their geography.

QUESTIONS FOR DISCUSSION

1. Ireland and Puerto Rico are both distinctly Catholic countries. What is the role that religion plays in the lives of the characters? How does that role adapt and change as each generation becomes more American?

2. "He said he loved biology and the way there were so many animals and how some of them resembled each other and how they inherited the same characteristics from each other" (page 207). Discuss inheritance, both genetic and psychological, as a theme in the novel. How much do you believe the characters are a product of what they have received from their parents? How much is independently earned and expressed?

3. Discuss the ambiguity of adversaries in *Blood Fugues*. How does the author choose to portray stereotypically villainous entities—wolves, terrorists, drug dealers? How does their depiction differ from the characteristically heroic portrait of a police officer? What, if anything, do you believe is truly the greatest enemy for the characters in the novel?

4. How does the author juxtapose the themes of birth and sacrifice? Discuss this as it relates specifically to the maternal figures in the novel—Fran, Mary Boyle, and the calf's mother. How do preconceived notions of motherhood affect the choices made by Fran and her mother?

5. Claudia's family secret is a source of great worry to her, and requires an enormous amount of courage to divulge to Kenny. What about her life would cause this seemingly disproportionate fear? Do you think others would have responded in the same manner as Kenny?

6. Discuss the notion of hybrid vigor—the vitality and strength expressed in the offspring of two genetically dissimilar parents—as it relates to the revolution of the Boyle–Romero clan, and the American family as a whole. How do the similarities of Ireland and Puerto Rico compliment each other in this enterprise, especially in relation to Kenny?

7. How does the structure of the fugue translate into the rhythm of the novel? How do we come to understand developments and expositions against the backdrop of Kenny's struggle to save the life of the calf? Whose struggle or secrets do you identify with most?

8. What is the significance of the epigraph in *Blood Fugues*? How do the quotes by Colum McCann, Milan Kundera, and Timothy A. Smith help inform your reading?

9. "We are the sum total of all the causes and all the effects we've made lifetime after lifetime. If you want to know the kinds of causes you made in the past, look at the effects you're getting now" (page 221). Does this philosophy hold true for each character in the novel?

10. Except for the last chapter, Memoir, the narrative is told in the third person. Why do you think the author chooses the first person narrative of Kenny for the final chapter? Do you think this is a fitting end? From whom else might you have enjoyed hearing?

READ INTO IT!

Join ClubRayo by emailing rayo@harpercollins.com